Jan. 9, 2011

*To Angie —
my favorite Critic —
It's more fact than fiction
Enjoy, Ray and Jewell
AKA Nate Tolar*

SHADRACH

NATE TOLAR

This is a work of fiction. While, as in all fiction, the literary perceptions and insights are based on experience, all names, characters, places, and incidents are either products of the author's imagination or are used fictitiously. Any reference to organizations or locales are intended only to add authenticity to the fiction.

Copyright ©2006 by Nate Tolar

ISBN 0-9777290-1-X

All rights reserved.

Cover Design byJennifer Wehrmann

Published and distributed by:
High-Pitched Hum Publishing
321 15th Street North
Jacksonville Beach, FL 32250

Contact High-Pitched Hum Publishing at info@highpitchedhum.net

Contact the author at: PO Box 50546, Jacksonville, FL 32240

No part of this book may be reproduced or transmitted in any form or means, electronic or mechanical, including photocopying, recording, or by any information storage and retrieval system, without permission in writing from the publisher.

Then Nebuchadnezzar, in a terrible rage, ordered Shadrach, Meshach and Abednego to be brought before him. Daniel 3:13.

SHADRACH

NATE TOLAR

High Pitched Hum
Publishing

CHAPTER ONE

The accusations of extortion and rape were frightening, and the gold lettering on the frosted window in the door did nothing to ease Ron's anxiety. HERSCHEL BIRDWELL, ATTORNEY-AT-LAW. The impudence of the words just added to his bitterness. The outrageous charges had hurt, and then began to rankle when he learned that Herschel had been assigned to defend him.

Ron knew Herschel, knew the caustic little lawyer was merely an Assistant Legal Counsel who worked exclusively with transportation contracts. As far as Ron had been able to determine, Herschel had signed on with the Postal Service right out of law school, even before he passed the Bar.

At the sound of the door Herschel turned from the coat rack and extended his hand. "Good morning, Ron." His voice was firm, trying to project a confidence he didn't actually have, and felt sure that it was also lacking in Ron, his first real client. "I appreciate you coming in so we can get started on this thing."

"Hello, Herschel." Ron glanced around the room's barrenness. A desk, a filing cabinet and a couple of chairs. "I didn't know you had a private office. I mean away from where you work downtown."

The sparsely-furnished office was just one main room with a storage closet and rest room, the doors to each slightly ajar. A sharp disinfectant, not quite overriding the mustiness, drew attention to the limited capacity of the suite.

Herschel grew solemn. "Oh, you never know about me. I dabble in a lot of things." He nodded toward the coat rack, then the straight chair by the desk. "Put your jacket over there and have a seat. This is going to take a while."

Ron slipped out of his blue poplin windbreaker and hung it next to the gray, elbow-sprung suit coat still swinging on its hanger. Herschel plopped into the old swivel chair behind the desk, raising his arms to fold back the cuffs on his sleeves while Ron hitched up his pants and tucked in his shirttail, then eased himself down onto the proffered chair.

"I was surprised to learn you're going to defend me." Ron didn't wait for an answer, or even try to smile. "I wasn't aware you had any trial experience."

Herschel continued to fuss with his sleeves, patting the crooked folds until they were flattened. If their roles were reversed that would have been his first concern, too. He looked up, in keeping with his resolve to be above board with Ron about everything. "I don't."

"Then why did Mr. Jordan assign you to the case?" Ron waited, his breath coming in short spurts. Did Hiram Jordan, General Manager of the Logistics Division, know something about Herschel? Everyone knew Mr. Jordan was more of a politician, just a figurehead, but the man had to have his reasons for appointing Herschel to something that was apparently beyond his area of expertise.

Herschel glanced down at the desk as his thoughts drifted back to his old law professor, Sam Whitley. The man had managed to aim a lot of law students in the right direction with the small sign so proudly displayed on the corner of his desk. *"Your mind will handle the truth, but anything else requires a superb memory."* And God knows a lawyer has enough trouble just keeping up with the truth. Herschel, trying to make light of his suspicion of how he had been picked, flipped his hand with his usual candor. "Probably Jake's idea."

The remark brought a frown as Ron's shoulders sagged. Mr. Jordan's letter informing him of the charges, and transferring him to the Distribution and Routing Section until further notice, really was sort of curt. There had been no mention of his defense until right at the last, as if it were an afterthought, and then only that Herschel would contact him.

The fact that Herschel was usually all business, hardly ever made jokes, caused a chill to settle between Ron's shoulders. "What would Jake Marshallton have to say about my defense?"

"Aw, come on, Ron." The question raised an annoyance in Herschel. "You've been around. You're not that goddamn naive?"

"I'm serious." Ron's voice rose at the thought of his accuser having that kind of influence. "What would Jake have to say about it?"

Herschel placed his elbows on the desk and rested his chin in his hands. He sat there, looking across the room for a moment before he turned. He had never heard a breath of scandal about Ron, but surely the boy was at least aware of what went on in the boardrooms and backrooms, and yes, he thought with disgust, the hotel rooms. "You're not shitting me? You really don't know?"

Ron slumped back, shaking his head. Jake did come in the office a lot and throw his weight around, but everyone just laughed about it.

Herschel swiveled around to face Ron and placed his elbow on the desk, letting his hand dangle in front of him. "I would think you've been in transportation long enough, but maybe not?" He flipped his hand and let it fall back. "You are familiar with Jake's contracts, though?"

"Yes." Ron cringed at the thought of the man's huge trucking business. Jake Marshallton was their biggest contractor. "There's eight."

"And they're worth what?" Herschel flipped his hand again. "Two million?"

"Yes." Right now, Ron thought, but the fuel savings should bring them a little under that. "That's about right, altogether."

"And you're aware of Jake's resort, the convention center he owns down in the Ozarks?" Herschel cocked an eyebrow.

"Rockmarsh Lodge?" Ron began to nod. "Yes, I've heard of it."

Herschel dipped his head. "Then you have probably heard that a few of the transportation officials from headquarters, and," his voice rose in emphasis, "some of them here in St. Louis, have been there. Have partaken of Jake's hospitality at one time or another." He chuckled softly at the story of Bill Warden's first trip down there to one of Jake's weekend fishing parties. The dumb bastard actually took his fishing gear along.

Ron frowned at Herschel's insinuations. "I've heard some of them talk about being there, but I wasn't aware they went as Jake's guests."

Herschel flipped his hand again, blinking at Ron as he tried to decide where to start in trying to explain Jake Marshallton's business world. It was such a whirling, gaudy carousel.

"Ron, Jake Marshallton inherited a fortune from his father, which included the corporation holding those contracts." Herschel's head began to shake at his inability to decide whether the inheritance was the cause, or merely contributed to Jake's delusions of grandeur. "The man has never had any responsibility, any pressure, nothing to worry about, so he's spent his life perfecting the role of the cat in a game of cat and mouse, particularly with the Postal Service."

Herschel's tone reflected his hostility toward such a twisted, wasted life. "You're aware, I'm sure, of how obnoxious the sonofabitch can be, but are you aware of how far the man's got his demented claws buried in some of the mousy-assed people you work for?"

A sinking sensation caused Ron to blanch. Could there be any truth in the stories he had heard? He watched Herschel slump calmly against the desk, raising his arm to touch his fingertips to his temple.

"Remember when you were a kid, Ron, and played *king of the hill?*" Herschel waited for a nod. "Then as you got older you left the kid stuff behind and went on to other things, like any normal person. Well, there are people who don't do that, don't follow a rational pattern."

Ron's expression grew quizzical. Herschel's opinion of anybody was usually limited to just a few choice words.

"Psychologists have a name for it, which escapes me at the moment, but there are people who become so fascinated by a particular phase of their life, actually obsessed with it, that their minds never develop beyond that point."

Herschel glanced up and began to nod. "Jake Marshallton is a prime example of that theory."

Ron continued to frown. He had never taken Herschel's ramblings too seriously, as the two of them had prepared for previous contract violation hearings, but the gruff attorney's perception had never been that deep before, either. "What's that got to do with me? With this case?"

Herschel leaned forward, letting his hand dangle from the desk again. "The arrogant bastard must have gotten his nuts off playing *king of the hill* because that's where his narrow little mind apparently stalled on him. He's still playing his childish games, and somehow, you've managed to piss him off."

"I can't imagine how. I have very little to do with the man, himself."

The very idea was ridiculuous to Ron. Jake never spoke to anyone in the office below Mr. Warden, and not even to him when there were District or Regional people around. Ron usually talked to Jake's bookkeeper, Mervin Sandler, or one of their terminal foremen.

Herschel's head began to shake. "With a person like Jake, God only knows. It doesn't take much with a domineering bastard, but that's where we are right now." Herschel leaned back and turned to his desk. "The silly sonofabitch is in the process of having you officially thrown out of the game."

The leaden weight in the pit of Ron's stomach became even heavier. "What do you think his chances are of doing something like that?"

Herschel shrugged and lunged his chair up to the desk. "Until we've picked his allegations apart and scrutinized them, we'll give this thing our utmost respect and attention." He reached over and tapped the file with his index finger. "We're going over this thing with a fine toothed comb, approach it from every angle, but until such time as we have reason to believe otherwise, we will assume the man's got you by the balls." Herschel's left arm raised with his fingers grasping upward, as though reaching up to pick a pair of plums from a tree.

Ron frowned and drew away. He had cringed at that very feeling as he read Mr. Jordan's letter, and certainly didn't appreciate the theatrics.

A smile softened Herschel's features as he pulled the yellow pad into position and took a ballpoint from his shirt pocket. He hadn't really meant to be so dramatic, but actions often drew more attention than words. "But I think we can handle it."

Ron's expression remained harsh, as well as the tone of his voice, at Herschel's apparent levity. "Would you feel that confident if you were in my place?"

Herschel sobered, twiddling the ballpoint between his fingers for a second before he glanced over. It rankled him to have his ability questioned, even when there was cause. "If I hadn't felt capable of defending you properly in this thing I would have refused the assignment."

"I'm sorry, Herschel." The sincerity of the response made Ron aware of his growing belligerence. The man had always thrown himself into every hearing they worked on together, and Ron had advised him on the terms of the contract concerned, but this was something else entirely. "I've got nothing against you personally, but this whole thing scares me to death."

"And it should. It's enough to scare anybody, but let me tell you something." Herschel turned, lowering his voice confidentially. "I've had this office about ten years. Jake is aware of that, as well as the people you work for, but they think it's nothing more than a tax office." He cocked an eyebrow in sincerity. "Oh, I'll admit I do some tax work, but I also do a lot of reasearch and investigative work for Holland, Bradford and Ashcroft. And that, I'm damn sure Jake is not aware of, otherwise he wouldn't have wanted me on the case."

The words raised a panic in Ron. It horrified him to think of Herschel handling the case alone, of being his only defense against the charges. "I'm sorry, but I'm just not happy with any part of this…, this trumped-up mess."

"Listen to me, Ron." Herschel nodded sternly. "Jake and his eminent counsel, Walter Hardesty, have to get this thing by the hearing judge first. I see no reason why we can't nip it in the bud at the hearing. No reason at all. But," he sighed as he drew back, "just in case we don't, and mind you I said just in case, and it goes to trial, we've got Ned Ashcroft to fall back on. I'm sure you're aware Ned is considered the sharpest trial lawyer in the midwest."

Ron's body sagged as he scowled and turned away. "I couldn't even begin to afford Ned Ashcroft."

"You won't have to." Herschel's head shook. "Since I've been assigned to defend you at the hearing I'll continue in the event of a trial, and Ned will step in with us as a favor to me. I've already discussed it with him."

"But you don't think it will get that far?"

"No, not really," Herschel's head continued to shake. "But if we don't get to work on it, by God it might."

"Well, okay." Ron looked down at the file. The admonishment had only served to heighten his anxiety. "What do we have to do?"

"Trust me, goddammit. I'm not in the habit of wading where I can't see the bottom." Herschel clicked the ballpoint and pulled the yellow pad into position, then opened the file. "Let's start with September 23rd. I believe that's the day Jake claims you came to his house to pick up the money, the ten grand, and forced yourself on his wife."

Ron frowned. "Yeah." The date had alarmed him. It was more than just a coincidence that they had picked a day Ron had been in Cape Girardeau.

"Yeah what?" Herschel grinned mischievously. "Yeah, it was September 23rd, or yeah, you fucked his wife?"

The frivolity of the question grated, causing Ron to almost shriek. "Yeah, Jake claims it was September 23rd." He leaned forward angrily. "I've already told you it's all lies, Herschel. I don't know what else I can do."

"Now, now." Herschel reached over and patted the air above the desk. "Don't get your constitution in an upheavel. I'm just trying to make you understand you have to give precise answers." He raised his arm to point across the room, as though indicating a higher realm. "When you get up there on the stand you're going to have to keep your wits about you and concentrate. Particularly on what might appear to be just a simple question. Think, dammit, or Walter Hardesty will slide this thing right into a trial."

Ron wilted back at the reprimand. He hadn't meant to sound whiny. "I'll try, Herschel. I'll try to answer as honestly as I can."

"Just trying is not going to be good enough, goddammit. You're going to have to concentrate, think about each question before you respond." Herschel held him in his stare for a second before he turned back to the file. "Let's get back to September 23rd. Do you remember what you did that day? Where you were?"

"Yeah." Ron nodded. He had already begun to feel as though he was trying to claw his way out of a hole. A deep hole in the ground. "I was in Cape Girardeau. I had an appointment with Oren Witcher. His contract was expiring and I had to talk to him about a possible renewal."

Herschel began scribbling. "Was there any way Jake could have known you were going to be in town that day?"

Despair tugged at Ron as he nodded down at his hands. "Yes. Jake came to the office the week before to leave some fuel certifications we had requested. I think it was on a Wednesday. I told him then I would be down there on the twenty-third, and tried to set up a time to talk to him about his Kansas City contract. It was expiring, too."

Herschel continued to write without looking up. "Did you meet with him?"

"No." Ron felt as if the walls of the hole just crumbled everytime he tried to pull himself up. "Jake said he was going to make an inspection trip on his route up to St. Louis that day, then ride his Chicago route that night."

"So?" Herschel paused, nodding down at what he had just written. "Jake knew you would be in Cape Girardeau on the twenty-third, and also, he has witnesses to the fact that you knew he would be away from home that night?"

Ron's voice was subdued at the thought of being trapped so easily. "I guess you could say that."

"Guess, hell." Herschel's voice rose as he turned to glare. "Doesn't this tell you anything?"

"Yes." Ron nodded, his expression reflecting his inner trauma. "This whole thing tells me I'm being set up, being thrown to the wolves."

"You're goddamn right." Herschel's eyes blazed as he thumped his finger on the letter of charges resting on top of the file. "This is not just some trumped up charge to embarrass you, Ron, and maybe get your wrist slapped. This man is after your *ass*."

Ron's voice began to tremble. "You think I don't know that?"

Herschel continued to glare and tap the letter. "He's not accusing you of just accepting a gratuity, or even a bribe, either of which could get you demoted and stuck in a shit job on a back dock somewhere. The sonofabitch has accused you of *demanding* money, and that borders on extortion." Herschel's eyebrows rose as he hesitated a second. "Then when you came by his house to pick up the money, he claims you made his wife spread her legs. That doesn't *border* on anything. That *is* spherical rape."

The last two words brought a shocked stare. Ron considered himself fairly knowledgeable about sex, but conceded he wasn't all that familiar with the terms the courts used for categories of rape. He had never heard that description before. "What do you mean, spherical?"

Herschel's head began to shake sternly as he drew out the words. "An-ny wa-ay you look at it."

Ron cringed at the sudden realization he was now an accused rapist. He couldn't generate any sympathy for Mrs. Marshallton because he had never met the woman, and she hadn't been raped anyway, not as far as he knew anything about.

His voice rose with anxiety. "But it didn't happen, Herschel. It's not true, any of it."

Herschel just nodded, indifferent to the emotionally charged words. "And that's what we have to get through to the judge."

Ron huffed at the thought of being in such a predicament on the strength of a letter. And no one had bothered to ask him if it was true. Not one of the transportation officials, his boss, Mr. Warden, or even his own defense counsel. These were the people he worked with and supposedly knew, who knew him, yet they had so readily condemned him. He mulled it over, studying his tightly clasped hands. "What happened to the thing about a person being considered innocent until proven guilty? Isn't that good anymore?"

"Oh, sure." Herschel stopped writing. "That's the good old American way, unless you work for the Postal Service. Particularly in transportation."

Disgust overcame Ron as he looked away, letting his shoulders sag.

Herschel turned back to his pad, but not before he caught the show of hopelessness. "I know, I know. It's enough to make a buzzard puke, but let's get back to this." He nodded down at the yellow pad. "What kind of car is that you guys drive? Your office car?"

"It's an Oldsmobile." Ron's tone reflected his indifference. "A cutlass."

"Color?" Herschel waited without looking up.

"It's white. A four-door. I don't know the license number offhand, but I can get it for you."

"That won't be necessary. They surely won't coach her that far."

Herschel chuckled to himself as he wrote. He was sure that sonofabitching Hardesty would give Alice Marshallton a crash course in *the truth, the whole truth and nothing but the truth* before she got anywhere near that stand.

Herschel smiled at the thought. "If I should bring the car into it, they are aware that it would sound better for her to simply say it was a white, four-door something. A woman wouldn't ordinarily be that precise in identifying a car. Women just don't think that way."

Ron frowned, becoming serious as he leaned forward and placed his elbow on the edge of the desk. "Who's *they*?"

"They?" Herschel hesitated, confusion wrinkling his brow. He had been so intent on taking his client through the case the way Ned Ashcroft suggested that he had apparently not been listening to what he had just said.

"You said *they* would coach her." Ron glared as he spit out the word that could include any one of a bunch of people he was beginning to despise.

"Oh." Herschel raised his head when the question registered. He had assumed Ron was aware that the case had settled down to *us* and *them*, and would understand who their immediate adversaries were. "Jake and Walter Hardesty."

"Walter Hardesty?" Bewilderment twisted Ron's features. He had heard enough about Jake Marshallton to not be surprised at anything the man would say or do, but an attorney? "You mean..?"

"Don't let Walter Hardesty fool you." Herschel nodded at the thought of Jake's pompous attorney, with his pinky rings, foppish vests and gaudy bow ties.

The only honor the man had was to his own bloated ego, and the pursuit of the long green. It was that kind of shit that put the stink on their profession. "That bastard's got the scruples of a sober wino."

"You mean a lawyer would encourage someone to lie?" Ron's brow wrinkled further at the thought of a witness taking the oath, with their hand in the air. "On the stand?"

"You're damn right." Herschel rolled his eyes. "That sonofabitch would, if that's what he feels it will take." He finished writing and began to review the page.

The admission of deceit frightened Ron, causing him to lean stiffly back in his chair. Were they going to have to verify what he did that day, in order to prove what he *didn't* do? He squinted, trying to visualize his travel voucher for that day in September. It, and the file on Oren Witcher's renewal, was the only written record he had. As he recalled, the day had started out bad and gotten worse. Because of the trouble with the office car he didn't have time to stop for breakfast, and... He began to mumble, almost to himself, as the thought blossomed up through his chilliness. "I didn't drive the Olds that day."

Herschel stopped, his eyes studying the far wall for a moment before he turned slowly. "Say that again."

Ron's face softened. Could something as simple as that possibly be his salvation? "I said I didn't drive the office car that day."

"Are you certain?"

"Yes, Herschel. I'm certain." Ron dipped his head. "We had been having trouble with the alternator, and when I started the car that morning the light stayed on." The incident was becoming clearer, almost funny now. Strange how something so frustrating at the time could be so welcome now. "I drove around the lot for a minute, circled it at least twice, but the red light wouldn't go off so I parked it, put a note on the dash that it still needed to be fixed, and drove my own car."

"Can you prove that?" Herschel turned, hoping the transportation office didn't have a policy of reimbursing one-day travel out of the impress fund. "Is there anything in writing?"

"Well, yes." Ron frowned. Weren't the people in the legal department reimbursed for their travel. "I claimed POA mileage on my voucher."

"And they allowed it?"

"Yes." Ron nodded irritably. How was he going to convince Herschel he was innocent of Jake's charges if he couldn't even get the man to believe something he had in writing?

"I'll need a copy." Herschel turned and started writing. "A complete copy. Front and back of each page."

Ron slumped back in his chair. "It was only one sheet." Either the legal department didn't use travel vouchers or Herschel never went anywhere.

"Whatever." Herschel shrugged as he folded the page over.

"I'll get you a copy."

"Okay." Herschel flattened the fold at the top of the tablet and pulled it into position. "Describe the car you drove."

Ron's eyebrows lifted at the question. "I told you I drove my own."

"Describe it, Ron." Aggravation dripped between Herschel's words. "I'm not familiar with you damn car."

Ron leaned forward, speaking distinctly. "It's a Firemist Thunderbird."

"A what?"

"Firemist Thunderbird." Ron smiled at the way Judy had fallen in love with the car when she saw it on the showroom floor that day. "Firemist is a dark metallic red, and Thunderbird is a sport coupe that Ford makes."

Herschel mumbled as he wrote. "Red. Ford. Two-door"

Ron shrugged. Judy would have a fit if she heard her car described so casually. "You want the license number?"

Herschel just shook his head. "Now. Since Jake's letter claims this all took place at his house I guess I'd better go down there and have a look. At least circle the block. What's Jake's address?"

Amazement struck Ron. He had been so concerned about what he was accused of doing that he had given no thought to where it had supposedly happened. "I don't know, Herschel. I really don't."

"What do you mean, you don't know?" Herschel scowled. "Eight goddamn contracts you've been through how many times? And you don't know his address?"

Ron's voice rose. "Jake's business address is a post office box."

"And you're telling me his home address is no where in those contracts?" Herschel waited. It was absurd, with the redundancy in government paperwork, to think the man's place of residence wasn't mentioned somewhere at least once.

"Not that I know anything about." Ron went over the contract format in his mind. The first page and the Order of Award or Renewal was the only place a contractor's address ever appeared. "Any correspondence with Jake is through the post office box and any personal contact is always on postal property. Either at our office here in St. Louis or the post office in Cape Girardeau."

"And you don't know his home address, don't know where he lives?" Herschel felt a slight relief even though he wasn't sure why.

"No." The word was sharp. It was beginning to irritate Ron to have to argue with Herschel on every little detail. "I've never had any reason to know Jake Marshallton's home address."

Herschel tilted his head as the idea unfolded before him. If it was true, then that goddamn Hardesty wouldn't be able to finagle Ron into saying something about the house that might mislead the judge. "You don't know where Jake lives and have never had any reason to know?"

"That's right." Ron looked away. He had never given Herschel any reason to believe he would lie about anything.

"Good." Herschel started writing again. "And be sure you keep that in mind if Walt Hardesty starts asking you about the house."

When he got to the bottom of the page, Herschel stopped and reread what he had written. He sat thoughtfully for a moment before he scratched out a word and wrote in a replacement, then folded the page over.

"Do you have ten thousand dollars, Ron?"

The question caught Ron unaware, bringing a sharp intake of breath as he wilted back. "I don't know what else I can tell you, Herschel. I *did not* take any money from Jake Marshallton."

"Let me put it to you this way, then." Herschel tapped the ballpoint against his upper lip, studying the far wall a moment.

"Imagine yourself on the witness stand, right up there under the judge's nose, and Walter Hardesty asks you if you've got ten thousand dollars. What would you tell *him?*"

"Oh." Ron looked down. He kept forgetting there was more to this than just him and Herschel.

"You damn right, Oh." Herschel blurted the word. "If you give that judge any indication you're even thinking about taking the red ass over the mention of money, you're going to flush everything we're trying to do."

"I'm sorry." A gripping fear began to squeeze Ron's confidence again. "I'll try to remember that."

"Listen to me, Ron." Herschel's voice was soft. He realized he didn't have the diplomacy of Ned Ashcroft, but he didn't have time to worry about that now. "There are things I need to know if I'm going to defend you. You've been accused of taking some money so it's necessary for me to be familiar with your financial situation. By familiar, I mean aware of every last nickel you've got."

Ron listened, nodding without looking away. He and his wife had worked so hard to have a down payment on a house someday, and now it could be his downfall. "Yes. I've got that much. Our savings account, mine and Judy's, has a little over twelve thousand dollars in it."

Herschel swiveled around and started writing, his words almost accusing. "I hope to hell ten thousand of that hasn't been deposited in the last six weeks."

"No." Ron's head began to shake as his mind went back to the night before he and Judy got married. They had sat across from each other at her mother's kitchen table while they consolidated their funds. It seemed like just last week. "Judy and I had about four thousand dollars between us when we got married eight years ago. We've deposited the rest since then. Fifty, sometimes a hundred a month, and we always put our tax refund in the savings." His head continued to shake. "No, it's been deposited over the eight years we've been married."

"Good." Herschel watched him. "And you don't have any other money? CDs, bonds, investments of any kind?"

Ron just sat there. He and Judy had discussed putting some of their money in a CD, or even buying double E bonds, but all the mutual fund brochures they saw had the same small print about understanding your investment could be more or less than the original amount at maturity. They had wondered how any of these companies could get any takers. He turned to look at Herschel. "Just a checking account."

"How much do you usually keep in that?"

Herschel was becoming disturbed at Ron's reluctance to talk about money. It sounded like he might be hiding something? From all Herschel had been able to determine, Ron was one of those doting husbands who trusted his wife to handle their finances, and apparently didn't know that much about it. But he had to be sure.

Ron raised his eyes to the ceiling as he thought. It was going to be difficult to get it down to the last nickel. "I'd say..."

"Roughly." Herschel looked up. Didn't the boy's wife ever give him a financial report, ever tell him anything?

The gruff word was confusing. A moment ago Herschel wanted the exact amount. It frightened Ron to think he was going to have to pay more attention to Herschel's questions and make sure everything was clearly understood by both of them.

"I was going to say a thousand, but it's not that much very often. We make sure it never goes below five hundred, so it probably averages six, seven hundred dollars."

"And there's nothing else?" Herschel continued to frown.

He didn't enjoy being a prick, but most people had no idea of the damage an *unknown* could inflict when it was introduced by the right person at the wrong time, or was it the wrong person at the right time. He supposed it would really depend more on relevance and timing.

"No." Ron's mind went to Judy's leather pouch of old coins her grandmother had left her, but their value was immaterial because she considered them keepsakes more than anything else. "Not that I can think of."

"Not that you can think of?" The words were sharp as Herschel slumped forward on the desk. "I sure hope this isn't too much of a goddamn bother." He hung his head in exasperation for a moment before he raised up in anger. "*Think, goddammit.* I don't need any fucking surprises while I'm trying to pull your ass out of the crack it's in."

The outburst seemed to ignite the very air, and the small room fell into the hush of a deserted morgue. Their hard eyes held each other for a long moment, until Ron drew in a breath and turned away. He had completely forgotten the small disability check from the Veterans Administration that was direct-deposited each month.

While he considered ignoring the small amount of the check, a toilet flushed somewhere in the building. The rush of water didn't quite drown out the piercing wail of a distant siren, then both faded away.

Ron cleared his throat as he turned. It was money so he really didn't have a choice. "I almost forgot the disability pension I get from the VA. It's not much."

Herschel's eyebrows lifted. "What kind of disability?"

"It's nothing, Herschel." It embarrassed Ron to even talk about it. "It was an accident, not an act of war."

But you're okay?"

Ron nodded. "I don't consider myself crippled, if that's what you mean?"

"That's exactly what I mean." Herschel turned to his yellow pad. "What do you do with the money?"

"It's direct-deposited in our savings account." Ron sighed and slumped back. It was almost as if Herschel believed he had actually taken the money, and wanted to make sure it wasn't where it could be found.

"There's nothing else. The savings and checking account. The car is financed and we just rent. That's everything, Herschel."

"Good." Herschel nodded without looking up. It wasn't exactly a success story, but it was good enough to keep Walter Hardesty from insinuating the boy was in a financial bind or had any reason to resort to extortion. "We shouldn't have any problems in that area then."

The sudden piercing trill of the phone caused Ron to stiffen. Hershcel flinched, then snatched it up, stifling the second ring with his hasty answer. "Hello." His scowl quickly relaxed into a grin. "Oh, hi. Yeah, I'm working on that thing I talked to you about last week." He blinked while he listened. "I didn't? Are you sure? Hold on a second and let me look."

He placed the phone on the desk and got up, turning to his filing cabinet. He pulled the top drawer out, fingered back half way and pulled a folder up. He took a sheet from it, studied it a moment, then pushed the folder back into place and closed the drawer.

"Ned. I knew I made two copies. I was sure I left one with you, but it seems your copy got back into my folder here. I've still got two." He started to laugh, then sobered. "Yeah. I'll probably be another hour or so, but I can drop it off on my way home. Okay?" He listened a moment. "Sure, no problem. Sorry about that, Ned. See you."

Herschel took an envelope from a drawer, folded the sheet and slid it in, then got up and stepped over to the coat rack. He placed the envelope on the narrow shelf above his coat and turned, adjusting his sleeves. "I put things up there so I'll be sure and see them when I leave."

Ron frowned as he crossed his legs and placed his elbow on the edge of the desk. "You said Ned. Is that like in Ashcroft?"

Herschel nodded as he dropped back into his chair. "That man works all the time." He pulled the legal pad over into position and picked up his pen. "Now. Where were we?"

He touched the pen to each paragraph down the page, then picked up the pad and folded the page over as he turned to Ron. "What do you know about Jake's wife?"

CHAPTER TWO

Judy's mind was in complete chaos as she stood at the kitchen window, watching the street for Wanda Simmon's blue Dodge. She felt as if her whole world had crumbled.

She couldn't remember ever *not* knowing Ron Hamilton. They had grown up next door to each other here in Affton, their families close enough to cause her to wonder about some sort of kinship. She had more or less accepted him as a cousin even though she had never tried to determine which one of her parents was related to which of his. It wasn't until a few days before her thirteenth birthday, while she and her mother were getting things ready for her party, that she learned she wasn't related to him at all. The closeness of the two families was nothing more than a friendship, fostered by the fathers working together at a chemical plant across the river in Illinois, the mothers being active in the same community projects and both families attending the same church.

Judy remembered trying to be disappointed at the news, and not being able to understand why she wasn't. If anything, she had experienced an air of relief, a degree of ebullience that was almost dizzying at times. And it had eluded her for over two years, until that summer Ron insisted she go with him to the Fourth of July Picnic at Carondelet Park, in spite of the cumbersome walking cast the doctor had put on her left foot the week before. She had slipped rounding third base in the final game of the South County Softball Tournament, and twisted her ankle under her as she fell. It didn't hurt enough to warrant the unsightly cast, but Dr. Palmer had insisted.

She had managed well enough that day, hobbling around, right up until the storm hit. The sudden downpour caused everyone to scatter, holding newspapers, plastic tablecloths, or whatever they could find above their heads for protection from the large, pelting drops. Ron had scooped her up in his arms and ran to the weathered gazebo at the center of the park.

With her arms wrapped around his neck, and her body pressed so tightly to him, she could feel their hearts beating in unison, and the tempo accelerating rapidly. As he eased down onto the bench, settling her so protectively on his lap, she had attributed his breathlessness to the exertion of running with her in his arms, but she couldn't explain her own exhilaration. Her breath, too, was reduced to short gasps as he gently drew her to him and kissed her. At the time she had thought the scintillation was from the static electricity in the heavy air of the storm, but she still tingled the same way when he kissed her.

As Judy reached up and brushed a tear away with her knuckle, her mind went back to the day Ron came home and told her he had been accused of taking some money. She was so ashamed of the way she had reacted, of the way she had tried to justify the offense in her own mind. Her first thought was that he had incurred a debt of some kind, then she recoiled at the possibility he might be getting the mental disorder, whatever they call it, that causes a person to steal. Her mind had raced, trying to put together the proper words to reassure him, but he had noticed the doubt in her expression, and dropped his head as he turned away. He wouldn't even look at her while he told her the rest of the charges.

The whole thing became so perversely funny she had wanted to laugh, but the tears welled up instead, and she snuggled up behind him to place her cheek against his back. She had felt so foolishly inadequate as she clung to him, wondering how she could have ever doubted him in the first place. It was preposterous, so utterly ridiculous. Her own darling, affectionate husband, forcing himself on another woman. A stab of jealously pierced her very soul at the thought of Ron's tenderness, his sensuous lovemaking. He would never have to resort to anything like that.

Then when her tears had begun to soak through his shirt, he had turned and gently nestled her head against his chest, holding her close, one hand lovingly massaging away the tenseness in the muscles in her shoulders and neck. She remembered thinking how it was all so wrong, so completely absurd. Not only the accusations, but the fact that *he* was the one in trouble and had to console *her*.

Two short beeps of a horn shattered Judy's reverie, making her suddenly aware that Wanda's car was sitting in the driveway, and she hadn't even seen it come down the street.

A sigh escaped as she turned and reached for her purse, then leaned down for the large shopping bag of supplies for the romper room. She had always enjoyed her Saturday afternoons with the women's club, helping to ready the church for Sunday, but it had become a real chore the last few weeks, since word of the allegations against Ron had gotten around.

The way some of the women smirked and giggled was bad enough, but the open caustic remarks were uncalled for. They were all adult christians who were supposedly friends and acquaintances. As she went out through the garage, Judy couldn't help but recall Marlene Howell's comment as they left the church last week. It had embarrassed her at the moment, but then, when she got home and thought about it, she realized the woman was merely defusing the tension created by the other women's snide remarks. The snickering had abruptly stopped when Marlene, always so jovial, had said she would gladly share her husband with another woman if he could command a stud fee like that.

Judy cringed at the thought of facing the same women again as she set the shopping bag on the rear seat of the Dodge, then got in the front. "Thanks for picking me up, Wanda. I really appreciate it."

"No trouble at all. Glad I could help." Wanda made no effort to put the car in gear. She waited while Judy got in, moving as though all the woes of the world were on her shoulders. "And don't let this thing get you down, honey."

"Oh, I'm not." Judy smiled weakly. "I was just going back over the list of supplies, trying to make sure I didn't forget anything."

"Sure you were." Wanda nodded, her tone overly sweet. She put the car in reverse and turned to look both ways before she started backing out. "You stand at the kitchen window every Saturday, so concerned with how many crayons and coloring books you bought for the nursery that you get tears in your eyes."

"Was I that obvious?" Judy looked down, wiping a fingertip under each eye. She hadn't meant for Wanda to know how much it was bothering her, even though they did confide in each other, but she had no intention of giving any of the other women reason to believe she gave the matter any credence at all.

"Not really." Wanda shook her head as she pulled up to the stop sign and checked both ways before she pulled out into a left turn. "You do real good out in public, honey. You really do. It's when you're alone that worries me, like today." She nodded back toward the house. "It seems as though the stronger the feelings a man and woman have for each other, the worse it becomes when there's a problem. You're letting some silly little thing fester into a cockamamie idea that you've let Ron down in some way."

Wanda lifted her hand from the steering wheel as her brow wrinkled. "Well, maybe not actually failed him, but you're kicking yourself at the way you reacted to something about these charges against him." She shook her finger at nothing in particular. "And if we had any way of knowing, any way at all of finding out, I'd almost bet your husband is walking around with a knot of guilt that he has embarrassed you with this.., this farce, and he didn't have anything to do with it."

When Judy turned away, blinking back her tears, Wanda continued, but in a much softer tone. "And it won't serve any purpose to agonize over it, either. But, if I know you two lovebirds, know you and Ron at all, he is no more likely to share his problem with you than you are to share yours with him. You'll both just live with it and try to do better the next time."

Judy gave each eye a swipe as she turned back. "I don't know what I'd do without you, Wanda." She smiled, massaging her fingertips together, then clasped her hands and dropped them to her lap. "You and Agatha Hendley. You've both been so nice."

Wanda's eyebrows shot up at the mention of the wealthy widow, the unofficial matriarch of the Southgrove Baptist Church. She wouldn't have thought the woman had a speaking acquaintance with Judy.

When Agatha's husband, a cardiologist, died in the crash of his private plane nearly five years ago, on his way home from a medical convention in Dallas, she had gone into official mourning for a full year. She had donned the widows weeds, and, after the funeral, only left the large house on Hampton Avenue to shop and attend church services. No one had a chance to do more than just nod, though, because she aways arrived a moment after the services had started, sat near the back, then slipped out the door at the close of the benediction.

The woman's concern amazed Wanda, causing her eyes to dart back and forth between Judy and the street. "I wasn't aware you knew Agatha that well."

Wanda couldn't recall ever seeing the two of them together. Mrs. Hendley was at least thirty years older than Judy and in a different Sunday School class, so they would have very little in common at church, and that was the only connection she was aware the two of them had.

"I really didn't until this thing with Ron came up." Judy shook her head, still in awe of how friendly the woman had been at the South County Mall the day she walked right up and said hello. "I was shopping one morning, right after word got out about Ron's trouble, and happened to run into her. She was real nice. Told me how sorry she was about it, and to not pay any attention to what people say."

Judy's eyes lost their solemnness as she recalled how gracious and warm the woman had been. "Agatha said some people become addicted to scandal the same as others do to alcohol or tobacco. She said if I didn't believe that I should consider how people discuss the soaps, dwell on every lurid detail. She said most of them haven't missed an episode in years."

When Wanda's features began to grow stern, it reminded Judy of the rumors that started going around a year or so after Mrs. Hendley had come out of mourning. At first it was only a brief trip to Jefferson City or Cape Girardeau, then the stories expanded to an overnight stay in Springfield or Kansas City. With the woman being such a pillar in the church, though, Judy had brushed the insinuations aside. But now, with the way Wanda reacted, she wasn't too sure anymore.

Agatha Hendley couldn't be any more God-fearing than Great-Aunt Matilda had been, and Uncle Ferdie always insisted that his little sister Matty, as he called her, was obsessed with something more than just religion. He said that when a church woman got on a cross-country bus and sat up for two days and a night, several times a year, to go to a camp meeting over in Ohio to listen to a man read from the same book she held in her lap, a book she had already read herself more than a dozen times, she was seeking a blessing of a more earthly nature.

But that was a long time ago, Judy thought, and Uncle Ferdie had such a fertile imagination. He used to poke fun at just about everything, but he was also a gentleman. He would have undoubtedly known of something in the Bible that would explain Mrs. Hendley's alleged trysts.

Judy broke from her retrospection and grabbed for the dash when Wanda suddenly stiff-armed the steering wheel and stood on the brake. The tires squalled as they slid up behind a stopped car, its left indicator blinking while the driver waited for a break in the traffic. Wanda glanced over at Judy, then back to the turning car as she accelerated gently, her mind still on the Widow Hendley's sudden interest in the matter. "Does Ron know he has a friend in Mrs. Hendley?"

"Yes." Judy nodded. "I told him about running into her at the mall. Told him what she said."

"But she's never spoken directly to him about it?" Wanda kept her eyes on the street.

"No. Not that I'm aware of."

"Does Agatha talk to Ron at all?"

Judy hesitated, squinting. "I don't really know. He did tell me a day or two after I ran into her at the Mall, though, that when he passed her house on his morning run she had stepped out on her porch to pick up her paper. He said she just nodded, so he nodded, too. He said they were too far apart to speak, anyway."

"Had she ever nodded to him before?" Wanda never knew of Mrs. Hendley ignoring anyone. The woman wasn't at all snobbish, but Wanda had never heard of her showing any interest in the younger church members.

Judy continued to shake her head. "He said she had never picked up her paper that early. It was always there on the porch."

Wanda wanted to feel good about Mrs. Hendley's interest in Judy and Ron, and knew she would have to suppress that sprig of suspicion she harbored about the woman intentions. It was possible that Agatha could be sincerely concerned. "Well, it can't hurt Ron's cause any to have Mrs. Hendley in his corner."

"That's what I thought, and the people Ron works for are behind him, too." Judy turned with an eager smile. "His big boss, the one in the Region, has already assigned one of the Postal Service's attorneys to defend him. That's why Ron needed the car today, to meet with the attorney over in Kirkwood."

"The Postal Service has an attorney in Kirkwood?" The implication puzzled Wanda. Why would the Postal Service have attorneys stationed in every suburb? No wonder postage kept going up.

"No." Judy turned, shaking her head. "The man works downtown in the Federal Building at Twelfth and Market where Ron does. The office in Kirkwood is the man's private practice. It has nothing to do with the Postal Service." She waited but Wanda continued to frown. "Ron said he didn't know anything about the private office until the man asked him to come over today."

"Ron knows the guy?" Wanda's harshness faded but she kept her attention on her driving. It certainly couldn't hurt to have an attorney in your corner, too.

Judy continued to shake her head. She hadn't meant to give that impression. "I'm afraid I'm not putting this very well. Ron never talks about his work at home. He explained it isn't that he doesn't trust me, but that transportation contracts are awarded throught the competitive bid process, and most of what he does is not public imformation. What little bit I do know is what he's told me since all of this started."

She waited for Wanda to nod before she continued. "Ron said this attorney represents the Postal Service when one of the contractors complains."

"Complains about what?" This was becoming much more involved than Wanda had ever imagined.

"Well," Judy faltered. "Whatever it is contractors complain about. That his rights have been violated, I suppose." She shrugged and waved it away. "When something like that happens they have to have a hearing. Ron handles the contract part of it, and this attorney handles the legal side."

Wanda nodded without taking her eyes from the street. Judy had told her about Ron's promotion a year of so ago, but she hadn't gotten the idea he was into anything that big. Rubbing shoulders with lawyers, and particularly the one who had been assigned to defend him. But why was Judy worried? "What makes you think Ron doesn't know the attorney?"

"I'm sorry." Judy suddenly realized she had digressed, hadn't answered the question. "I didn't mean to give that impression, but it's, well, just that Ron doesn't seem to be too enthusiastic when he talks about it."

"My God, honey." Wanda lifted her hand reprovingly as she stopped at the red light. "I doubt that any man would be overly thrilled about being charged with extortion and rape."

"No, I didn't mean that." Judy looked down at her hands. The way Ron frowned when he mentioned Mr. Birdwell had worried her. "I mean when he talks about the attorney. I've tried to think he's, well, maybe embarrassed to discuss the charges with someone he works with, someone he probably knows and respects. I don't know what it is, but there was something about going to see the attorney that bothered him."

"You could be right." Wanda started nodding, then, at the short beep of a horn, lifted her eyes to the traffic light. When she saw it had turned green she moved her foot to the accelerator and caught up to the traffic. "I'm sure I would be horrified if I had to discuss charges like that with someone I knew."

Judy nodded, but only that she would be uncomfortable, too, not that she felt her husband's problem was that simple. Her intuition, and the years she had known Ron, told her it was more than that. The fact that he chose to keep whatever it was to himself, to not confide in her, caused her to cringe and her voice to quaver. "I pray it's nothing more than that."

"I'm sure it isn't." Wanda reached over and patted Judy's arm. "And don't you worry. With the Postal Service standing behind him like that, even assigning a lawyer who knows him. He's going to be okay."

The remark brought a smile to Judy's face as Wanda turned into the church lot and swung into a parking space. It had reminded her of what Ron told her at breakfast. Even if he didn't seem to be anymore excited about it than he was with Mr. Birdwell, it sounded good to her. "Ron told me that Mr. Warden, the Contracting Officer, is driving down to Cape Girardeau today to talk to the contractor about the charges."

Wanda drew back as she unbuckled her seat belt. "On Saturday?" His boss is willing to do that on his day off?"

"Yes." The smile grew wider as Judy let her seat belt retract out of the way. "Ron said he heard Mr. Warden talking to someone on the phone yesterday, and he told whoever it was that he was going down there today to talk to the man."

"And you're still worried?" Wanda looked back as she pushed the door open. "With the way all those Postal Officials are ganging up on that contractor, why," she shook her head, "the man doesn't have a chance."

They retrieved their shopping bags from the back seat and headed across the yellow striped lot toward the nursery room door. The thought of a man falsely accusing someone, and then having the sky fall in on him intrigued Wanda. It tickled her to think of some blowhard getting his comeupance, but then it crossed her mind that it could be difficult for Ron after this was all over, especially if the man was someone he knew, and still had to work with.

"Does Ron know the man, this contractor?"

"Yes." Judy nodded. "He has to work with all the contractors."

Wanda began to blink as she shifted her purse to the hand with the shopping bag, and reached for the doorknob. She had watched actors face each other on television, in staged courtroom dramas, but this was real people, a friend's husband who was being accused. Ron would have to face this man, his accuser, but then it occurred to her that he would probably have to face the man's wife, too.

"Does Ron know the man's wife, this... alleged victim." She had almost said floozy. With the man it was just an accusation of Ron taking some money, but with the woman it was something else entirely. Wanda despised a woman who had no more self-respect than to flaunt herself, especially in a courtroom.

Judy turned, shaking her head. "He said he doesn't."

It irritated Wanda to think of a nice young man like Ron Hamilton being accused by some loose woman, but it could be worse. She somehow felt it might be easier to face a person over something so intimate if you *didn''t* know them.

"He's never even met her?" Wanda frowned as she pulled the nursery room door open.

"No." Judy looked over her shoulder at Wanda as she stepped inside. "Ron told me this morning that he wouldn't know the woman if he passed her in the middle of the street."

CHAPTER THREE

Apprehension gnawed at Bill Warden as he headed south out of St. Louis in the white Oldsmobile assigned to the Transportation Office. It always thrilled him to head down I-44 toward Table Rock, and Rockmarsh Lodge, but he was on I-55 this morning, headed for Jake Marshallton's office in Cape Girardeau.

When Bill was promoted to Manager of the Transportation Office, and designated Contracting Officer, he felt he had arrived. Had finally paid his dues. As a member of the upper echelon he was in a position for people to start kissing *his* ass. No more dipping into his own pocket for ticket money to the fund raisers the State Committeemen held for every tacky poitician who came to St. Louis. That obligation had now been passed down to the aspiring members of his staff.

On stepping into the position of Manager, and Contracting Oficer, Bill had become the *boss*, and he intended to make that abundantly clear. He knew he would be signing all office correspondence, in addition to the transportation contracts, and had started immediately to practice his signature. Sometimes two or three hours a day. He couldn't think of anything more impressive, more authoritative than the flawless Palmer Method signature of William P. Warden.

He never used his middle name of Percival anymore. When he finally reached high school there were already several Bills, so everyone called him Percy. But only until the girls began to shy away, turned off by his lecherous hands. Then the kids began to laugh and slur the name among themselves until it sounded more like *Pussy*.

Bill wore the name with an arrogance until he began to realize the girls were actually avoiding him. They moved in groups of never less that three, and were always so engrossed in conversatrion, talking so incessantly that they passed him right on by. It didn't really sink in, though, until he spent a dateless, and danceless prom, and finally understood there was nothing flattering about his status. That was the night he vowed to be somebody someday, to do whatever it took to reach a position that would make people look up to him, especially the women.

And now that he had attained his goal, life was good. The female contractors and supervisors, as well as those on his staff, were so nice, especially Maggie, his secretary. She made sure his candy jar had butter scotch drops in it, kept his office in order and even brought his morning coffee right around the desk and set it in front of him. His heart quickened at the thought of how she teasingly drew away when he ran his fingertips up the back of her leg.

While Bill dwelled on the feel of his secretary's leg the Oldsmobile angled slowly off the road, until a wheel thumped over a fragment of truck tire tread on the shoulder, and he gave a startled jerk. With tires squalling, the car careened back and forth across the slight drop-off several times before he managed to regain control and bring it back to the highway, and his thoughts back to the task at hand. Talking to Jake Marshallton about this thing with Ron Hamilton.

Bill had been appalled that morning, several weeks ago, when he read his copy of Jake's letter of charges. To think Ron, his Transportation Officer, had brazenly taken Jake Marshallton for ten thousand dollars, while he, the damn boss, had been satisfied with an occasional weekend party and a hundred dollar bill in his Christmas card.

Then he had reached the part about Ron supposedly raping Alice Marshallton, and started to wonder. According to Hiram Jordan she didn't have to be raped. Hiram had been meeting her for lunch now and then, and said it never took more than a couple of martinis to slide her panties right into her purse. The very idea was ludicrous. Bill was sure that Ron never drank anything more than an occasional beer, and didn't have the reputation of being a womanizer. That would refute the rape charge, as far as he was concerned.

And besides, Bill was more than just a little partial to his Transportation Officer. While Ron was Superintendent of the Truck Terminal out in Hazelwood, he had instigated more than one project that produced both savings and improved service. Then when Bill promoted him to head up the Transportation Department, Ron had dived right in with his fuel savings program and earned Bill an Outstanding Merit Increase the first year. That's why Hiram, while they were on the phone yesterday discussing the charges against Ron, had suggested that Bill should at least drive down to Cape Girardeau and talk to Jake about it.

Bill knew he had better do it right away, before he lost his nerve, and besides, Herschel Birdwell was going to sit down with Ron this afternoon to start preparing for the hearing. If he could make some kind of deal with Jake today it would save everybody a lot of trouble.

A twinge of jitters touched Bill as he came up the ramp from I-55 and headed for the frontage road. Jake's large service facility, where he maintained an office, was just over the hill. Jake was an exemplary host at the weekend parties he threw at his Convention Center in the Ozarks, near Table Rock, but in his ofice sometimes, the man could be a real bastard, a raving tyrant.

As Bill rounded the last curve he leaned forward, hoping the place would look deserted, even though he had called yesterday to make an appointment. Bill's guts tightened, though, at the sight of the dark green Cadillac Coupe, with its glittering gold wheels and trim, setting in the lone parking space to the left of the office door. The car was headed into the small, ornate sign with the calligraphic inscription, *MR. MARSHALLTON*.

Bill cringed at a stomach cramp as he shut off the engine and released his seat belt, then sat hunkered over the wheel, waiting for it to pass. That happened sometimes when he was forced into a situation he wasn't too crazy about. Like confronting Jake on this thing about Ron, and trying to work out a compromise without pissing him off.

If they could just reach a solution, some sort of an agreement, without jeopardizing his own position with Jake. Being stricken from Jake's guest list, and giving up Helen, the redheaded vice president at Rockmarsh Lodge, was not a negotiable item.

When the knot in his stomach loosened enough for him to trust his intestines, Bill got out of the car and crossed the parking lot. He would have gladly bought a *dozen* tickets to a fund raiser for even a dog catcher, but he was above that now, and had to start acting like it.

Jake Marshallton got up from his desk when the familiar white Oldsmobile pulled into the lot. He stood back from the window, chuckling softly to himself as he watched Bill get out of the car and head across the blacktop. Jake was aware that it wasn't Bill Warden's idea to be here.

It tickled Jake to know the powers that be weren't any more concerned about his charges against Hamilton than to offer up a mere third lieutenant. He had expected Calvin Donaldson, the District Manager, at least. But, then, Jake kind of liked C.J. The man was even more of a party animal than Bill Warden, but he wasn't mealy-mouthed. C.J. never hesitated to call you a son of a bitch when it fit, or forgot to smile while he was doing it.

Jake realized it wouldn't serve any purpose to antagonize Bill Warden, though. After all, Bill *was* the Contracting Officer, and a person never knew when they might need a favor. Jake stepped around behind his desk and eased into the huge leather chair as he heard the outer door open. He would just let Bill do the talking, see how long it took the simple bastard to broach the subject. Helen had told him Bill had about as much tact as an appointed politician.

At the sound of the door being closed, Jake slipped on his horn-rimmed glasses, then picked up several papers from his desk and began to study them. Jake Marshallton never *waited* for anyone. You didn't maintain the high ground by giving the impression you even thought of making concessions.

Jake gave the appearance of being engrossed in the pages he held as Bill Warden stopped at the office door, and just stood there. Jake watched out of the corner of his eye but gave no indication he knew anyone was there. He studiously went over the top letter a second time, a piston ring advertisement, and had about decided to look up when Bill reached over and meekly tapped a knuckle on the doorjamb.

The timid gesture sent Jake's dander into orbit. *Judas H. Priest.* Where in the hell does the goddamn Postal Circus get these fucking clowns. A Contracting Officer, for Christ's sake, standing there in the door like a school boy with a gut full of green apples.

Jake seethed for a moment, then dropped the pages face down on his desk and placed his glasses on them. He pushed up from his chair, inconspicuously tugging at one trouser leg to make sure the cuff caught on the top of his brown and white lizard skin cowboy boot.

"Come in, Bill." Jake ambled across the room, extending his hand. "Cindy's never here on Saturday. Hell of a note when the employees have more privileges than the damn boss."

"I know that's right." Bill stepped forward eagerly and gave the proffered hand a shake. Jake didn't always acknowledge his presence, especially when Hiram or C.J. were around. "It was good of you to see me on a Saturday afternoon."

Jake motioned to the guest chair as he turned back to his desk, glaring as he sank into the big chair and picked up his glasses. It wasn't in Jake's nature to be considered *good* about anything. "If I didn't have business, hadn't already intended to be here this afternoon I would've damn sure told you yesterday."

"I realize that, Jake," Bill gave a weak smile. He had heard people joke about Jake's defensive bluster, and how to handle it, but he had no intention of provoking the man, not if he expected to get any consideration this afternoon. "I meant it was good of you to take the time to see me. I know how busy you are."

The *harrumph* rattled in Jake's throat as he looked away. The poor son of a bitch had kissed so much ass to get where he was that he didn't know how to do anything else. It wouldn't serve any purpose to lean on the man, but damned if he would make it easy for him, either. Jake turned back. "What brings you all the way down here on a Saturday, Bill? Some of my people been fucking up?"

"Oh, no." Bill shook his head. He didn't need to mention the altercation on the dock the other night, or the unscheduled stops some of his drivers continued to make. One of the Specialists would handle that with Jake's terminal foreman. "We have no complaints with your service."

Jake's eyes rolled back in his head. What a crock of divine shit. If he had wanted a massage this morning he would have gone down to the damn lodge. He pitched his glasses on the desk and leaned back. "Bill, I can't believe you drove all the way down here just to tell me what a great fucking contractor I am. Hell, I already know that."

Jake tilted his head and waited. As a boy, he used to walk along the stream running through the pasture on their ranch, searching for crawdads. When he found one at the edge of the water he would put his foot on it and push it down into the mud, push until it was buried, then step back and wait. He always admired the ones that managed to claw their way back to the surface, even though he would just step on them again, and again, for as long as it took.

Confusion wrinkled Jake's brow when Bill Warden slumped forward, an arm across his stomach, his watery eyes seeming to bulge.

Bill took in a long breath. "No, it isn't that, Jake. I wanted to talk to you about..." he hesitated nervously. "Well, about this thing with Ron Hamilton."

"Oh?" Jake drew back with a show of indignation, subconsciouly putting his foot out to the crawdad again. With Bill Warden coming in here with his goddamn hat in his hand, those pussy-whipped bastards in St. Louis had rolled over, had turned their back to this thing just as he had expected. "Where does it say I'm supposed to give a fuck what you want?"

"Nowhere, Jake. Not that I know of, but it isn't just me." Bill straightened, the cramp easing off with his decision to take the matter to a higher level. "Hiram and I discussed it on the phone yesterday and he suggested that I come down here today and try to work something out with you."

The low chortle in Jake's throat almost squelched the belligerent image he was building. That goddamn Jordan, sitting up there in his ivory tower, had the au-fucking-dacity to send this pussy-brained ass kisser down here to argue the case. To rescue their sorry asses. To Jake, executive grovelling was like nectar from the gods, better than an orgasm. It stirred him to a frenzy.

"So?" Jake glowered. The very idea of these two crotch wimps willing to eat shit rather than stand behind their boy was fodder for his fury. "You and Whorem Jordan already held the hearing?" He dipped his head with a glare. "Is that what you're saying?"

"No, Jake. I didn't mean that." Bill began to shake his head. This wasn't going at all well, and he couldn't seem to concentrate. The way Jake slurred Hiram's name sent Bill's focus off into a harem of undulating bodies, an orgy of nude females that kept swamping his reason for being here. It was next to impossible to keep his mind on Ron's dilemma.

Bill had never really put it all together before, but Hiram *was* seeing more than one woman, and more than just for an occasional lunch, too.

It seemed as though Alice Marshallton was in town for lunch every time you turned around, and then there was the blonde vice president who always hung onto Hiram down at the lodge. What was her name, Emily? And she came to St. Louis now and then, too. Could it be that he could work something out with Jake that Helen might come to St. Louis sometime, that he could be with her more than just an occasional weekend party. The very thought of the woman's red pubic mound excited him, sent his blood racing.

"I, ah, only meant that we were talking yesterday, and the subject came up." Bill looked down, picking at his fingernails. "We, well, Hiram actually." Bill looked up, smiling wanly at the way he had been snookered. That goddamn Jordan had put him in the hot seat so the bastard should at least take the blame for his being here. "He thought if we could work something out on this it would save a lot of time and trouble."

"What do you mean, *work something out?*" Jake scowled. It wasn't the first time Hiram Jordan had sent one of his bootlickers out with a gutless suggestion to settle something.

"Ah." Bill drew himself up, trying to ignore Jake's sarcasm. "We've transferred Ron to Distribution and Routing, completely away from Transportation. We're willing to leave him there."

Jake's eyebrows shot up in disbelief as he went into a scathing stare, leaning farther over the desk. "The son of a bitch puts the touch on me for ten grand, then plays house with my wife, and I'm supposed to be thrilled all to hell that you've transferred him across the hall?"

The heat of Jake's eyes caused Bill to cower back, searching for something to appease the man. He and Hiram had discussed cutting orders for different amounts on each of the eight contracts, to cover the ten thousand, but their only mention of Mrs. Marshallton had been Hiram's remark that if Ron had actually crawled into bed with her, he wouldn't bet a damn dime on just who in the hell had ended up on top. The money would be easy to cover, but the...?

Bill frowned. Jake hadn't used the work 'rape,' but how had he said it? The words slipped out limply. "Played house?"

"*I said played house.*" Jake leaned even farther over his desk, stabbing a finger toward Bill with each blurted word. "And I don't mean the son of a bitch put on a fucking apron and took the goddamn throw rugs out on the side porch to shake 'em, either."

It scared Bill for Jake to fly into a tantrum. The man's temples throbbed and his eyes held you like two laser beams. Bill couldn't recall hearing that Jake had ever went beyond waving his arms and shouting, but that was more than enough as far as he was concerned. He hadn't the slightest inkling now of which way to turn, or even if he should, when Jake settled back and began to smile.

Jake's furor quickly dissolved when he realized he might have gone too far, that the man could possibly be reaching the limits of whatever it was that sustained him. Bill wouldn't be the first one to crumble, but it wouldn't serve any purpose to alienate the poor bastard. He was Hirams' butt boy, true, but he was still the Contracting Officer. And besides, Jake conceded, you can cultivate a toady much better with sugar than you ever could with horseshit.

He tilted his head and spoke in his best fatherly manner. "Bill, it's the principle of the goddamn thing. It isn't the fucking money. I keep more than that in petty cash, for Christ's sake. And there's nothing wrong with fun and games, a little horizontal refreshment once in a while, but I can't have this self-righteous son of a bitch sticking his fucking nose where it doesn't belong, dictating how I'm to run my own goddamn business."

Bill Warden began to loosen up, started to breathe again as Jake glossed over the charges, particularly the rape, but tensed again when he realized Jake was treating that part of it so casually. The thought of Ron, his own damn subordinate, crawling into bed with Alice Marshallton had been festering in the back of his mind since that morning he read his copy of the letter. And now, with Jake being so unconcrned, he didn't know *what* to think.

"But you said he raped your wife?"

Jake's harsh demeanor turned into a playful grin. "Did I say that?"

"It was in your letter."

"No." Jake began to shake his head slowly at the man's gullibility. "That letter was prepared by Walter Hardesty, my attorney. He would never use the word in a letter of charges." Jake's voice became low, confiding. "Walt will tell you that rape is merely an opinion. An opinion that is never expressed until after the fact, hardly ever mentioned before the overall performance has been evaluated and found to be lacking in some way."

Jake chuckled inwardly at the poor son of a bitch's utter confusion. "What difference is there between rape and seduction anyway, Bill?" Jake settled back with delight as he watched the man, aware that the simple bastard didn't have a clue. His eyebrows lifted facetiously as he spoke. "Just a little salesmanship."

Bill's brow wrinkled, oblivious to Jake's banter as he tried to recall what the letter *did* say. How it was worded exactly? He remembered it said Jake felt he really had no alternative but to agree to the ten thousand dollars, but then, when Bill got to the part about Ron mounting Alice Marshallton's body, the very woman who gave him the slobbering hots, his mind had virtually exploded.

With Bill's features twisting so harshly, Jake began to fear he was losing him, and that would never do. Not now. He needed the simple son of a bitch to plant more credence in the craven minds of those cocksuckers in St. Louis.

Jake leaned forward on the desk again, speaking in a consoling manner. "Rape is a woman's word, Bill. A word they use when the fever of the tussle didn't quite lift them to the pinnacle of their fantasy. It could mean the poor son of a bitch failed to go deep enough to touch her passing gear, or something as trivial as the inconsiderate bastard not kissing her while she dropped her rocks. Most of the time, though, it only means she didn't get paid."

The longer Jake talked, the tighter Bill's features grew. Jake's rationale was only managing to convince Bill that the mere presence of the accusation meant there really had been something to base it on. Told him that goddamn Ron had *done* it. Had fucked Alice Marshallton bigger than shit.

Jake gloated quietly. He could just imagine what was going through the man's horny little mind. The versions he had heard of Bill's escapades never included any dalliance, any tenderness or terms of endearment. From what he had been told, every piece of ass the man ever had could be considered rape. He couldn't help but chuckle at the way Helen shook her head that day when she said the poor son of a bitch probably thought foreplay had something to do with golf.

And it was all falling so nicely into place. The afternoon he and Walt worked up the charges, and decided to go a step farther and accuse Ron Hamilton of forcing himself on Alice, they were sure both Hiram and Bill would buy the story. Hiram was seeing Alice regularly, and Bill wanted to so bad his eyes watered every time he thought about it.

"Bill." Jake's voice was still soft, almost sympathetic. "We've got a good operation going here in our Region. Before you brought that self-righteous bastard into your office we were just one big happy family. We concentrated on hauling the mail, not a lot of bullshit paperwork that's going to cost a hell of a lot more than the few pennies you think you're going to save." He waited for a nod, then grew stern again. "We work hard, Bill, and we play hard. We can't let a goddamn Shadrach come in here and start fucking things up."

Bill Warden began to stir, blinking as he nodded.

It was all so confusing. Jake could be so erratic. Ranting and raving over the least little thing, like filling out a few simple fuel forms. And then, well, today. Making light of ten thousand dollars. Said he kept more than that in one... No, not a pocket, but it made you think of pocket change, of having that much money on hand. And Mrs. Marshallton's involvement in this thing had never really been an item with Bill. He had always felt that a woman who bed-hopped was fair game.

Jake began to relax as Bill loosened up and started shifting around in his chair. These little Caesars were all alike. Come in here tilting at windmills, then fade and fall back when the goddamn blades start to turn. It didn't take much to remind the pricks just who the hell was in charge.

And Jake Marshallton doted on watching Bill Warden's last shred of propriety dissolve into a leer when he added the kicker.

"We let somebody like that come in here, Bill, and start throwing his goddamn wieght around, start setting examples, why you would only have occasion to see Helen once a year, at the State Convention in Jeff City." Jake paused with a smirk. Timing was everything when you stroked a dickhead. "I'd hate to have to be the one to tell her that. She's rather fond of you."

Bill's face lit up as his thoughts swung back to Helen, and the last weekend party at the Lodge. She was such a tease, the way she slapped at his hands, as if she really meant it. He smiled as he stood, boldly thrusting out his chest. "She's a nice young lady, and I would miss seeing her, too."

Jake pushed his chair back and stepped around the desk, the trouser cuff still caught on the top of the gaudy boot. "I'll tell her you said hello, and that you're looking forward to our next little get-together."

"Okay." Bill beamed at the invitation, as indirect as it was, and the man's jovialness. Jake wasn't really as bad as a lot of people would like for you to believe. "And tell her," he spoke with more confidence now, "to give me a call if she ever gets up to St. Louis. I know some really good lunch places."

The remark sent a quick chuckle through Jake. With some of these guys it was damn near boring, the way they kept their minds tucked in between their goddamn testicles. "I'll do that Bill. I'm sure she'll be tickled." He could just imagine Helen's reaction as he walked Bill across the office.

Jake stopped at the door and pulled a money clip from his trouser pocket. "I realize there are certain procedures you and Hiram are obligated to follow, that you have to stand behind your employees. I can respect that."

He looked down, moving his fingertips across the ends of the folded bills while he talked. "Somebody said Hiram was in the process of appointing legal counsel to represent Hamilton."

"Yes." Bill was relieved that Jake didn't appear to be offended. "He put Herschel Birdwell on it."

"Who?" Jake glanced up innocently, his thumb and forefinger clamped on the end of a bill in the center of the fold.

"Herschel Birdwell." Bill frowned at the question. He was almost certain Jake knew who Herschel was. "He's the Assistant Legal Counsel assigned to Transportation."

"Oh, yeah." Jake nodded as he pulled a bill from the wad and returned the clip to his pocket. "The little guy. I've seen him around."

Bill just stood there, mesmerized by the sight of the hundred dollar bill. "I believe Herschel is meeting with Ron this afternoon."

Jake doubled the bill over and creased it, then doubled it over again. "I'm just sorry you had to waste your Saturday on this." He reached out and slid the folded greenback into the breast pocket of Bill's coat, then tapped the pocket with the back of his fingers. "The least I can do is spring for lunch on your way home."

"Why thank you, Jake." Bill pulled his chin in severely to look down at his breast pocket. He could have said it wasn't necessary, that he reimbursed himself for things like that out of the office impress fund, but Jake didn't need to know that. "Thanks a lot."

"My pleasure." Jake flipped his hand to wave it away. "Tell Hiram I appreciate the way he's moving on this thing. We need to put it behind us and get on with our business."

"I'll do that Jake, and you have a nice weekend." Bill stopped at the door and raised his hand, then stepped outside. His fingers tingled at the thought of reaching into his pocket for the bill, but he would wait until he got in the car. He didn't want Jake to get the wrong impression.

Jake stepped back to his desk, out of line with the window, breathing noisily through his nose as he watched Bill Warden walk across the driveway to his car. If he ever had reason to believe he had a two-faced cocksucker like that working for him he would mark some office money and have it slipped to the simple prick, then put the cheap son of a bitch out on the street so goddamn fast it would make his fucking head swim.

CHAPTER FOUR

Herschel had kept Ron in the corner of his eye when he mentioned Mrs. Marshallton, watching for a show of emotion, any indication of discomfort as he moved them into the more scandalous side of the charges.

The old chair groaned as Herschel waited, still holding the ballpoint in position. If the boy had some touchy spots in this area he needed to know what they were. Walter Hardesty would damn sure use the slightest reluctance to talk about that part of it, any hesitation or sign of bashfulness, to make Ron look guilty as hell to that judge.

Ron grew serious at the mention of the contractor's wife. With the way Herschel had phrased the question concerning Mrs. Marshallton, as if he might be part of the rumors circulating about her, but they were merely that as far as Ron was concerned. Just office gossip. There was nothing in the stories that he knew to be the truth, but he was beginning to realize he needed to concentrate on what he *did* know about the woman, which wasn't very much. He shook his head as he looked up. "I've never met the woman, Herschel."

The innocence of the remark caused Herschel to slump over the desk, his head hanging dejectedly for a moment before his returning anger began to draw him up. "What the hell's that supposed to mean?"

Ron frowned at Herschel's surliness. What else *could* it mean? Judy didn't have any trouble understanding it when he told her he had never met the woman.

When Ron continued to stare, Herschel realized he was pushing, getting much too edgy. "Do you mean you've never been formally introduced to the woman or you've never even seen her?"

"I mean I've never seen the woman," his words were stern. The way Herschel insisted on a literal interpretation of everything was becoming a bit tiring, but if that's what it was going to take he would have to go along with it. He would make his answers as clear as he could. His remark to Judy this morning crossed his mind. "I wouldn't know her if I saw her in the middle of the street."

Ron's growing pluckiness pleased Herschel. Now they were getting somewhere. He grinned impishly down at his pad as he began to write. "Or spread-eagled on a bed?"

Ron's face flushed, the veins in his neck becoming engorged. There was nothing humorous about his predicament. "I told you it's all a bunch of lies, and I don't appreciate your insinuations. I haven't done anything wrong."

Herschel's ballpoint plopped onto the yellow pad, the old chair giving a tortured squeak as he swiveled around. The time for pussyfooting, for tiptoeing around the charges, especially the more sensitive side of it was long past.

"If you'll take the goddamn chip off your shoulder and bear with me for a minute, just one fucking minute, I'll try to explain where we stand." Herschel cocked his head impatiently. "Okay?"

Ron's mouth dropped open at the reprimand. The man had a lot of gall, trying to be so flippant about something that wasn't a joking matter, then flaring up when he was called on it.

Herschel placed his arm along the edge of the desk and let his hand dangle, his eyes still intense even though his inner wrath was starting to subside. They *were* making progress.

He blinked rapidly, gathering his thoughts. "As far as I've been able to determine, you're a nice young man. Highly regarded by just about everyone I talked to, but *naï*-eve as hell about the more salacious side of life."

He stifled a smile at Ron's attempt to glower. "You married your childhood sweetheart, and people tell me you're in the process of living happily everafter." Herschel paused for Ron to grasp what he had said, to understand where they were headed.

"You've got her picture on your desk and go straight home from work. You two probably still eat supper by candlelight, and I wouldn't be surprised that you help her with the dishes, then either take her to a movie or snuggle up on the couch to watch television."

Herschel's brow wrinkled as he looked away. He wasn't sure if he was still talking about Ron's life, or describing what *he* had always thought a marriage should be.

During the long years of working his way through law school he had thought about marrying someday, but when he had finally graduated and passed the bar, the burden of the debts he had acquired kept him from reaching out for a woman's hand. He had always felt the first step in courting a woman was to hold her hand, and now, with the goddamn libbers, taking a woman's hand without shaking it was considered harrassment. He was glad, though, as he turned back to Ron. Glad there were still a few around who felt the same way he did about marriage.

Herschel nodded his admiration. "In your private world sex is part of the love process, something that goes with marriage. And fidelity is more than just a damn word you see somewhere on the back of a sound system."

Ron's displeasure was beginning to ease, but his frown still held. He didn't care for the way Herschel was delving into his personal life, particularly the way he had started including Judy. It was one thing to ridicule him, but he would not allow anyone to talk about his wife, or his marriage. "What's wrong with that?"

"Nothing, Ron." Herschel hesitated. The look on Ron's face made him realize he might be treading dangerously close to the edge of matrimonial intimacy. A man's home and family was his own private domain. He knew his would be if he ever found a woman who would have him.

"Not a damn thing." Herschel's head began to shake. "What's wrong is that you're being sullied, being snatched from your warm place in Eden by some sleazeballs and slung into the degeneracy of the business world, and you're going to have to defend yourself."

The last two words frightened Ron, drawing his brow even tighter. "I thought that was your job?"

"No." Herschel's head continued to shake. "I'm merely handling your defense. That is to say, question their witnesses, keep the illustrious Mr. Hardesty in line, make sure he adheres to the principles he no longer has or probably even remembers. You're going to have to face these people alone. When you're up there on the stand you'll be on your own. You're the only witness we have on your behalf, and it's my responsibility to have you ready."

Ron drew back, a long sigh escaping. Herschel's explanation made him feel as though he had shrunk, and was sitting in a huge witness chair. He feet weren't even touching the floor, and he was cowering under the scathing stare of an enormous man in a black robe and white powdered wig. Ron was waiting for those glaring eyes to blink when he realized Herschel was still talking.

"I don't believe you have the slightest idea of what's going to happen when Walter Hardesty gets you on the witness stand, up there in front of the judge and a live audience." Herschel hesitated but Ron didn't look up. "You'll be on *his* turf, the main attraction in the man's own private circus, and believe me, that sonofabitch is a master. He'll be on your ass like a pair of wet shorts."

Ron picked at his fingernails, his voice barely above a whisper. "I'll just tell them the truth."

"Aw, bullshit, Ron." Herschel scowled, falling back in his chair as his voice rose. "The only time you ever hear truth mentioned in a goddamn courtroom anymore is when the clerk swears you in."

Ron looked up with a frown. "I hope you're not trying to tell me I'm going to have to be deceitful, going to be expected to lie."

Herschel grabbed the corner of the desk angrily, his voice more piercing than the squeals from the old swivel chair. "Have I ever given you that impression, ever told you to lie?"

Ron stared in awe of Herschel's outburst for a moment before he remembered the question and started shaking his head.

"Have I ever told you *anything* to say?" Herschel glared as he continued to breathe heavily, a few strands of graying tousled hair moving in tempo with the throbbing vein at his temple.

Ron finally broke eye contact, still shaking his head as he slumped back, looking down at his hands.

"You can bet your ass I haven't, and don't, by God, forget it." Herschel released his hold on the desk and duck-walked his chair back a couple of steps. "That's part of *Mister* Hardesty's repertoire." His chin rose and waggled with each syllable of the word, giving it a certain arrogance.

Ron looked up warily, raising a hand to place his fingertips on his chest. "He's going to try to make me lie? Surely the man doesn't believe I'm that gullible."

Herschel raised his chin, as if to rise above the misunderstanding, and started moving his head from side to side. "No, no. I mean make you react in such a way that the judge will believe you are being less than truthful. That judge is going to be swayed a hell of a lot more by your reactions than he ever will by anything you say."

Herschel paused for some kind of response, but Ron just stared.

"Walter Hardesty knows better than to attempt to influence an official of the court, play with the mind of a judge, so he's going to have you do it for him."

Ron began to blink, his brow drawing even tighter at the remark. "I'm not sure I understand."

"Think back a minute." Herschel slid his elbow along the desk again, leaning closer. "Every time I mention money or pussy you start to swell up. Take the red-ass. If that sanctimonious sonofabitch had you on the stand right now he'd play you like a country fiddle."

Ron's face flushed as he looked down again. He was sure he could discuss money in a courtroomt without getting flustered, but he wasn't too sure he could openly talk about sex with Mr. Hardesty in front of a lot of people, especially if Mrs. Marshallton was going to be sitting there looking at him.

"You've got to understand what's going on, realize what they're planning to do." Herschel's tone grew softer. "They've stated their case in writing, and the judge will have familiarized himself with that. Walter Hardesty is sure to call Jake and his wife to the stand, and God only knows who else, to give credence to their accusations. He'll present his case step by step, like a goddamn theater production, mainly to justify his retainer to Jake, but he'll know the judge is concerned only with the allegations in their letter. It will be up to that goddamn Hardesty to substantiate the charges, so he will use you to give the judge reason to believe you are being less than truthful when you say you never went to the house, never picked up the money or stuck a dick in that woman."

He hesitated but Ron didn't look up. "That's why we have to get ready to cover your ass all the way from the bank to the bedroom."

Ron sighed at the gravity of his predicament, and began to nod . He was in the big chair again, and the domineering judge still hadn't blinked.

"To begin with, Ron, there isn't a dime's worth of difference between a flush of anger and a blush of embarrassment. And from where that judge will be sitting he won't be able to tell the difference, anyway. You're going to have to condition yourself to face Walter Hardesty, to sit there and not get excited about anything the man might bring up." Herschel tilted his head quizzically. "You see what I'm saying? Understand what I'm talking about?"

"I think I do." Ron remembered their last hearing, the one where the attorney from Kansas City tried to claim the contractor was entitled to the same hourly rate the Dept. of Labor Wage Determination in the contract specified for drivers. It gave Ron a good feeling to recall how the lawyer scowled when he stood to explain that the Wage Determination was written for hired drivers, and that the contractor had set his own wage rate at the time he prepared his bid.

Ron's hesitation, and his complacent smirk worried Herschel. The boy's knowledge of transportation contracts was phenomenal, and he had testified very well at the other hearings, but this had nothing to do with contracts, per se. There would be no ground rules this time.

Herschel looked away, scratching thoughtfully at the back of his head. "I'm not too goddamned sure." He was well aware that Walter Hardesty was not your *run of the mill* legal whore. Ned Ashcroft had referred to the man as a prostituting attorney, but then, Ned was the only person he knew who could vilify somebody without being vile about it.

Ron drew himself up. "What is there to understand about answering a few tricky questions?" He had done okay the times he testified at other hearings. "I'll just take my time and think before I answer."

Herschel leaned back in the noisy chair. What was the story Sam Whitley used to tell, about one of the ancient philosophers who could stand out in the street all day and recite from the book of knowledge, but if it started raining you'd better send a lesser mortal to go out there and bring him in, other wise the poor bastard might drown. Sam insisted that arrogance was a person's worst enemy.

"Ron." Herschel turned and looked at him. "They tell me you can make that...," he flipped his hand helplessly in the absence of a name, "that computer you all use, you can make it produce a transportation system for a given area that's just short of genius. You've even used it to identify the major points of wind drag on a semi, and produced a fifteen percent savings on fuel usage."

"Yes. I have." The sudden change in direction brought a frown. He was worried about Herschel's ability anyway, and all this jumping around certainly didn't help. "But what's that got to do with this?"

Herschel began shaking his head, his eyes still on Ron. "It never ceases to amaze me that a man can program a computer to do anything from measuring the goddamn solar system to counting the hairs on a mosquito's twat, but the poor sonofabitch can't train his own mind worth a shit. Doesn't use his head for much more than just creature comforts."

Herschel's small, dark eyes were becoming sullen under his shaggy brows as he continued to move his head from side to side. "It gripes my ass that man is born with a glob in his head no bigger than that," he raised his clenched fist and turned it as though talking to it, "a brain that shames the most sophisticated computer, yet the poor bastard just lets the damn thing vegetate because it didn't come with a set of instructions."

Ron's apprehension continued to grow. Herschel was still drifting away from the subject. "I'm not sure I'm following you."

"That's what I just said, but let me see if I can throw a little light on it." Herschel turned back to his desk and began to scratch at the crown of his head.

Ron sat rigidly, waiting, almost afraid to breathe. He had never seen Herschel get so involved before.

Herschel finally looked up and turned to Ron, letting his hand drop to the desk and leave his sparse hair even more disheveled. The boy had no idea, had not the faintest clue.

"When Walter Hardesty gets you on the stand, up there in the spotlight, you're going to think he's Clarence Darrow, Count Dracula and Pope John the twenty-fucking-third, all rolled into one. The man is going to come at you like a truck load of frenzied turkey gobblers."

Herschel's eyes narrowed when Ron flinched, and his tone grew more exacting. "You're going to have to program yourself to face a professional bully. To sit there composed and ignore all the bluster, the pompous bullshit, contrived innuendoes, and keep your wits about you."

The chilling heaviness settled in Ron's stomach again, like it did when he had finally realized the charges were real. That he was actually being brought into court. "You have any suggestions?"

"Yes." Herschel nodded, now that he felt he had the boy's attention. "The first thing you're going to have to do is pull yourself up out of your snug little world and quit feeling sorry for yourself. You're in trouble, Ron. *Big* goddamn trouble."

"I'm not feeling sorry for myself." Ron drew in a breath, resentful of the attempt to blame him for such a travesty, for a farce the legal profession apparently sanctioned because they were acknowledging it, they had provisions for handling it.

"I told you I'm scared. It scares me to death to think a person can be accused of something like this and brought into court."

"Damn right you're scared." Herschel nodded. "Anybody would be."

He didn't want to overdo it, now that they were facing in the right direction, now that the boy had the proper perspective. He just wanted Ron frightened to the point of paying attention, not terrified.

"What do I have to do?"

Herschel turned and placed his elbow on the edge of the desk. "You have to stay just like you are right now, Ron. Scared enough to remember what's going on, and scared enough to stay alert. When Walter Hardesty approaches you in all his professional fervor, in all his brilliance, he'll be prepared to literally destroy a scrupulous young married man."

Ron cringed back into his chair at Herschel's words and the menacing tone of his voice.

"Oh, yeah." Herschel's eyes grew wide as he began to nod. "That sonofabitch will know more about you than you ever knew about yourself. He'll make a point of knowing how to flatter you, how to piss you off, how to embarrass the shit out of you, and all at the precise moment he needs to sway the judge one way or the other."

Herschel drew in a breath and leaned forward, anxiously raising a forefinger and his eyebrows.

"*But*, if you stay in control of yourself and let the bastard see that you truly are, let him see that you're an honorable man, a conscientious employee and faithful husband, even though you *are* scared shitless, you might establish some sort of an edge."

Ron nodded, the plausibility of Herschel's strategy causing a faint smile, which brought Herschel's finger even higher.

"And don't even think about getting any cute ideas of matching wits with the man. The sonofabitch is way out of your class. Just confine your answers to yes or no, and don't volunteer a goddamn thing. You're not after his ass, but you do need to stay alert to the fact that he *is* after yours."

Ron gave a sigh of disgust. He was learning that transportation contracting was a lot more involved than he could ever have imagined. He wouldn't forget this mess if he lived to be a hundred.

Herschel leaned closer again, tilting his head grimly. "You can't lower your guard for a goddamn second or the unethical bastard will nail your ass. The prick will crucify you."

The air in the small office was becoming heavy, hard to breathe.

"You can't trust the man, Ron." Herschel's voice suddenly grew softer, almost intimate. "When Walter Hardesty smiles at someone he's questioning, especially someone he's got on cross, it has nothing to do with compassion. It's merely the man's colossal ego spilling over."

Ron blinked as he drew in a labored breath. All these warnings about Mr. Hardesty were making the word *unethical* as frightening to him as the word *maimed* had always been. They both sounded so cruel.

"Forget the polite, civilized world you live in." Herschel ran his hand through his hair again, ignoring the groan of the swivel chair as he leaned back. "Step down into the infernal realm of jurisprudence, the cesspool of deliverance. Forget that shit about turning the other cheek."

Ron glanced up, blanching at the gruesome description of the legal system. He already had the sinking feeling of being pulled into some kind of quagmire, but he had only thought of it as quicksand.

Herschel continued to loll back, satisfied with the effect of his words. "I wouldn't think you'd need anything other than the fact he's a ruthless sonofabitch, a first class prick who's trying to hoist your ass up to the world as an example." He pitched forward, raising his finger again. "Not an example of how bad you are. You know you haven't done anything. He's using you merely to demonstrate the resplendence of the mighty Walter Horatio Hardesty."

Herschel dropped his hand back to his lap, his inquiring eyes still on Ron. "Doesn't that piss you off? I know it would me. I'm afraid I'd have a little trouble even being civil to the sonofabitch."

Ron sighed as he looked down at his hands. He hadn't been brought up to be rude, not to *anybody*. He felt sure he could explain anything they wanted to know, yet the whole thing was so awkward. If he just knew what this was all about, why he was being so wantonly accused and brought into court.

"Work on it, Ron. You'll be surprised how easy it is to despise the man.

Why, with a little effort you might even learn to loathe him. That's when you'll be able to handle yourself on the witness stand."

"I don't hate Mr. Hardesty, Herschel." Ron's voice was calm. He was beginning to realize it wouldn't do any good to shout, though he already had a couple of times. "I don't even know the man, but I am shocked that an attorney, a member of the legal profession, would stoop to something like this."

"I know, Ron." Herschel nodded. It did him good to know there were still decent people in the world. Maybe someday the honest ones, the Rons and Judys would prevail, would manage to tip the world far enough to their side to jettison the Walter Hardestys and

Jake Marshalltons. It was a good thought, despite the fact it would put a lot of honest lawyers out of work.

"If you can't hate the man, then throw a little effort toward hating what he's trying to do. Trying to do to you and your wife. Think about *her*." The idea of having a wife still stirred Herschel. The thought of having someone to come home to, someone to care for, who cared for him. The idea comforted him while he waited for Ron to nod. "He's trying to screw up your *happily everafter.*"

"I realize that, Herschel." Ron nodded solemnly. "I think I understand it a little better now. You don't have to worry. I'll be able to answer Mr. Hardesty's questions when the time comes."

Herschel swung around to the desk again. "Well, don't let your heart bleed too much for that bastard. He's sure as hell not going to lose any sleep over you, but I think you have some idea now of where we're headed." His features softened as he picked up his ballpoint. "There's no limit to what a person can do when they get their head on straight and know where they're going."

He scooted up to the desk and reached for the yellow pad. "Now, let's see." He looked the page up and down for a moment before he clicked the pen and started writing. "You're sure you don't know Alice Marshallton."

"Is that her name? Alice?"

"Yeah." Herschel nodded without looking up. "I've got Ned's investigator working up some background on her. Her and Jake both. We'll talk some more when I get that." He stopped writing and turned. "But you wouldn't recognize Jake's wife if you saw her?"

"No." Ron began to shake his head blankly.

A mischievous grin blossomed as Herschel turned and started writing. "From either end?"

"No." Ron frowned in spite of his best efforts. It bothered him to think about being questioned like this in front of a judge, and whoever else might be in the courtroom, but he would just have to tolerate it. He supposed he could respond to their gutter talk in a civil manner. "I wouldn't recognize her from either end."

Herschel folded the page over and continued writing without looking up. "And you said you don't do any sportfucking?"

"No, Herschel." He shook his head with the calm denial, then took in a breath, as if to draw himself above it all. "I told you I don't"

The tediousness in Ron's words caused Herschel to stop and glance over. "Now don't get disgusted. You're doing just fine, but I have to be sure about these things. Have to be sure that you're above reproach."

Herschel waited but Ron just stared, as though he had steeled himself against the offensive questions.

"If I'm going to present you to that judge as the original Mr. Clean, I've got to make damn sure they're not going to bring in some squeegee you've been stroking and poking. You see where I'm coming from?"

"Yes." Ron nodded. He kept forgetting Herschel didn't really know him all that well, had no other way of being sure he hadn't been fooling around. "I understand what you're doing, and I appreciate it."

"Just bear with me and we'll get through this okay." Herschel turned back to his legal pad. "You know yourself that transportation people spend a lot of time on the road, and there *have* been those who found themselves in a bit of a sweat over the partaking of horizontal gratuities."

"Yes, I'm aware of that." Ron had always thought the stories of chance encounters and clandestine meetings were merely the product of someone' boastful imagination, but he guessed he really knew a certain portion of them, at least, must have had some sort of basis. "I know what you're talking about."

"Then you understand what we're up against." Herschel turned. "You realize I've got to know everything. Every little incident, regardless of how innocent it might seem." He used his ballpoint like a baton. "Walter Hardesty can build a goddamn mountain out of nothing more than a turd in a fucking mole hill."

Ron cringed at the sudden chilliness. The impact of the words had caused that awkward incident to zoom up out of his subconscious like a bad dream. He had never mentioned it to anyone, not even Judy.

A stifling heat rose out of his shirt collar, causing him to turn his head from side to side. The memory of it had haunted him even though he was sure no one saw them that night, and he would just as soon forget the whole thing, but now he had no choice. It would be better for Herschel to hear it from him.

He looked down, tightly gripping the sides of his chair for a moment before he took a breath and raised his eyes to Herschel. "There *was* a woman at the Holiday Inn in Cape Girardeau."

CHAPTER FIVE

Ron's sudden admission, in such a plaintive tone, caused Hershcel to wilt forward over the desk. He held his head between his hands, letting his ballpoint plop onto the yellow pad. Sonofa *Bitch.* They hadn't even taken the white suit out of the cleaning bag, and the goddamn thing already had pecker tracks on it. It would appear that defense attorneys dwelled in a world of ulcers and assholes.

Herschel shifted slowly onto one elbow and turned, scratching irritably at the back of his head. Sudden about faces pissed him off. Made him want to puke. "I thought you said you didn't fuck around?"

"I don't, Herschel." Ron shook his head. It wasn't supposed to have sounded like a confession, like it had been a.., a clandestine meeting. He wasn't sure he even knew how to pronounce the word.

"Oh." Herschel drew back, his eyebrows arching in a pretense of innocence. A him, a her and a motel. Just who in the orgiastic hell did the boy think he was trying to shit? "You mean now we're going to have to convince the judge you met this skirt at the Holiday Inn for a game of tiddlywinks?" His eyebrows lifted even further with contempt.

Ron's head continued to shake as he looked down at his hands. "It wasn't like that." Why did everybody always jump to the same conclusion? Most of the travel stories going around the office had probably been built on nothing more than something like this. Well, he would have to make sure they *un*built this one.

"Then what *was* it like, pray tell?" Herschel gave the words a snippish tone as he turned to his desk, reaching for the pen. He loathed deceptiveness.

Ron drew in a breath at the censuring words. He could see now what Herschel meant by not being able to tell the difference between embarrassment and anger. It wasn't clear, even to himself, which it was he felt right now, but he was beginning to understand how easy it would be to rile him over this. And no one was going to believe him anyway, so he might just as well detach himself from the whole thing and not allow Herschel to goad him. Or Mr. Hardesty either, when the time came.

When Ron continued to blink, studying the floor, Herschel began to relent. The boy was already carrying a big enough burden. He didn't need an extra ration of sarcasm to go with it, but this could sabotage their entire case. "When was this.., this encounter, tryst, whatever you call it?"

Ron looked up, his mind stymied by a veil of fog. He had dismissed the incident when he decided to not tell Judy. There had really been no point in bothering her with it, and now just about everything had faded into the distance except the image of the woman. "I don't remember, Herschel. It was back in the spring. March or April."

"You'll have to get a lot closer than that, Ron. I'll need a date, a day." Herschel sighed. From the sound of this, he couldn't be sure there wouldn't be another secluded rendezvous or two dredged up from somewhere before they were through, and he would need to keep them in some kind of order.

The statement caused Ron's head to shake as he looked down. He always stayed at the Holiday Inn when he went to Cape Girardeau, but he couldn't place this particular time. "I'm sorry. I just can't seem to think."

Herschel nodded. The mind *will* rebel at self-incrimination. Once a person has managed to explain something away they will consider themselves exonerated, even if it still keeps them awake at night. There were even things in his life he would just as soon forget, and hadn't, but he would still need to know when this innocuous little orgy took place. "Can you figure it out from your travel vouchers?"

"Probably." Ron nodded as he glanced up. He wanted to think it was the last week in March, but he could go through the vouches and make sure. "I'll get the day and date for you."

"Okay." Herschel reached over and scribbled a couple of words, then turned back. "You want to tell me about it?"

Ron blushed as his pulse quickened at the thought of that night in the deserted bar. The woman had been several years older than him, and quite attractive. He liked to believe it was honor that restrained him, but he hadn't hesitated to admit there had been some fear. Fear of not being man enough to handle such a superb woman. He had never entertained the thought of being unfaithful to Judy, but he still hadn't been able to get the woman out of his mind. "There really isn't much to tell."

"I'll be the judge of that." Herschel's voice was gruff as he pulled the yellow pad into position.

He recalled Ned Ashcroft saying that men were always so casual about things like that *after* the fact. And Herschel had agreed. Most men do tend to ignore how the surge of an erection drains all the blood away from their brain, flushing any common sense they might ever professed to have right into the head of their dick.

"You just tell me what happened." Herschel nodded sternly. "That's all Walter Hardesty would need to contaminate you, to sully the shit out of you in the eyes of that judge. Bring in some fucking floozy you songed and pronged in a goddamn motel."

Ron frowned. It was irritating for Herschel to not believe him, to insist on making it sound as if he had smuggled the woman into his room, but he needed to stay calm and make sure Herschel knew he didn't. "It was in the bar."

Herschel scowled suddenly, the veins in his neck bulging as he lashed out. "I don't give a big rat's ass if it was in the bar, the restaurant, or out in the fucking driveway. In a courtroom the word *motel* is synonymous with unauthorized ass. Now *tell* me about it, goddamnit."

Ron drew back. That was exactly what he was talking about, blind assumption. He would have to make sure everyone understood the situation perfectly. Make sure the judge, at least, knew the whole thing had happened innocently enough in the lounge.

He sighed as he studied the ceiling. This was going to be the same as the other hearings. It would be up to him to keep the details straight, and trust Herschel to tend to the letter of the law, if there was one for something like this.

Ron placed his elbow on the edge of the desk and drew in a breath. "I went down there to conduct some seminars for contractors."

"Cape Girardeau?" Herschel stopped writing.

"Yes." Ron nodded. He was sure he had already said it happened in Cape Girardeau. "I had finished for the day and went to the bar. I like a bottle of beer sometimes at the end of the day. It relaxes me."

"This was at night?" Herschel wasn't sure he knew what constituted a *day* for transportation people in a travel status, with mail trucks operating around the clock. He waited, the ballpoint still poised over the pad.

"Yes." Ron thought about it as he watched Herschel write. After supper he had finished his paperwork and arranged things for the seminar in Sikeston the next day. He had gone over it again, made a few last minute notes, then decided to visit the lounge before he went to bed. "I'd say eight-thirty or nine."

Herschel just nodded and kept writing. "Go on."

"Well, I was sitting at the bar." From his memory of the woman, herself, the rest of it was coming back now. "There wasn't anybody there but me and the bartender, and he was down at the other end washing glasses." Ron hesitated at the thought of the way the woman stepped through the door. Nonchalant, not as though she was lost, or looking for anybody. There had been a physical radiance about her, a sort of seductiveness. "I hadn't been there long when she came in."

"Alone?" Herschel still hadn't looked up.

"Yes, she was alone." Ron had watched her in the large mirror behind the bar as she crossed from the door, then kept her in his peripheral vision when she turned toward him, walking along the edge of the small parqueted dance floor. With the way she moved, and the short split in the front of her skirt giving a flash of thigh with each step, it was difficult to keep from turning and openly admiring her. "She stopped at the stool beside me."

Herschel's shoulders lifted impatiently. If the boy wasn't any better at seducing a woman than he was at getting to the point of a story, then the charges, the dipsticking part at least, *was* a lot of bullshit.

Ron looked down. He had been embarrassed by the woman's attention, and tried not to show it, but he wasn't too sure he had managed to pull it off. Not with the way she had smiled at him. "She asked if anyone was sitting there?"

The words piqued Herschel's tolerance, causing a scowl. Nothing had apparently changed in the game of grab ass in a hundred years. "Was there something to make her think there *was?* On the bar, or the stool?"

"No." Ron was beginning to understand now why Herschel had been so explicit with the word *naive*.

"And you say the place was empty?" Herschel turned back to his pad and began to scribble.

"Yes." Ron just sat there. It was beginning to sound a little too obvious. He hadn't really thought of it that way at the time, though. "She asked if I minded if she sat there."

"And you helped her up on the stool?" Herschel couldn't help but chuckle to himself at Sam Whitley's little joke. The old man brought it up anytime a discussion or one of his lectures so much as even hinted at the subject of chivalry. Sam would raise a finger and tilt his head. "And remember. In this day and age, when you see a man open a car door for a woman you can rest assured that it's either a new car or a new woman."

Ron drew back at the way Herschel seemed to gloat. He wasn't sure whether Herschel was smirking at him or the woman's question, but he wasn't going to let it bother him. "I just told her I didn't mind."

"What happened then?" Herschel folded the page over and slid the heel of his hand back and forth to flatten it.

Ron recalled his quandry over whether he should motion for the bartender. It could be taken as meaning to buy her a drink, but when he turned the man was already headed their way, so he had stayed out of it. "The bartender came over and she ordered a drink."

"Did you pay for it?" Herschel waited. Even the purest mind would interpret buying a woman a drink as the first step of intent.

"No." Ron had still not been sure of whether he should offer to buy when the woman discreetly placed a bill on the bar. "She paid for it herself."

Herschel began to write. It really didn't matter. The fact that Ron was cozy with some broad at a motel bar would be tarnish enough, especially if that sonofabitching Hardesty knew about it and put the woman on the stand. "Did the bartender act like he knew her?"

Ron couldn't recall that the bartender had even spoken to her. The man had merely nodded when she told him what she wanted. "He just fixed the drink, collected for it, then went back to what he was doing."

While Herschel continued to write, Ron's thoughts stayed on the woman. She had pulled the drink to her, swirled the ice cubes a couple of times with the swizzle stick, then withdrew it and placed it on the bar. She had been so friendly, smiled so easily. "After the bartender left she asked if I had had a busy day."

The remark stopped Herschel, bringing his eyes around. This was becoming much cozier than just two strangers passing in the night. "She acted like she knew you?"

Surprise illuminated Ron's face. He hadn't thought of it that way at the time, but yes, she actually had. The way she looked at him, and talked so readily. And she hadn't attended the seminar that day, yet she knew there had been one.

When Ron continued to stare, Herschel threw up his hands. She either did or she didn't, and he could give a shit less, but if the boy did know who the woman was he needed to know that, and her goddamn name. "Did she know you? Did she introduce herself?

"No." Ron shook his head, almost afraid to mention the hackneyed introduction that had become such a joke in the world of transportation contracting. And Herschel already had him in bed with her, anyway. "She just said we had a mutual friend."

"Did she say who the mutual friend was?" Herschel glared. There was a dozen different ways to go from *that* overture, and they all led right back to Pandora's box, or Pollyanna's, or who'th fuck-ever she was.

"No. And I didn't ask." Ron settled back in his chair. He was as tired of the trite introduction as everybody else. "I didn't want to know."

Herschel made a brief entry on the pad. "What happened then?" He had sort of hoped to find out who the mutual friend was, know who besides Jake was dabbling in the bush market.

"Nothing. We just talked." It annoyed Ron for Herschel, his own attorney, to keep inferring there might have been something between him and the woman. "I told you there wasn't anything to tell."

"What did you talk about?" Herschel wrote listlessly. This immaculate encounter had about as much chance of going unnoticed by Walter Hardesty and his people as a limber dick at a nudist wedding.

"Oh." Ron shrugged. She had been so easy to talk to. He hadn't realized how long they had sat there until he got back to his room. "We talked about the weather, the seminars, the fuel savings program. Stuff like that."

Astonishment brought Herschel upright. *Stuff like that* wasn't public information. He would have sworn Ron knew better. "Do you usually discuss contracting business with strangers?"

"She brought it up." Ron bristled. "I just said the seminars were going okay, and we were still working on the fuel savings. I didn't go into detail about anything, Herschel. I'm not a blabbermouth."

"I was going to say." Herschel leaned back. "You've never given me that impression, but I had to make sure."

Herschel's trusting tone had a calming effect on Ron, brought his mind back to the story. "When we had finished our drinks she said there was a little place, I believe she said it was on the highway south of town, that had live music and entertainment."

"And?" Herschel's face blanched. That was all he needed, for Walter Hardesty to have a witness place the boy in some fucking dive. A married man in one of those places, with a goddamn hooker on his arm, might just as well go ahead and dip his quill in the well of iniquity. His name would be engraved in the great book of transgressors anyway.

"I just told her I'd better not." Ron had considered explaining that even though his wife didn't always know where he was or what he was doing, she did know what he *wasn't* doing, but he didn't. He had learned that faithfulness was something you kept to yourself. When you start trying to explain it to people their minds have already moved on to something else.

The answer pleased Herschel. Pleased him that Ron hadn't tried to go into some big virtuous spiel. The boy was coming along okay. He would do just fine on the witness stand.

"What did she say to that?" Herschel waited. A woman could be a real bitch about something like that. The old saw about a woman scorned could even include a whore with the mutual friend's money already tucked away in her reticule. He chuckled quietly to himself at the word. It sounded like something that goddamn Hardesty would use, hoping some of the jurors might think he was referring to one of the woman's body openings.

Ron shook his head. "She didn't say anything. She didn't get mad, if that's what you mean." The woman had left a tip, then put the rest of the change in her purse and slid from the stool. Her friendliness hadn't changed. "She told me she had enjoyed talking, then said good night and left." Ron shrugged. Surely he wasn't the only man who had ever turned down a proposition, it that's what it was. "I went to my room."

"And you'd never seen her before?" Herschel smiled with admiration. Had the boy actually wandered into that notorious garden, sat under the apple tree with an ambitious strumpet, and walked out with his moral cherry still intact?

Ron shook his head. Herschel's smugness was inscrutable, almost as if he thought Ron was leading him on about the woman, and approved. "I don't remember ever seeing her before."

Herschel grew solemn. There was always a first time for everything, but right, wrong or somewhere in between, he would have to at least *try* to sell this dubious story to the judge if Walter Hardesty chose to go that route. He turned back to his desk.

"What did she look like?" Herschel felt he should have some idea of just what the hell to expect if that sonofabitching Hardesty should happen to know who the woman is, and puts her on the stand. That bastard had been known to make a silk purse out of a sow's ear, so there was no telling what the man might do when he had the whole pig.

"Well." Ron could still see her walking away from him, along the edge of the dance floor. "She was kind of attractive, for an older woman." He couldn't remember a split in the back of her skirt, but there didn't need to be. Her body curved in all the right places, and she walked as if she knew that.

When the image of the woman faded, Ron looked up. "She was in her mid, maybe late thirties."

Herschel leaned over the legal pad, writing intently. When had young people started considering thirty to be the end of the road? He couldn't remember. When he was growing up he had eagerly looked forward to reaching twenty-one, and when he got there he had been so busy establishing himself that he had never thought to look back.

Ron didn't wait for Herschel to finish writing, not with the vivid memory of the woman welling up out of his subconscious like a fountain. "I believe she was wearing a dark blue suit, you know, skirt and coat. I do remember her blouse was red. Bright red, with the collar out over the jacket."

"No split skirt or naughty neckline?" Herschel didn't stop writing. He realized today's strumpets had abandoned the mesh hose and jet skirts that barely covered the cockpit, but a business suit? He shrugged at a second thought. What the hell, it *is* considered a business, a *big* fucking business.

Ron frowned at the way Herschel had of making things sound vulgar. The split in her skirt hadn't been all that provocative, and her blouse was the usual button-up kind, certainly not what you would call revealing. In good conscience, though, he began to nod slightly at the memory. She could have maybe fastened it one button higher. "Her blouse *was* open some."

"Throw a little cleavage on you, did she?" Herschel glanced up impishly. He had never heard of a woman approaching a man, especially at a bar, without flashing something, even when she wasn't on the make.

"No." Ron grew solemn. "I didn't get that idea."

It hadn't occurred to Ron at first that the woman wasn't wearing a bra, but it wasn't as though she was flaunting herself. Several times, when she reached for her drink, he had gotten a glimpse of her breast, and the one time, when she picked the glass up and swirled the ice cubes around, he had watched the dark nipple jiggle against the satiny material of her blouse.

The thought caused him to smile. "She did have nice breasts, but I think her blouse was open like that more to show off the pendant she was wearing."

"What kind of pendant?" Herschel looked up. Even if they knew who she was there wouldn't be a chance in hell she'd be wearing the damn thing if they put her on the stand, but it was worth making a note of.

Ron became serious. He remembered the delicate gold chain, but he couldn't recall whether there was a cameo set in the top of the small locket, or if it was just filigreed engraving. He couldn't even be sure of the shape.

"I'm sorry, Herschel. I really don't remember." He shook his head. "It's been quite a while."

Herschel twiddled the ballpoint between his fingers while he watched Ron's inner turmoil. It was funny how the mind worked, registering what a person really considered to be the most important without them even being aware of it. "You remembered her tits."

A blush engulfed Ron. Yes, he admitted silently, he could still see the blouse, and the chain jiggling as he watched the erotic nipple, but he just couldn't place the pendant.

Herschel brushed some imaginary debris from the desk. "It's nothing to be ashamed of, Ron. There's nothing wrong with looking." Herschel's tone had lost its harshness. "That's why the Good Lord extended your eyesight out past the end of your arms. It's a natural reaction. Show's you're not frigid."

The last word brought a smile as Ron looked down. Maybe they should work on trying to convince the judge that he was. "Is it important for you to know what the pendant looked like?"

"No, not really." Herschel turned to his desk. Even if they did put the chippy on the stand it was a hundred to one shot she'd be wearing the fucking thing, anyhow. And it wouldn't serve enough purpose to make an issue of. "I was just checking your memory before we started working our way up to her face."

Ron nodded, his features beginning to soften. He hadn't really thought of the woman as pretty, but, to him, a face was only a part of a woman's physical attraction. A pleasant personality made a lot of difference. "I remember her face."

"Then you *did* look up." Herschel grinned at the calm answer. He was pleased with the way Ron was shaping up. By the time Walter Hardesty got a shot at him, the boy just might be ready to engage in a little crotch talk without acting like he was looking at one.

Ron continued to nod at the memory of the woman, and how easily she smiled. "She struck me as a nice woman. Her hair was dark and curly, down almost to her shoulders, and there was a mole..." He raised his finger to the outer end of his left eyebrow as he hesitated. Was it above her left eyebrow?

"A mole?" Herschel stopped writing. The dark suit and bright-colored blouse hadn't quite been relegated to coincidence yet, and now there was the goddamn mole. Herschel had felt it accented her face very well, and hadn't been sure if it was real or just a beauty mark the day Ned Ashcroft pointed her out to him. They were waiting for a table at the Ben Franklin Hotel dining room when she came out of the elevator and crossed the lobby to the front doors. "There was a mole on her forehead?"

"Yes." Ron nodded, more serious now with Herschel's interest. He remembered it was small and flat, not one of those ugly kind, but it *was* a mole. "It was just above her left eyebrow."

Herschel continued to squint. The fingers of understanding were beginning to fondle this thing, beginning to give it some kind of order. Like Sam Whitley used to say. All of a sudden you'll realize you've got a bird's eye view of a cat's ass in the moonlight. "Did she have sleepy eyes, you know, heavy lidded, and lips that were... Was her mouth sort of pouty?"

Ron continued to nod. "Yes. You could describe her that way." The word *sensual* came to mind, but he tried to ignore it. With the way Herschel had reacted, as if reading his mind, he didn't want to even think sexiness, but the man's sudden insight bothered him. "Do you know her?"

Herschel slumped back in the noisy chair, twiddling the ballpoint, mulling it over, letting the cat move clearly into the moon's silvery glow. Mutual friend my ass. Did that cocksucker really have the unmitigated gall?

His voice was calm as he looked up. "Are you and Jake at odds over something, stalemated on some issue?"

"Yes." Ron nodded absently. He had been at odds with Jake Marshallton over one thing or the other ever since he came into the job. Maybe Herschel was right about the *king of the hill* thing. Jake had balked at every proposal, no matter how minor, and there was nothing minor about the fuel saving program. The other contractors, even the larger ones, had readily agreed to certify their fuel costs, but not Jake. Mervin Sandler told him that Jake went into a tantrum every time the program was even mentioned. "Jake is being terribly difficult about the fuel savings program. Why?"

"How *much* difficult are we talking about?" Herschel's expression emphasized the word. It didn't have to be a whole hell of a lot to raise Jake Marshallton's hackles, but to create a hullabaloo such as this was another story. He was well aware of the man's temperament, knew the sonofabitch could be as stubborn as a deaf mule.

"Well." Ron frowned at the question. Jake was being his usual self, about as difficult as he could be. He wouldn't even discuss examination of his fuel costs. "Jake won't agree to *any* revision of his fuel costs."

"Money, Ron. Money, goddamnit." Herschel's tone dripped with aggravation. He almost felt sorry for Walter Hardesty. The man was going to have to show the boy to be a horny, greedy bastard, and Ron just didn't dwell on those levels. "What kind of *money* are we talking about?"

"Oh." Ron looked down, his mind going back to the estimates he had prepared on Jake's routes. There were eight different sets of paperwork, one for each contract, and he had never progressed far enough on any of them to worry about a total. As he recapped his fingers curled into fists, gripping and ungripping slowly, as though he were doing isometric exercises. He turned calmly when he finally reached a total. "It would probably be in excess of a hundred thousand dollars, altogether."

Herschel began to nod gravely, as though he had just had the trinity explained to him. "I think I'm finally beginning to get a handle on this thing. Finally beginning to see what the fuck this is all about." He looked up. "Yes, sir. I've got a sneaking suspicion that the woman who approached you in the bar that night at the Holiday Inn was Alice Marshallton."

"Jake's wife?" Ron's voice rose at the suggestion. Why, Jake had to be in his sixties, and this woman couldn't be more than half that. He tensed as a chilliness began to creep up on him. According to the gossip Jake had been married more than once. In fact, he was supposed to have been married several times. The thought of the man's casualness toward marriage caused Ron to almost whisper. "You think it might have been..? You really think Mrs. Marshallton would do something like that?"

"I'd damn near bet on it." Herschel was becoming more confident now. Everyone knew she came to St. Louis for an occasional *business* lunch, and there were rumors that she had even been to Washington a couple of times. "From what I hear, it wouldn't be the first time the sonofabitch sent her out to limber up somebody's negotiating tool."

"But his *wife?*" The very idea was abhorrent to Ron. He had heard the stories about Mrs. Marshallton playing around, how she met Mr. Jordan for lunch now and then. It was bad enough that she did that sort of thing, but for it to be at her husband's direction was more than his principles could accept.

Herschel was still nodding. "That'll give you some idea of how far that sonofabitch will go." Hershel looked down at his pad. It was the same old shit. The bastard used his wife to clamp a ring in the wimp's nose, then turned the leash over to one of his round-heeled vice-presidents. "That ornery bastard sent her over there to initiate you into the fold, to get him a handful of short hair."

Ron just stared. The stories about some of the transportation people's conquests at Jake's parties crowded his mind. He had preferred to consider it as wishful bragging, or at best just whoring around, not something like this, not a contractor's planned control of administrative personnel.

Herschel's eyebrows lifted. "With a hundred thousand dollar jump start, only the Good Lord knows what that peice of ass could have cost the Postal Service." Herschel began to nod. "This thing is getting clearer by the minute. Alice Marshallton's miscarriage," he paused with a smirk, "her fucking failure at the motel bar that night could very well be what instigated this whole goddamn mess."

The chill that had settled around Ron began to seep into his body. He was being accused of forcing himself on this woman, the very woman he had found so bewitching that night. And it was beyond him to even imagine her, such a personable lady, even if she was Mrs. Marshallton, being involved in these phony charges, or any of the other stories he had heard about her. The mere thought of being caught up in something like this made his insides shrivel. He cringed as Herschel became more excited.

"Yes, sir." Herschel nodded almost gleefully, now that he was getting a handle on this thing. "That bastard sent her over to that bar, and you turned her down. Had the unheard-of-fucking-integrity to say thanks but no thanks."

Herschel's eyes fairly snapped at the thought of Jake Marshallton flying into one of his rages. "That must have really scalded his ass. I'd give my left nut to have been a little mouse hiding in the corner that night when she came home."

"Why?" Ron didn't find anything comical about any of this.

"*Why?*" Herschel looked up, amazed that the boy didn't understand. He thought he had made it abundantly clear. "Can you imagine the look on that sick sonofabitch's face when she walked in and told him you turned her down. Told him you wasn't putting out." His knees suddenly clamped together and his body stiffened with a jerk, forcing a squall from the old chair. "*Gott-damn,* that's rich."

It still wasn't funny to Ron. Jake Marshallton was playing with his career, threatening his entire future, and there was certainly nothing frivolous about it. He waited for Herschel to recover from the attack. "Do you think they'll bring that up at the hearing?"

"Oh, you can bet your ass they'll bring it up." The words were sweetly musical as Herschel pulled himself up in the chair. "Walter Hardesty will make a goddamn production out of it. That prick will undoubtedly bring in the bartender to verify the incident, and the guy will just happen to remember that you insisted on buying the lady a drink. Then, when that goddamn Hardesty gets a shot at you, his questions will be phrased to lead the judge to believe you accosted her at home because you felt she still owed you a fuck."

The chill gripped Ron tighter. He would have to tell Judy about it after all, and about how Herschel thought they would try to make something of it, but she would understand. He hoped. And he was going to see that everyone else did, too. "I'll make sure the judge knows I didn't buy her a drink, then."

"You'll do nothing of the kind." Herschel turned, using the ballpoint for a baton again. "Walter Hardesty is no fool, Ron. After that sonofabitch establishes the fact that you've met her, and just lets the judge assume you knew who she was, he'll very innocently ask if you had a drink with her at the Holiday Inn on..," he hesitated, his brow furrowing at the lack of a date, "on such and such a night, and you will tell him the truth. You will merely say, *yes.*"

Ron drew back, not willing to accept what the answer would imply. "I don't consider that as having a drink."

Herschel slumped back in his chair. The thought of a young man like Ron living in this old world twenty some-odd years without ever being a part of it stretched his patience to a thread. "Ron, when two people sit at the same bar, on adjoining stools, partaking of a little libation while they giggle and wiggle and talk," his composure suddenly abandoned him and the thread snapped, propelling him forward angrily, "they are *hav-ving* a *fuck-king* drink."

The outburst had no effect on Ron whatsoever. His expression didn't change, and his voice remained calm. "But I want to make sure the judge knows I didn't buy her a drink."

"I'll make sure he knows that, for Christ's sake." Herschel slumped against his desk. "I'll bring all of that out on redirect. I'll make sure the judge knows what went on." He took a deep breath and let it out. "And what didn't."

Ron began to breathe easier. He had forgotten that your own lawyer got a chance to clarify anything raised on cross-examination. "Just so the judge knows I didn't do anything."

"I'll *handle* it, Ron. I'll *handle* it." Herschel lifted his elbow to the desk. He would need to talk to Ned Ashcroft about this latest development. Refuting whatever Walter Hardesty might try to build out of this could be tricky, and it might be a chore, too, just keeping Ron from screwing anything up. "I'll make sure the judge knows you *didn't* buy her a drink, *didn't* get in her pants, and, if it will make you feel any better, I'll make sure he knows you didn't even help her up on the goddamn stool." He turned to his pad angrily. "Okay?"

Ron nodded as he eased back in the chair. Now it was Herschel who was losing his cool, and that couldn't be too good, either. "You don't have to be sarcastic."

"I have to be whatever it takes." Herschel pulled the pad to him and clicked the pen. "And I'll need the day and date of this attempted deflowering."

Ron grew solemn at the thought of trying to explain the encounter, not only to a judge, but to Judy, too. "I'll get it from my travel vouchers."

Herschel nodded. "Just so I have it." He had no choice but to stay ahead of Walter Hardesty on this little skirmish. He would discuss it with Ned, get his opinion on how to approach Alice Marshallton on the stand. He wouldn't have any qualms about leaning on the bartender, but this woman would be something else when that sonofabitching Hardesty got through instructing her on the agonies and ecstasies of a desecrated damsel.

He finished writing and pulled the pages back into place as he glanced up at the clock. "This throws a whole new light on the subject. Gives us a clue to what they're trying to do, and why. I'd better run this by Ned while it's still fresh in my mind. I have to stop by there anyway."

Ron pushed himself up from the chair. He hadn't realized they had been at it so long, but he was glad Herschel was beginning to believe him. And that Mr. Ashcroft was helping Herschel. It made him feel a lot better.

He stepped over and lifted his jacket from the hanger. "I do appreciate what you're doing, Herschel, and I'm glad Mr. Ashcroft is helping, too."

"Don't let it get to you, Ron. We're going to do just fine." He pushed the squeaky chair back with his knees as he stood, tapping the desk top with the edge of the long yellow pad. "And be sure to call me if you think of anything else."

"I will, Herschel. And thanks again."

As Ron left, Herschel lifted a worn leather briefcase from the floor and placed the legal pad inside. The very thought of having this conscientious young man's future in his hands scared him, twisted his guts until he thought he was going to puke. And he wasn't sure whether it was the arrogance of the charges, or the degeneracy of his own goddamn profession.

CHAPTER SIX

The modest white house, with the profusion of flowers around the small front porch and down the sides, had always been so inviting when Ron turned the corner each evening walking home from the bus stop, but not today. It was almost ominous as it came into view. He cringed at the thought of trying to explain the woman in the bar to Judy at this late date. He touched the garage door opener and turned into the driveway, pacing the Thunderbird until the overhead door had retracted all the way.

He eased the car carefully into the confines of the garage, the closeness adding to the gloom of the charges hanging over him, and the turn the case had taken. He had hoped to get this thing settled and get on with his life, but that seemed highly unlikely after today's session with Herschel.

Judy would have to know about his encounter with the woman, and he hoped she would understand, but there was no point in bothering her with a lot of detail. He would just tell her about it, and why he had felt he should tell Herschel. If it was ever established that the woman actually *was* Mrs. Marshallton, and it appeared the incident was going to have a bearing on the case, he would try to explain what it was all about to her then.

It irritated Ron to think of his wife sitting in a courtroom, listening to Mr. Hardesty fabricate a story of him trying to seduce a woman in a bar, then later assaulting her in her own home. The very idea was repulsive. It had never entered his mind that such a harmless incident would come back to embarrass him, or require that he give his wife some sort of explanation, but he hadn't considered ever being in such a predicament, either. He would prefer that Judy didn't even attend the hearing, but knowing her, that was just wishful thinking.

Ron got out of the car and closed the door, then touched the wall button and waited while the garage door crawled back down into place. The thought of Mr. Ashcroft being interested in his defense, and willing to advise Herschel, lifted his spirits enough for him to manage a smile as he stepped into the kitchen.

Judy had already set the table, and started filling the glasses with ice from the freezer door when she heard Ron come into the garage. Her talk with Wanda today had partially relieved her doldrums, and now, with Ron back home, she felt even better. She set the glasses on the table and turned as he reached out and pulled her to him.

She raised up on her tiptoes and touched his lips with a kiss, then drew back, her voice hoarely low. "How did it go?"

"Good." He held her close and nuzzled her cheek and ear, speaking softly. "I think it's going to be okay."

"What did Mr. Birdwell think about the contractor's accusations?" She snuggled in closer, holding him tightly, but he could feel her tenseness as she became still, waiting.

"He said he thought we could handle it." Ron held her protectively, to reassure her while he massaged her neck and shoulders. She didn't need to know this was Herschel's first case. "Herschel said he considers any charges to be serious, and always gives them his complete attention. He said he sees no reason why we can't be ready for the hearing, so we shouldn't worry."

And Ron was sure Judy would appreciate knowing about Mr. Ashcroft, but he didn't intend to give her false hopes or drag her into this mess any farther than was necessary. If what Herschel said was true, if the woman at the Holiday Inn that night *was* Mrs. Marshallton, and Mr. Hardesty was going to use it at the hearing, then he would do his best to keep Judy as far away from the whole thing as possible.

Judy reached up and gave him another quick peck as she drew away. "Now, you see. All that worry for nothing."

Ron managed a faint smile, but only at the thought of having her. She was his whole life, the very center of his private world, and he intended to keep that world as far as possible from the contamination of the one he worked in, the tainted world of transportation contracting.

"No, we're not there yet, honey." He withdrew his arm from her waist. "We've got a long way to go before we're out of the woods on this, but I think Herschel is going to be able to handle it."

"I'm glad." She turned toward the cabinets straightening her clothes. "Now you hurry and do what you have to while I put supper on the table, then you can tell me about it."

While Ron put his jacket in the closet, then washed his hands, he went back over his meeting with Herschel and what had been accomplished. Judy would expect to know why he was being accused, and what Herschel intended to do about it, but she didn't need to know all the lurid details.

He had never mentioned the rumors of who was supposedly sleeping with whom, any of the subtle *slips* about something that supposedly happened to someone while they were *on the road* or at one of the weekend parties at Rockmarsh Lodge, and certainly not the *business* lunches he had heard about that often lasted past quitting time. The only thing he had mentioned to his wife was the fifth of whiskey that had been left on his desk last Christmas, and he had let her think it was returned to the contractor. There was no point in telling her that Mr. Warden had volunteered to take care of it for him.

The aroma wafting through the house drew him back to the small formica-topped table in the breakfast nook where they ate most of their meals. They usually had a light meal on Saturday evening, soup and a sandwich, but Judy seemed to be outdoing herself lately. The meat loaf and mashed potatoes, one of his favorites, was certainly welcome. He hadn't realized how hungry a person could get just sitting around talking.

When Ron and Judy were both seated, they reached out and clasped their hands together across the table, then reverently bowed their heads while Ron gave the blessing. Before the *amen* they both sat quietly for a moment with their own private thoughts.

Ron never asked for any personal consideration, just guidance in his daily endeavors. He realized that the people he dealt with, and the Jake Marshalltons and Walter Hardestys of the world, had the same opportunity to pray that he did, and he didn't intend to put God in a position to have to choose sides. Judy's mind, however, operated more along the lines of feminine logic. With God being a man, she thought no more of asking Him for a special favor than she did of asking Ron. And she would go to any length to protect her man, the man she had known for so long and loved so dearly.

With a respectful amen, they released their grip and looked up with a smile. As Ron dipped into the steaming mashed potatoes, Judy looked down, adjusting the napkin across her lap while she put her thoughts together.

"You didn't say what Mr. Birdwell really thought of the charges?" It bothered her when she got the feeling Ron was deliberately being vague or trying to bluff his way around something.

Ron stuck the spoon back in the bowl of potatoes, then lifted a slice of meat loaf onto his plate. He hadn't realized how little he knew about the justice system. How indifferent a lawyer could be to what supposedly happened, or if, in fact, it even happened at all. "He never actually said, honey."

"You mean he didn't even ask whether you're guilty or not?" She flashed an injured pout, hesitating with a spoonful of potatoes in midair.

"He didn't have to." Ron shook his head as he pulled a roll apart. "I made a point of telling him that to start with."

Judy looked down as she plopped the potatoes onto her plate. "I would think that would be a lawyer's first concern."

"Well." His mind groped for an answer, something that would give her some idea of court proceedings. "I believe the law says a person is entitled to representation whether they're guilty or not."

Her expression registered concern as she placed the spoon back in the potatoes. "You mean Mr. Birdwell would have to defend you even if he knew you were guilty?"

"Now *that* I'm not sure about." He hesitated, his fork halfway to his mouth with a piece of meat loaf. His mind went back to what Hersched had said about Jake and Mr. Hardesty coaching Mrs. Marshallton. Herschel hadn't commented on the legality of it one way or the other, just that they would do it. "But Herschel did say that if he had any qualms at all about the case he would have refused the assignment." Ron's conscience sent a twinge through him at the way he had paraphrased Herschel's statement to answer her question.

Judy frowned at the slice of meat loaf she was lifting to her plate as if it was some kind of foreign object. Her opinion of the legal system was not very good to start with. It irked her to think of the way all those attorneys in that big murder trial last year had contradicted each other. It was all over the papers and television. One or the other of them *had* to know they were being untruthful. "All I can say is, if that contractor's lawyer had anything to do with writing that letter of charges he ought to have his face slapped."

A surge of pride rose in Ron. He had never known Judy to sound so belligerent before, but he hadn't intended for her to get so wrapped up in this case, either. Before he realized it he was around the table, easing down onto one knee beside her chair.

"Now, honey." His arm slid around her shoulders. "We can't be sure the lawyer knew the charges were contrived." His fingers worked lightly on the back of her neck. "Can we? We can only be sure of the contractor and his wife. We know they're aware that they are not being truthful."

The woman in the bar flashed through his mind again. She was too personable, seemed too nice to have been Mrs. Marshallton. That woman would never agree to be a party to such accusations.

Judy turned and pressed her cheek to his as a tear welled up in her eye and spilled over. Here he was consoling *her* again. She brought her hand up to his chin and gave him a fervently wet kiss in spite of the salt in the tear and the onions in the meat loaf. She was not going to allow those people to mistreat her husband.

"I'm sorry, Ron, but it makes me furious everytime I think about it." She raised her napkin and patted her tears from his face, then touched the napkin to each of her eyes. "There just doesn't seem to be any common decency in the world anymore."

"I know." He got to his feet, then leaned down and kissed her on the forehead before he returned to his place on the other side of the table. "But Herschel said it will be their lawyer's responsibility to convince the judge that their accusations really happened. All we have to do to refute their story is catch them in a lie. That would show the judge their charges are not true."

"And how does he propose to do that?" She looked down as she spread the napkin on her lap again, then picked up her fork.

"We went over everything in the letter today." Ron's thoughts went back to the thing with the car. Maybe that would make her feel better.

"We started with the date this all supposedly happened." He took a small bite and chewed hurriedly while he thought. "You remember last September when I used our car to go to Cape Girardeau? The day you had to come and get me, and I dropped you off at home on the way out of town?"

She hesitated a moment before she began to nod, solemnly chewing a piece of meat loaf as though it had no taste.

He leaned toward her. "That was the day Jake's letter claimed all of this took place."

Her expression didn't change as she swallowed arduously, looking down at her napkin with a sigh of resignation. "A day you just *happened* to have been down there."

"Yes." Ron's voice rose with his enthusiasm. "And Jake's wife won't know I was driving our car."

Judy bristled as she looked up, her eyes beading and her words full of contempt. "What does that woman know about our car?"

"Nothing, honey. Nothing." Ron's voice rose another octave under her stare. "That's what I'm talking about."

When Judy continued to glower, as if she had caught him sneaking out the back door of a brothel, Ron hurriedly wiped his mouth. It hurt to have her look at him that way.

He managed to keep his voice calm. "They will have to put Jake's wife on the stand to testify to what they claimed in the letter." He would have reached out to take her hand but she had them clasped together in her lap.

"Herschel said Jake and his lawyer will coach Mrs. Marshallton until she's word perfect. Herschel says they are good at that sort of thing, but the only car they will know to use when they brief her on their story will be the office car. I had never driven anything else to Cape Girardeau before that day. If Jake's lawyer doesn't bring up the car, then Herschel will when he cross-examines her."

Judy turned away and dabbed at another tear that had welled up and started to make its way down her cheek. "It will just be his word against hers."

"No." Ron shook his head. "Herschel won't do anything at that time but ask her what kind of car I was driving when I came to her house, and the court recorder will take down her answer. Then," Ron drew himself up, "when I get on the stand, Herschel will ask me about the car and I will tell him the truth."

Her voice was low, almost muffled as she raised the napkin to her eye again. "They could save a lot of time and trouble if they put me on the stand. I would tell them the truth."

"I know, honey." Ron almost shivered at the suggestion. He didn't even want her in the courtroom, and surely not up there where Mr. Hardesty could make a fool of her. "But you weren't there that day."

"You weren't either, but they're going to put you on the stand, so it will just be your word against hers."

"Oh, no." Ron smiled. "When Herschel asks me about the car, he will then enter a copy of my travel voucher in evidence, showing I was reimbursed for using a privately owned automobile that day, not the car she would have previously testified I had been driving. Remember? Our office car was grounded in St. Louis that day with a bad alternator."

A slow smile crept across Judy's face as the scene began to unfold in her mind. This Mr. Birdwell probably didn't even resemble that lawyer on television, the old gray-headed one who had a different trick up his sleeve every week, but he was evidently just as sharp. It thrilled her to imagine the woman's embarrassment. "I can't hardly wait to see the look on her face when she realizes she's been caught with her pants..."

She stopped abruptly, hoping Ron hadn't caught what she almost said. But he had, and it was suddenly hilarious. As he erupted with laughter, she smiled sheepishly and slid one hand across the table, dabbing at her eyes with the other. "I didn't mean that the way it sounded."

Ron took her hand to let her know he wasn't insinuating he thought she was burlesquing the subject. She needed to loosen up, not be so edgy. "I know, honey, and I wasn't laughing about that particularly. I'm just happy we're getting to the point where we can talk about it. Herschel said we need to be able to discuss these things without being embarrassed. He said the judge will pay more attention to the way I act than to what I say."

He sobered at the thought of Judy sitting in the courtroom listening to Mr. Hardesty question Mrs. Marshallton about what supposedly happened that day. Herschel seemed to think there would be nothing sacred in their attempt to discredit him in front of the judge, and he didn't want his wife subjected to anything like that.

Judy touched each eye with her napkin again, then dropped it back to her lap when Ron became so serious. It worried her when he did that. She wanted so desperately to believe him, but she couldn't help being upset when he talked about the contractor's wife.

They both sat quietly for a moment, each with their own thoughts, while the gravity of the matter closed in on them again. Her attention, even though she had never actually doubted him, dwelled solely on finding a clue that would convince her that Ron had *not* been with that woman.

His thoughts, however, were directed wholly toward shielding his wife from embarrassment. It was one thing to attempt to drag him down to their level, but exposing Judy to their world of depravity was something else entirely. The first thing he had to do was find a way to keep her away from that hearing.

Ron toyed with the food on his plate. If he could manage to talk her into staying home, then there wouldn't be any need to tell her about the woman at the Holiday Inn in Cape Girardeau.

He continued to concentrate on his plate, moving a forkful of mashed potatoes around in a pool of gravy. "Herschel is familiar with the contractor's lawyer, aware of how he operates, and says there is no limit to what the man will do to win a case."

A frown wrinkled Judy's brow.

He caught her concern without even looking at her. "Herschel seems to think they will make a big production out of their accusation that I forced myself on Mrs. Marshallton."

"What do you mean, production?" Her brow drew tighter.

"Well." Ron looked at her now. "You know how you and I kid around about some of the guys at the office, about what casanovas transportation people are supposed to be?"

She nodded cautiously, still serious.

"Like the time last summer when you went to Chicago with me to give my fuel savings presentation to the people at the Logistics Management Seminar in Oakbrook." It became easier for him when she began to relax. "Remember that Wednesday evening we went to the steak house? Remember when we left the hotel how I pointed out some of the guys from the other Transportation Offices around the country as we crossed the hotel lobby?"

Her face softened as she listened, looking down to smooth the napkin across her lap.

The scene at every seminar was the same to Ron, no matter who the men were or which office they were from.

He swirled gravy through his potatoes as he talked. "Remember how a couple of them were reading the bulletin board, two or three were browsing in the gift shop, picking their teeth, and several roamed the lobby as if they were lost." He hesitated but she just sat there. "Remember how we laughed that some of them would go back to their office and brag about what a great time they had in Chicago. Talk about all the booze and broads in the Windy City?"

She raised her eyes with a faint smile, making her cautious nod unnecessary.

"The casanova stigma is probably based more on things like that, but transportation people *do* have a reputation of being rogues, and that's what Herschel is talking about. The contractor's attorney will build their case around that to convince the judge that I'm just another Transportation Romeo who took advantage of a defenseless woman."

Her features remained stern. "No one would ever believe anything like that about you, Ron. Not any of our friends, or even the people you work with."

"I know, honey, but that judge won't be one of those people. He'll be from the Board of Contract Appeals, one of six judges who serve a two year term, and are assigned cases from the top of the stack, in turn. To him I'll be just another transportation person, and

Herschel says Jake's lawyer will certainly not allow the man to forget that."

"You mean the judge won't make any effort to check any of this beforehand? Won't even bother to inquire into your background?"

"Not that I'm aware of." He looked down. The judges at these hearings were always so grave, so strict, as though they had no feelings about the charges or the people, one way or the other. "Herschel said the judge would familiarize himself with the charges, but from what little I know about it the only thing he will have is a copy of Jake's letter."

"I would think he'd at least want to know if there was any basis for the accusations." She had given up on the food on her plate, which was now cold, and pushed it away from her.

"That's what the hearing if for, honey." Ron touched his mouth with the napkin and placed it on the table. "To determine if there is any truth in the matter, any reason for the contractor to bring the matter to trial."

"Does Mr. Birdwell think there's a chance they might get away with it? A chance that you will have to go through a trial"

Ron drew in a breath. Maybe Herschel was right about the sheltered world he and Judy lived in. "Hershcel said there is no way of knowing what Jake's lawyer will come up with. That's why I don't want you to go to the hearing."

She leaned forward determinedly, raising her eyebrows to him. "Ron, I'm not a child. I've heard sex discussed before. What do you think women talk about when they're together?"

He rolled his eyes toward the ceiling. "The only women you get together with are the ones you see at church."

Her head began to nod in concurrence, phrasing her reply before he even finished talking. "Yes. And we talk about sex."

Yes, he thought. Church women talk about getting pregnant and having babies, and having to endure the plague and the anguish of PMS, but Judy had no idea of the kind of talk he meant. Gutter talk. He drew in a breath to fortify himself as he placed his elbow on the table.

"Judy. The hearing is going to be held in an open courtroom. Do you think you could sit there in public while an attorney questions a woman about me? Goes into intimate detail?" He paused but she just stared. "Could you sit there and listen to the woman describe what I supposedly made her do in her own bedroom, talk about the way she claims I fucked her?"

She turned away, recoiling as if she had been slapped. "You don't have to be so crude."

He didn't relish shocking her like that, but she needed to understand the seriousness of his predicament. "Herschel questioned me about everything today. And because I've been accused of taking some money, he wanted to know everything about my financial situation, and because of the other charge, he said he needed to know if I've been doing any fooling around. He called it sportfucking."

Her brow drew tighter, her voice low as she looked down at her napkin. "How utterly disgusting."

"I assured him I hadn't, but he said he wouldn't put it past Walter Hardesty to bring in some woman anyway, one who would testify that I had been seeing her, had been intimate with her."

"What would that prove?" Her voice had become hoarse, her eyes wet again from the unfairness of it all.

"Just, I guess," he shrugged, selecting his words very carefully now, "help convince the judge I'm just another transportation Don Juan, capable of doing what they claimed in their letter."

She dabbed at her eyes without looking up. "Where would they find a woman who would lower herself to do something like that?"

Ron's thoughts flashed back to the woman in the bar. She had been much too nice to be one of those people, to be a prostitute, or Jake's wife either, from the stories he had heard about the woman. He wished he had discussed things like this with Judy before, had told her about the incident when it happened. It would have made it a lot easier now.

A sigh escaped as he watched her. There was no point in keeping it from her any longer. "There are more people like that around than you realize, honey. While Herschel and I talked about it, and him being so insistent on knowing everything, no matter how trivial, I remembered something that happened in Cape Girardeau while I was conducting seminars last spring."

Judy looked up slowly, a twinge of fear causing her brow to wrinkle. "What kind of something?"

"Now, honey." Ron slid his hand across the table but she made no effort to take it. "It wasn't anything to get excited about, but I thought I had better tell Herschel about it anyhow."

When her eyes didn't waver, even so much as to blink, he drew back, shifting uncomfortably in his chair. He could tolerate the way Mr. Jordan and Bill Warden looked askance at him over this, and laugh at the uncouth remarks of his so-called friends at work, but Judy's reproachful expression hurt, pierced his very being like a flaming arrow.

"I didn't mention it before because there wasn't anything to tell." His lungs labored with the heavy air. "It was last spring at the Holiday Inn in Cape Girardeau. I stayed there the week I conducted Contractor Seminars around the southeast section of the state."

Her stare raised his defenses, made him feel as though he were already on the stand. Herschel had looked at him the same way at first.

"One night while I was having a beer in the bar there at the motel, a woman came in and took the stool next to me. The only reason I felt I should tell Herschel was that she apparently knew who I was because she asked how the seminars were going."

Judy continued to glower across the table at him, as if he had suddenly started breaking out with a bad case of the pox.

"Herschel said there is a slight possibility that Jake or his lawyer would know her, or even, somehow, know about that particular incident, and bring her in to testify that she had met me in a motel bar and had a drink with me."

"And that would make you bad?" Her head moved from side to side, as though prompting a negative reply.

"Herschel said when the word *motel* is mentioned in a courtroom it's synonymous with..," he hesitated. There had to be a better way of saying it. "Illicit sex, and would certainly plant a seed of doubt in the judge's mind."

The tears began to flow as she raised the napkin to her eyes. How dare that judge condemn her husband for just not being rude to a woman who took a seat next to him at a bar. A creeping iciness, however, was welling up in her like a geyser, bringing a shiver at the thought of a woman brazenly approaching Ron, but she couldn't quite form an image. Women like that had a way of making themselves so attractive. "Was she pretty?"

"Now, honey." His wife looked so small and defenseless over there by herself that he wanted to put his arms around her, wanted to reassure her. "I told you there was nothing to it. We just talked until we finished our drinks, then she left and I went to my room."

"Didn't she introduce herself?" Her voice became more tolerant at the realization she might possibly have been too hasty. Surely the woman would have introduced herself, at least given her name if she had anticipated anything, any kind of intimacy.

"No." His voice softened at her remorseful tone. "But Herschel seemed to think, with her knowing about the seminars, that she might have been sent by someone. That she might have been a call girl."

"A *what?*" Her tears stopped as she became offended by the audacity of it.

Judy bristled at the idea of someone thinking they could corrupt her husband. She suddenly realized that cowering and crying wasn't going to help Ron. What he needed now was a wife, a wife who would stand up to those people. Why, if she ever found out for sure that a..., she refused to say *whore,* it was such a deplorable word, that a woman like that had tried to put her hands on Ron she would snatch the hussy baldheaded.

Judy's sudden indignation surprised Ron. She was mad now, not hurt. More like she had been at the New Year's Eve party last year when the tipsy blond in the sagging strapless dress had insisted on cutting in, had pushed herself between them while they were dancing.

"Herschel said there is the possibility they will know who she is, and bring her in to testify to Lord-only-knows what went on that night." With Ron's own imagination able to place him and the woman together in a dark booth at a roadhouse, or on the smoky dance floor of some nightclub, there was no telling what kind of story someone like Jake Marshallton or Walter Hardesty could put together. "That's why I don't want you to go to the hearing."

Judy leaned forward and slid her hand across the table to grasp his, her reddened eyes never wavering. "There is no way I'm going to let you go into that courtroom alone, Ron." Tears began to make their way down her face again, but it was anger now. "I want that judge to know who I am, and I want him to know I don't appreciate what these people are trying to do to my husband. And I want that woman to look at me while she's testifying, while she's saying what she's been told to say, and know that I know what she is and that I feel sorry for her." Judy squeezed his hand, but made no effort to catch the tears dripping from her chin onto the piece of cold meat loaf on her plate. "Women have a way of understanding each other about things like that."

A lone tear slipped down Ron's cheek as he began to nod, even though he was smiling. As long as he had Judy he didn't need anyone else. "Herschel's got some people checking into all of this. He will know a lot more about the case, know more about these people long before the hearing. Maybe the woman won't even be there."

Judy raised the crumpled napkin to her chin, then dabbed under each eye. Her voice was low, but just as determined. "The contractor's wife will be there, and she's even worse. The woman has allowed them to use her, allowed them to disgrace her by putting those lies in their letter."

CHAPTER SEVEN

Alice Marshallton sat rigidly in the leather chair at the conference table in her husband's study, staring across the room at Walter Hardesty. He was sitting so pompously in one of the large easy chairs by the fireplace, talking to Jake. The man was such an arrogant ass. So typical of nearly all the men in any position of authority that she had encountered through the years. She had found it difficult to even be civil to him the few times she had happened to run into him at Jake's office, but now, here in her home, so blatantly helping Jake concoct a story to ruin that young man's career. She could understand a little subterfuge to fire an obnoxious truck driver or get rid of a sticky-fingered bookkeeper, but the very idea of what they were planning, the discrediting of an honest person, rankled her.

She had been aware of Jake's inflexibility, had some idea of Jake's callousness before she married him. With the number of people Jake employed, and the type of person ususally involved, she understood it was sometimes necessary to take drastic measures, but for Jake and his attorney to deliberately destroy an innocent person was more than she could tolerate.

And Alice had never denied her own degree of guilt in Jake's methods. She had always thought she could stop the travesty anytime, could talk some sense into Jake, but knew now that she couldn't. Not anymore. Not since Jake had allowed Walter Hardesty to invade his confidence, and the way he had begun to fly into a rage when she tried to question something he was doing. Or even something he wanted her to do.

It had started soon after they were married, when Jake told her about an obstinate truck driver he wanted to get rid of. Jake had explained the required procedure, the hearings and appeals that would be necessary, and the hellacious amount of time and money all that would take, but if she would just lead the driver on, lure the man into making a pass at her, then Jake could fire the guy without any fear of repercussions.

She glanced down at her hands as she realized how her involvment in her husband's deceptiveness had grown since that first time. How she was now keeping the important people in line and helping to cull out the troublemakers and the ones who became greedy, but there had never been anything as cruel as what Jake and his lawyer were working on now. The young man had merely refused to be a part of Jake's world, balked at being taken in by Jake's tactics and they were going to make an example of him.

When Jake finally pushed himself up, then turned and crossed to his armchair at the head of the table, Walter Hardesty, too, got up and came over to take the chair across from Alice. She raised one hand to her mouth and looked away as he approached, discreetly clearing her throat to keep from watching the man give that outlandish vest a tug, check the floppy bow tie, then run his fingertips over his lacquered silver hair. The way the man strutted around and preened all the time was so monotonous.

Walter Hardesty openly looked Alice over as he lowered himself into the chair. He waited for her to turn back and nod a greeting, then his smile became more of a sneer when she didn't. He wasn't comfortable placing so much responsibility on a woman, even one as greedily loyal as Jake claimed his wife was. The grandiose attorney readily conceded the woman was doing an excellent job of keeping the Postal Service hierarchy under control, but he had found that women were naturally capricious. They were much too quick to succumb to an emotional whim or the dictates of their heart.

"Alice." They both turned at the sound of Jake's voice. "They haven't assigned a judge for the hearing yet, but we need to start briefing you on how we're going to handle this." He waited a moment, but she just sat there.

"And the judge will set the date when he gets the case." Jake hesitated again, grinning immodestly as he slouched forward onto the table. "I've met a couple of the judges on the Board of Appeals, and they're just good ol' boys trying to make a living." He chuckled coarsely. "Just trying to get along. But," he straightened, nodding with deference to his lawyer, "just in case we don't draw one of these guys, Walt is going to have to be ready to earn his money."

Walter Hardesty drew a noisy breath in through his nose as he looked down at the table. The remark about knowing some of the judges was completely out of line, not something to be bandied about, but he had covered the man's loose mouth before. Many times before. He just billed additional hours, whatever it took to soothe his irritation at the time.

He turned, eyeing Jake sternly. "Friendship has no place in a courtroom, Jake. We will prepare our case and present it the same, regardless of whether you have met the judge or not."

Alice blanched at the stern words, waiting for the explosion, but Jake just sat there, grinning defiantly.

The two men eyed each other for a moment before the attorney turned slowly to Alice, his voice sharply precise. "And I'm going to insist that we hold everything in the strictest confidence. We will *not* chance jeopardizing our case. Is that understood?"

When Alice nodded, Walter Hardesty dipped his head and turned his glare back to Jake again .

"Aw, hell, Walt. This is just between us here." Jake scowled as if the issue was being blown all out of proportion. "And Alice knows better than to put my business on the street."

The attorney nodded slowly, satisfied his point had been made. Jake had a natural tendency to pop off, a need to feed his own ego, but Alice was a woman. And you never knew when a woman would find it necessary to embellish or improve some item of gossip, or who might possibly be within hearing distance when she did.

"Now." Walter Hardesty drew himself up, clasping his hands together in front of him, his eyes holding Alice Marshallton intently. "When they appoint a judge I'll have my people run a check on him so we'll know how to proceed."

Alice's questioning frown caused him to lean closer, tilting his head confidingly. "It's much easier to play to a person when you know a little something about them. Their likes and dislikes, their strengths and weaknesses, their opinions, their attitudes." He paused but she just sat there, her eyes staring blankly across the room. "In the meantime you will need to be made aware of your part in this hearing, and start preparing yourself accordingly."

"My part?" Her eyebrows lifted as she turned, drawing back indignantly, her fingertips pressed to the base of her throat.

"Yes, your part." Jake spoke harshly as he shifted in his chair and crossed his legs. "You know goddamn well what he's talking about."

Walter Hardesty lowered his eyes with forbearance, twirling first one pinky ring and then the other. Jake's coarseness was so annoying, but he waited. The man's tirades did tend to keep his wife in check.

Jake continued to scowl, his voice becoming gruff. "If you're going to make this judge believe you've been raped, you're going to have to know something about the son of a bitch who did it." He uncrossed his legs and scooted up to the table, breathing noisily. "I'll testify to the rest of it. We'll get Charley Ferguson from the bank and Frank Bedecker from across the street."

When Walter Hardesty started shaking his head, Jake leaned toward him angrily. "What do you mean, no? Charlie will get up on that stand and say anything I tell him to say, and old Frank sits out on his porch day in and day out. He'll swear he saw whatever I tell him he saw that day, and swear that he saw it for as long as I tell him we need for him to have seen it."

"Jake?" Walter Hardesty straightened in his chair, squaring his shoulders assertively as his stare held Jake. His face was solemn and his voice sternly soft. "Do you want me to handle this case?"

"Hell yes, I want you to handle the case." Jake's voice rose several decibels as he spoke, "Do I look like a goddamn lawyer?"

"No, Jake, you don't." Walter Hardesty spoke in his best courtroom manner, with subtle movements of his head emphasizing his words. "And you don't think like a member of the legal profession, either."

Jake grinned arrogantly as he settled back, ignoring the reprimand. It wasn't good to let a lawyer forget who wrote the fucking checks.

Walter Hardesty hesitated, allowing Jake time to gloat, then continued. He had known Jake Marshallton for a lot of years, and was well aware of the man's temperament. "The fewer people we use in our presentation the less chance there will be for a leak. With just the three of us involved there will be no chance of this judge, whoever he might be, or Herschel Birdwell to find a flaw in our case."

The explanation tickled Jake, drawing him forward in his chair with a loud guffaw. "Herschel Birdwell will do well to even find the goddamn courtroom."

"That may well be," the attorney nodded, his expression still serious, "but we never underestimate an adversary."

"Adversary? You can't be serious." Jake chortled huskily as he slumped back in his chair. "That little son of a bitch is nothing more than a glorified paper pusher. A goddamn government rubber-stamp."

"For the time being," Walter Hardesty's voice rose sternly as he nodded to Jake. "Herschel Birdwell is counsel for the defense, and we will refer to him as such." The attorney's eyes held Jake with a fierceness. He himself would do whatever blustering that he felt might be necessary on his side of a courtroom. "And for the duration of this hearing we will show Mr. Birdwell every respect due that position."

Alice sat tensely, her hands clasped tightly in her lap as she witnessed the exchange between the two of them. She had never heard anyone talk to Jake like that before.

"If you will recall," Walter Hardesty's voice became even more stern. "When we decided on our course of action, when we instigated this thing, I believe I told you I would handle it. And I will, but we're going to do it my way."

He waited, staring belligently until Jake finally looked away.

"When I have finished my direct examination of you at the hearing there will be no doubt in that judge's mind, no doubt whatsoever that you were unscrupulously relieved of ten thousand dollars, and highly infuriated over the liberties the young man took with your wife."

Walter Hardesty continued to stare for a moment before he dipped his head, as if to affirm what he had just said, then turned to look across the table at Alice. "And when I conclude my direct examination of Mrs. Marshallton there will be no doubt in the man's mind that she was," he paused with a shrug, "well, went through what we said she did in the letter."

He placed his elbows on the table, still frowning as he brought his hands together, absently twisting the pinky rings again. "That's why it's important that we put our story together very carefully, step by step, so each of you will not only be well versed in your part of it, but thoroughly familiar with our entire presentation. When we have accomplished that, then each of you will be able to testify convincingly enough to expunge any doubt the judge may have that all of this did, in fact, actually happen."

Alice clasped her hands tightly in her lap as she listened, an ugly loathing rising in her. The trial she had followed on television last spring was gripping her very soul. She had never doubted the honesty of the harsh prosecutor or the sincerity of the distraught baby sitter when the girl tearfully described how the woman had smothered her retarded child. Alice had been satisfied that justice had been served when the woman was given the death penalty, but now she wasn't so sure. How could she ever be sure about anything again?

Walter Hardesty continued in a serious vein as he lowered his hands to the table in front of him. "Now. Mrs. Marshallton, it will..."

"Aw, for Christ's sake, Walt." Jake waggled his head in disgust, his words sarcastically sharp. "You don't have to be so goddamn formal."

Walter Hardesty turned, slowly drawing in a breath to stifle his aggravation. "Jake, it's common knowledge that I've been your business counselor for a number of years. *Our* occasional show of familiarity in a courtroom can be understood, however," he nodded across the table to Alice, "that does not include your wife. I have no such relationship with Mrs. Marshallton." He paused, then continued when Jake's scowl held. "A strict deportment between the plaintiff's attorney and the plaintiff's wife, who *just* happens to be the victim in this case, will avert any hint of collusion, preclude any tainting of our allegations."

"Hell, I can understand that, Walt. At the hearing." Jake continued to bristle, waggling his head again. "But here?" He stabbed his finger down on the table. "Just between us?

"Most certainly." The attorney emphasized the words with a nod, keeping his voice calm. "In preparing a case I insist that everyone, at all times, observe the same rules of conduct as those required in the courtroom. That discipline assures a much more believable presentation."

Jake just shrugged as he lifted his hands in surrender and let them fall back to the arms of his chair.

Alice felt a shiver as Walter Hardesty turned to face her again. The man apparently had no qualms about what he was doing, had no concern at all that he was fabricating a story to mislead a judge and ruin a young man's career.

"In a courtroom, Mrs. Marshallton, every detail is of the utmost importance." He flexed his hands, watching the sparkle of the pinky rings while he talked. "A person's appearance is as crucial to the case as their testimony. One must dress in accordance with the image they are trying to convey."

Alice nodded, but only in agreement with his logic. Her aversion to his deceptiveness still gripped her tightly.

"You are going to appear before this judge as a housewife who has been violated in her own home." He smiled at the way she glared. "And as such you will come into the courtroom in flat shoes and neutral hose, and a dress that is not only long enough to cover your knees when you sit, but also be full enough to conceal the contours of your entire body." He lifted one hand toward her display of cleavage, and the way her blouse was open enough to show the small gold locket dangling between the swell of her breasts.

Her frown slowly turned into a look of disbelief at his austere instructions. She couldn't imagine going anywhere in such an outfit. "I don't have anything like that. Shoes *or* dress."

The sound of Jake's voice caused them both to turn. "If they don't have it here in town I'm sure you can find what he's talking about in St. Louis. You go up there often enough."

Walter Hardesty kept his eyes on Alice, disregarding Jake's interruption. "When you step up on the witness stand, and take a seat before the judge, I don't want him to see..," he hesitated as he tipped his head toward her open blouse, "I don't want the man to have a glimpse of anything that could remotely be construed as provocation for the attack."

"The attack?" The very idea startled Alice, causing her to blurt out. When she had agreed to let them include in their letter that the young man had forced himself on her, she hadn't imagined it ever coming to something like this. She looked incredulously at her husband for a moment, glanced at the attorney and then back to her husband again, her voice rising with disbelief. "Surely you're not going to expect me to testify that I was forcibly attacked?"

Jake nodded toward the attorney then looked at his wife as he spoke. "You're going to testify to whatever Walt tells you happened that day."

"But, Jake." Her voice softened to a pleading as she leaned toward him. "A lot of people know this young man. There's no way we're going to convince anyone that he forcibly attacked me."

"Please, please." Walter Hardesty raised his hand and brought it down in a slicing motion between them. "There is no reason to have to claim bodily harm. Rape is nothing more than the absence of consent. The act itself, however it was accomplished, is completely irrelevant."

Jake chuckled at the way Alice glowered, the sudden fire in her eyes holding Walter Hardesty in contempt. It never ceased to amaze him how a woman, created from the rib of a man, solely for man's pleasure and procreation, took herself so goddamn serious. She flaunted her bush as though it were the Golden Fleece, allowing those who curried her favor to take coital communion, and damn quick to cry foul if some guy attempts to dip into the nectar without doing any currying. And then they become disgruntled all to hell if some poor son of a bitch acts like he's not interested in the goddamn thing in the first place.

But there was something wrong with Alice's attitude. Jake frowned as he watched his wife. She hadn't been offended by the young man's refusal that night, and now she was becoming edgy. Much too edgy. She had been indifferent about the entire case before today. Jake sobered, trying to attribute it to Walt's domineering nature, but he couldn't be sure.

"Mrs. Marshallton." Walter Hardesty leaned forward on the table, clasping his fingers into a fist in front of him, watching the cluster of diamonds reflect their brilliance around the room. "In the commission of a rape, a compelling fear can be even more intimidating than physical force."

"Fear?" Her features contorted at the idea. Surely they weren't going to try..? "What reason could I possibly have to fear that young man?"

"No, no." The attorney's head shook. "Not fear of the accused. From the information I have been able to obtain on Mr. Hamilton so far it would be virtually impossible to cast him in the role of a..," he raised his eyes to the ceiling and shrugged, "shall we way, a ruffian."

Alice continued to grimace at the man's insolence, at his apparent lack of concern for what he was going to do. "Then what could I have possibly had to be afraid of?"

Walter Hardesty smiled, unclasping his hands in a gesture of concession. "We're going to use Jake."

She whirled toward her husband, then back to the attorney, as if there was some sort of crude joke between them. "What do you mean, *use Jake?*"

"Mrs. Marshallton." Walter Hardesty slowly settled back with a sigh, his expression and voice both now devoid of any trace of humor. "How long did the doctor keep your jaws wired together two years ago?"

The question stunned her. It brought a gasp as she drew back, surprised he even knew about it. She had stayed at home the entire time, under the pretense of suffering from a bad case of the flu. There had been several of the more serious strains making the rounds about that time.

When she just sat there, the attorney continued. "Three weeks, wasn't it? And what caused your injury?" He hesitated but she continued to sit there, staring in disbelief. "The reason for your fractured jaw?"

Alice recoiled at the thought of anyone, especially this man prying into her personal life. What right did he have to invade her and Jake's privacy, to openly discuss Jake's inability to control his temper? She thought she had managed to keep it quiet.

"I believe you had donated some money to the church." His voice had become calm, almost sympathetic. "Several hundred dollars, as I understand, without consulting Jake. Am I right?"

He continued when she slumped back in her chair and looked down at her hands. "And last year, in late October, I understand you supposedly fell in the bathtub and fractured some ribs."

Alice cringed at the man's impudence, at his apparent knowledge of the way Jake had angrily confronted her in the family room that night. She had never been able to determine how Jake found out she had been taking money from her house expenses to help her mother. Alice sat quietly, recalling the fury of Jake's wrath. She had never forgotten the sharp sound of her ribs cracking and the excruciating pain when he slammed her into the corner of their slate-topped bar.

Walter Hardesty leaned forward when she turned away, staring into space as if she were in physical pain. "And that, I understand, was also over money. Somewhere in the neighborhood of a thousand dollars."

He waited for her to turn back. "Now, if you will consider this little scenario, run it through your mind, you will understand how we're going to substantiate an absence of consent by convincing the judge that Mr. Hamilton forced himself on you by creating a compelling fear."

Alice's brow grew tighter as she turned, glaring as Jake cleared his throat and leaned forward. Her husband was apparently as anxious to hear Walter Hardesty's little stratagem as the egotistical lawyer was to tell it.

The attorney laced his fingers together in front of him, studying the brilliance of the two pinky rings as if they were a crystal ball. After a moment he smiled and looked across at her.

"To properly set the scene, and also preempt any defense allegations that the accused might possibly have been lured into the house the day he came by to pick up the money, we will establish that it was hot and humid in Southeast Missouri on September 23rd." He paused with a satisfied smirk. "We will make sure it's in the record that you invited the young man to step into the coolness of the foyer merely as a courtesy while you went to get the envelope."

Walter Hardesty studied the cluster of diamonds seriously for a moment before he raised his eyes to her and continued. "When you handed the envelope to Mr. Hamilton he slipped it into his briefcase without bothering to count it, or even look inside, all the while making small talk about Jake being out of town, having to be gone overnight sometimes when he inspects his mail routes."

Alice just stared when the attorney paused to glance at Jake before he continued. "You will testify that you innocently agreed with the gentleman that, yes, your husband would be gone for another day, and the accused then suggested you go into the bedroom with him."

He stopped with a pleased expression, then sobered and continued when he got no reaction. "And you, of course, became highly indignant and told him to leave, something to that effect," he shrugged it away, "we'll work that out later, and that's when Mr. Hamilton threatened you."

Jake was still captivated, listening eagerly, but Alice had slumped into her chair, moving her head slowly back and forth between the attorney and her husband in disbelief.

"When you tell the accused you think he'd better leave, he asks you if he is going to have to call Jake when he gets back in town and tell him there was only half the agreed amount in the envelope. Asks is he is going to have to tell your husband that he will not close the fuel saving files on the contracts until the rest of the money is received."

The way she shrank back in alarm pleased him. Emotionalism was an excellent instrument in the courtroom. It wouldn't show up in the transcript of the hearing, but it would be indelibly inscribed in the judge's memory. "What do you think Jake would do if he discovered you had skimmed five thousand dollars from a business transaction he had trusted you to handle?"

Alice turned toward her husband, her voice coarsely low, as though her vocal cords had constricted. "Are you going to let yourself be used like this? Allow your temper to be exploited in a public courtroom?"

Jake settled back, jovially waving it away. "Hey, I'm not on trial here. I'm just trying to expose the greed and corruption in the system, show what I have to put up with to make a dollar hauling a little mail."

Walter Hardesty spoke softly as he watched her. "Run that through your mind while you shop for an appropriate oufit, then we'll get together again when they appoint a judge." He smiled as he pushed his chair back and stood. "You and Jake and I will present a case that will be talked about for years, one that Mr. Birdwell will find impossible to refute."

CHAPTER EIGHT

A sigh of persistance escaped Herschel as he flopped into the noisy swivel chair and began folding his shirt sleeve cuffs back a couple of turns. He was proud of his progress so far, even though he was just getting started on the case against Ron Hamilton. Herschel couldn't help but feel the mechanical failure of the office car on that particular day was a good sign, but Ned Ashcroft said there was never room for complacency in a courtroom, especially when you're dealing with people like Walter Hardesty and Jake Marshallton. To effectively defend a case, and cross-examine witnesses, Ned insisted you need three things. Background, background, background. That's why he had asked his own confidential investigator, Elwood "Woody" Schoffner, to do some profiling on both Jake and his wife. Ned had assured Herschel that a defense attorney needed to know as much as possible about the people he was dealing with.

Herschel smiled at the thought of the way Woody had sat there that night, blinking stolidly, a slight nod now and then, while Ned went over the case for him, explaining what would be needed. The man had scribbled a few notes while he listened, then closed his small spiral notebook, put it in his pocket and slipped out the side door of the office. Woody never made a written report, just notes on the information he managed to ferret out on whoever, or whatever was involved. He was quick to tell you he was an investigator, not a scribe.

In briefing Woody on this case, Ned had told him that both he and Herschel were almost certain the woman who approached Ron at the Holiday Inn that night was Alice Marshallton. It was Jake's trademark, had become his first step with new transportation personnel, particularly when they started poking around in his contract's cost statements. And a hundred thousand dollars was considerably farther into Jake's business than he had ever allowed anyone to even think of going before.

Herschel's concentration was broken by two soft raps of a knuckle. He looked up as the nondescript man eased the door open just far enough to allow his pudginess to slip through, then pushed it shut as quietly as he had opened it. Woody Schoffner could be as inconspicuous as a pickpocket at a state funeral.

"Come in, Woody. Come in." Herschel half rose and extended his hand as he nodded toward the straight chair next to his desk. "And have a seat."

"Counselor." Woody nodded, giving the proffered hand a limp shake, then placed his battered shopping bag on the floor next to the chair as he eased himself down. His grayish white shirt and generic blue tie were as unobstrusive as his dark baggy suit. Woody contended that an investigator who even resembled one seldom got close enough to the keyhole of the matter to see anything.

Herschel tingled with anticipation as he lifted a legal pad from the drawer and pulled a ballpoint from his shirt pocket. "What's the good word?" He was anxious to know something about Jake and his wife, learn what drove people like them, and he was aware that Woody never tarried, never wasted a lot of time on small talk. The man preferred to just give you what he had and be on his way.

"I don't believe there is one." Woody glanced over at Herschel then back down to the shopping bag, rummaging as he talked. Researching the dregs of humanity seemed to keep hitting a new low. "Not with these scumbags you're hung up with."

"You don't think so?" Herschel chuckled to himself. Woody's vocabulary never left you in doubt about anything, either.

Woody lifted a worn manila folder to the desk and transferred the strained rubber band to his wrist. He never ceased to be amazed at the mendacity and insidiousness abounding in the world. Herschel had sure picked a dandy for his first appearance before the bench. "These sumbitchs you're fooling with are lower than buried snake shit, Herschel, and just about as twisted."

"Oh?" Herschel glanced up from smoothing the legal tablet. Ned had told him the same thing, in a nicer way, of course, and it had been gnawing at his confidence. "You really think so?"

"I know so." Woody nodded with a certaintly as he opened the folder and picked up the first page. "I'm going to give you what I've got, in the order I've got it, and you can run with it from there."

"Okay." Herschel pulled the pad into place. The click of his ballpoint sounded overly loud, almost like a starting gun.

Woody scanned the sheet of notebook paper in his hand for a second, then placed it face down on the left side of the folder. "We'll have to put that little tete-a-tete, that aborted orgy at the Holiday Inn on hold for the time being. This shady lady, if it is Alice Marshallton, apparently isn't a barfly. Around home, anyway. Nobody in any of the lounges around town seem to remember seeing a woman like her, and it appears that bartenders and barmaids are about as stable as itinerant fruit pickers. The lounge manager doesn't even remember who worked last month, let alone last spring. But I haven't closed that file yet. The motel manager I talked to hasn't been there but a few months herself."

Herschel nodded, trying not to show his disappointment as he watched Woody pick up the next page. He still felt the woman at the Holiday Inn that night was Jake's wife. It fit too well.

"Now." Woody looked up, his eyebrows raised with anticipation. "Who do you want first? Jake or his ol' lady?"

Herschel lifted his hands noncommittally, still miffed at the lack of information on their cute little attempt to shanghai Ron Hamilton.

"In that case." Woody flicked the page in his hand and pulled the folder into position. "We might as well start with Jake. That big-mouth sumbitch is cuckoo enough to tell time by."

"Cuckoo?" Herschel's brow wrinkled. He had heard Jake Marshallton referred to as crazy, but he hadn't taken it literally.

Woody nodded as he waggled the sheet toward Herschel. "And there's papers to prove it." He referred to the page in his hand for a moment, then turned it over and placed it to the left. "There's a place in New Mexico, an exclusive retreat tucked away in the mountains, where the raunchy rich go when their little jollies trolley jumps the track."

"An asylum?" The very idea startled Herschel, suddenly moving his case over into an entirely different arena. "You mean the indomitable Jake Marshallton has actually been commited, has been officially declared *non compos mentis*? A graduate goofus?"

"No, no, not an asylum." Woody frowned at Herschel's concern. "A sanctuary, retreat, and places like that don't *commit* people, Herschel. Mr. Marshallton was signed in as an overwrought guest."

"Well, *pardon* me all to hell." Herschel turned, looking down at his pad for a moment before he started writing. Crazy was crazy. He didn't care what they called it. "But Jake has been institutionalized, I mean officially?"

Woody began to nod as he reached and turned the last sheet back. "Oh, Yeah. Several times." He studied the paper a moment. "The first time was twenty-two years ago. The sumbitch went berserk when he found out his wife had taken their two girls and left. The fact that she had the audacity to leave him apparently tripped his toggle."

Herschel nodded as he wrote. He had heard that Jake had a couple of daughters, but that was all. There had never been any talk about them or mention of their mother. "Did you find out why she left?"

Woody's tone became gruff. "Her lawyer told the divorce court that it was to get the little girls away from the obnoxious prick."

"His own daughters?" Herschel glowered, revulsion elevating his voice several octaves. "The bastard was…?"

"No, no." Woody's head shook. "Jake never touched either one of the girls himself." He placed the page to the left and picked up the next one. "At the divorce hearing Jake's wife told the judge that the oldest girl had told her, the girl was six at the time, that Jake had picked her up and sat her on some guy's lap while they were sitting in his car, then bragged about the girl's potential charms while the man ran his hands around under her clothes."

Anger twisted Herschel's features even tighter as his breathing became heavier. Apparently nothing was sacred to the sonofabitch.

"Herschel." Woody's tone grew stern. "You need to know what you're facing here, need to understand the mentality you're dealing with. To Jake Marshallton, woman was created solely to pleasure man, therefore a woman, any female, is merely a life support system for a pussy." His eyebrows lifted for emphasis. "A pussy, to Jake Marshallton, is nothing more than a commodity, a common commodity that trades well."

Herschel turned away, abomination glazing his stare. To him, women were inviolable, and always would be even though he had never been too close to one. His mother had passed away when he was seven and his father never remarried. Herschel was sure he would feel the same way about any woman, particularly the one he hoped to marry someday.

When Herschel continued to sit there, breathing noisily through his nose, Woody reached out and took him by the elbow. "Herschel, Jake Marshallton didn't establish the puss trade. It's been going on since the beginning of time, ever since Eve throwed some leg on Adam." He paused but Herschel continued to sit there. "And if there wasn't a whole hell of a bunch of women out there who insist on perpetuating the game, who have discovered the damn thing they sit on can be even more lucrative than the Midas touch, Jake wouldn't be able to maintain the roster of corporate courtesans that he does."

Woody continued as Herschel heaved a sigh of disgust and picked up his ballpoint. "You're probably aware that Jake's present wife, and stable of round-heeled vice presidents, have compromised enough management personnel for the man to virtually control the Transportation Department of the Postal Service."

Herschel's words were curt. "I've heard rumors."

"They're not rumors, Herschel. That's why Jake Marshallton's got the unmitigated gall to try something like this. To think he can destroy this young man's career."

Woody started nodding when Herschel frowned at his reference to Ron Hamilton. "Yes, Ned asked me to look at your boy, too. You don't need any surprises when you're out there in front of the judge, and as far as I can tell, there won't be any. Not from that angle, anyway."

"I know Ron, and I've checked him out." Herschel continued to frown as he nodded. "And I've worked some hearings with him. The boy's okay, he's good people."

"That's what I just said, Herschel. Now let's get back to Jake." Woody looked down as he lifted the next page. "You need to understand the man, know where he's coming from."

Herschel turned to his desk. The thought of matching wits with a demented man, a certified lunatic with enough money to hire a shyster like Walter Hardesty, sent a fear through him. The very idea twisted his intestines until he cringed, until he felt like he was going to puke.

Woody referred to the page as he talked. "Jake didn't actually fly off the handle when he found out his wife had left. Losing her wasn't precisely what flipped his switch. That happened later, when her lawyer called to notify him that his wife had filed for divorce and wanted a lump-sum settlement of two million dollars." Woody looked up with a gloat. "That's when Jake threw the phone, and the family cat through the sliding glass door to the patio."

The room was quiet while Woody waited for Herschel to absorb what he had just said. Herschel finally spoke, his voice barely above a whisper. "What happened then?"

"Nothing, apparently". Woody's eyebrows raised noncommittally as his head began to shake. "His housekeeper called the doctor." Woody turned the page over and placed it on the stack to the left as he talked. "When the doctor got there Jake was curled into a fetal position on the family room floor, crying and mumbling incoherently."

"How long did they keep him out there?" Herschel nodded toward the pages on the left that Woody had turned over. "The place in New Mexico."

"I believe it was sixty days that time." Woody wet his thumb and forefinger on his lip and picked up the next sheet.

"Did his wife get the two million?"

"It doesn't matter." Woody scanned the page solemnly. If Herschel was going to start handling cases like this he was going to have to learn to distinguish between what was relevant and what wasn't. "The outcome of that case would have no bearing on your deal here."

Herschel shrugged. It really wouldn't, but he sort of hoped she did, and maybe a little something extra to bury the cat.

Herschel's disorganized attitude irritated Woody. That's why he liked working for Ned Ashcroft. The man never got away from the subject, never relented for a second, and Woody was almost sure Herschel had been around Ned long enough for it to rub off. He would mention his concern about it when he gave Ned this stuff.

"You're going to have to bear in mind, Herschel, that Jake Marshallton is not your *run of the mill* asshole. There is nothing sacred to the sumbitch. Absolutely nothing."

Herschel sobered at Woody's seriousness. He realized it came from being around Ned Ashcroft, but Ned did insist that every case had a weak spot, a chink of some kind, and it was imperative that he know where it was in Jake's allegations. He would just have to keep on until he found it.

"The man is an only child." Woody's voice was less emotional now as he got back to the subject. "He bullied his parents, and everybody else, with crying, threats, tantrums, anything that worked, all through his formative years, until he became incapable of handling rejection and denial. In any form."

Woody watched Herschel fume as he wrote. An abhorrence for what Jake Marshallton and his attorney were attempting to inflict on the young man would be a powerful incentive for Herschel. "By the time Jake was in his late teens the greed was deeply ingrained." Woody's head began to shake again. "Not a greed for money. The man's never been without it, or had to earn any, and it's certainly not a greed for love because he doesn't know what *that* is. Jake Marshallton has never had any respect for anybody, including himself, but the man does have an impassioned need to dominate."

He waited for Hershcel to take it all down. It was such a shame the man's first case had to be something like this, something so far outside the realm of common decency.

"The second time Jake went to New Mexico was over a bookkeeper." Woody paused while Herschel folded the page over and continued writing. "Jake doesn't trust anyone, especially the people handling his money, so there is quite a turnover in bookkeepers. And to avoid all the hassle of firing them, as well as the severance pay, Jake will finagle the poor bastard into resigning."

As Woody put the page aside and lifted the next one, Herschel stopped writing. His only outward sign of loathing was the engorged vein at his temple. It had began to throb as Woody delved deeper and deeper into Jake Marshallton's depraved business world.

"This particular bookkeeper, though," Woody glanced up and continued, "had apparently been aware of that, because the guy hadn't been gone long when the next one, the new bookkeeper, found that a tidy sum had been skimmed from several of the corporate accounts. That was when Jake come unglued."

Herschel nodded as he looked down and began writing. It was gratifying to know the overbearing sonofabitch wasn't infallible, but he still couldn't imagine Jake Marshallton crying, or curled up on the floor.

"The next time Jake ended up out there," Woody placed the page to the left and picked up another, "was when his second wife divorced him."

A sly smile spread across Herschel's face, causing him to write faster.

"How much did *she* get?"

Woody studied the page a moment, then turned it over and picked up the next one. "What she had asked for, but it was what her lawyer got that gave Jake his frequent-flyer points that time."

Herschel sobered and stopped writing, confusion wrinkling his brow.

"I found evidence that Jake slipped her lawyer a little something under the table, probably twenty-five percent of what she was asking for. Records show he had withdrawn that amount in cash a week before the divorce hearing." Woody stopped with a smirk.

Herschel's confusion tightened even further. "But you said she got..?"

Woody sobered, nodding graciously. "That I did. Her lawyer accepted Jake's money, then turned right around and won her the settlement she had asked for, and took half of that."

A hearty chuckle shook Herschel as he flopped back in the noisy chair. He should have guessed. Scum always attracts scum. You never see the damn stuff separated on the surface of a pond. "Was that how the sonofabitch met Walter Hardesty?"

Woody's nod became larger, and his words sweetly polite. "One and the same. The most honorable Walter Horatio Hardesty, and it was on that particular trip that Jake met his present wife."

"In a nuthouse?" Herschel pulled himself back to the desk and picked up his pen. He had never heard anything that would lead him to believe Alice Marshallton might be unbalanced.

"No, not the place in New Mexico." Woody went back to his notes, studying each page before he turned it. He went through several pages before he found the one he wanted. "Jake was only there ten days that time, then they transferred him to a sanatorium in Arizona. One of those rehab clinics that specializes in supervised convalescence and guidance." Woody looked up. "That's where Jake met her, but it was more than a year before they married."

Herschel blinked as he leaned down to write. He had never heard anything about Alice Marshallton having any kind of health problems, either. "What was the matter with her?"

"Oh, she wasn't a patient." Woody's head shook hurriedly. "She was in and out, visiting her mother."

Herschel nodded slowly. He knew he had never heard anything about the woman's health, mental or physical.

"Her mother went in two or three times a year for treatment of some kind of skin disorder." Woody looked up from the page. "Candy Carson, the name Mrs. Marshallton was using at the time, lived across the state line in Nevada. She was one of the painted ponies on a crotch carousel."

Herschel looked up at the mention of Nevada, and the indirect reference to the state's legalized prostitution. "You mean she worked in a whorehouse." His voice rose sharply on the last word.

"Not a whorehouse, Herschel." Woody flipped the page for emphasis. "She worked for an escort service. Those places don't have rooms, or women lounging around in silk nighties that are barely long enough to cover the product. There is just an office where they take the call, then notify one of their.., ah, escorts to cover the assignment."

Herschel had stopped writing. "Do you think Jake knew this when he married her?"

Woody began to nod. "Why hell yes. It was the reason the sumbitch did. Jake didn't start cozying up to the woman until he found out she wasn't too particular about who she fucked."

"But..." Herschel slumped back in his chair. The absurdity of it had no place in his own concept of matrimony. "To knowingly marry a whore?"

"Herschel." Woody kept his voice low, under control, aware that bachelors, especially the older ones, had such a sacred concept of wedlock. "The first time a man like Jake gets his nuts caught in the marriage mill he writes it off as experience. He consoles himself by claiming to have acquired a certain caginess from the encounter, but the second time," his eyebrows lifted, "the man's whole attitude will change. There is no more fascination with the fairer sex. To Jake Marshallton, this third marriage is nothing more than a fucking business deal. Literally."

When Herschel just sat there, his mind apparently wrestling with the concept of such an arrangement, Woody continued.

"Jake Marshallton had been providing postal officials with commercial pussy for years, yet when he went to negotiate a contract renewal, a cost of living or fuel adjustment, all he ever got was the glad hand and a morsel that was commensurate with the quality of the last piece of ass he had placed on the altar of appeasement." Woody's voice rose to penetrate Herschel's obvious aversion to the whole idea. "The man had no leverage."

Woody waited, watching Herschel turn stiffly to his desk and pick up the ballpoint as if it were dirty.

"Then," Woody's tempo accelerated as he referred to the page in his hand. "Six and a half years ago Jake met this enterprising doxy and the pubic hair growing on his brain began to quiver like an antenna. He recognized her as the opportunity for moving up in the world, for moving into the position of lead dog on the cold tundra of debauchery, and a complete change of scenery."

Woody tidied the sides of his file as he talked. "Imagine, if you will, the potential of being in a position to threaten to expose a postal official for using his authority to take advantage of a contractor's wife." He picked up the next page. "Minor officials only get one shot at her, to give her carnal knowledge of the poor bastard, then he's turned over to one of Jake's canvasbacked vice presidents for perpetual tethering." A sneer curled Woody's mouth. "The big dogs, however, are allowed a limited partaking of the enchanted nectar as a reminder of just who the hell," Woody stopped with a grin as the pun crossed his mind. "Or maybe I should say just who the *fuck* is in charge of who."

Herschel slumped farther over his desk. The road ahead was getting bumpier and dirtier. No wonder the Regional and Headquarters people had distanced themselves from this goddamn mess. He knew Alice Marshallton came to St. Louis occasionally, and had heard she made a trip to Washington now and then, but it hadn't entered his mind the bastards were running scared, trying to get their tainted peckers back into their pants.

Woody tapped the page he was holding with the tip of his finger. "With a ruthless bastard like Walter Hardesty on retainer, and a wife who has carnal knowledge or a firsthand experience with the personal quirks of damn near all the Postal Service hierarchy, the man's got more balls than a lotto game."

Herschel's voice was coarse. "The sonofabitch knows how to take advantage of everybody, especially the wimps." But there was one consolation, as far as Herschel knew. Alice Marshallton had no personal knowledge of Ron, carnal or otherwise. That is, if Ron hadn't overlooked anything about that night in the bar at the Holiday Inn. He'd have to make damn sure on that. "What kind of club does Jake hold over his wife?"

"He doesn't need one, Herschel. It's probably as much her idea as it is his. An aging strumpet wears her own mantle." Woody's head shook sadly. "No one is more aware of how age can tarnish the merchandise than a woman in the trade." Woody turned a couple of pages back, referring to them as he talked. "Six and a half years ago the woman was in her mid-thirties, thirty-four, thirty-five, a bit long in the tooth to compete with the tender flesh just breaking into the business. And she apparently had enough experience on the mat to know there aren't that many horny union officials around anymore, not enough seeking horizontal refreshment to make seniority much of an asset, anyway."

Woody chuckled to himself at the way he had worked the old story in, but Herschel was either not familiar with the joke, or hadn't understood. He hadn't stopped writing or even changed his expression.

Woody just shrugged and picked up the next page. "When she realized she had a man of means crowding her..." He hesitated when Herschel turned with a puzzled stare. "Oh, yeah." Woody nodded. "A call girl knows when age starts creeping up, and goes on the prowl for a retirement system. When this woman realized she had a successful businessman cozying up without trying to get in her pants, she recognized the opportunity and grabbed it."

Herschel spoke softly. "Alice Marshallton is a damned attractive woman, Woody. Regardless of her age. And I have heard talk that she moved around some, jumped in and out of bed here and there, but the idea had never entered my mind that it was at Jake's direction." He paused as he glanced down. The idea of such a marriage was still foreign to him. "Not until Ron told me about her approaching him at the Holiday Inn that night."

Woody drew back, not really sure Herschel understood the gravity of the situation. "You'd better be sure your boy's telling the truth, Herschel. You'd better be damn certain he didn't show her anything that night that could embarrass him in the courtroom."

Herschel nodded calmly. "I am, Woody, I'm convinced it happened the way Ron said it did, and I'm satisfied that he didn't know who she was."

Woody turned the pages back and closed the file, sliding the rubber band from his wrist to the folder. He reached into his shopping bag and exchanged the folder for another one. "And even if he did turn her down, Herschel, there's a good chance that she wasn't offended, didn't choose to push it."

The remark changed Herschel's frown to a curious squint.

Woody moved the rubber band to his wrist, then opened the file before him. "Let me tell you some things I found out about this woman."

CHAPTER NINE

Woody stared gravely at the file in front of him, straightening the edges of the pages as he gathered his thoughts for a moment before he looked up. His head tilted slightly as he glanced toward Herschel. "There's a general consensus that women who peddle their bodies, particularly the ones who make a career of it, are showing their contempt for society, or mankind, or whatever they feel will justify their participation in the crotch market. It's never for the money. That would be admitted prostitution."

The tone of his voice was startling. Herschel had never heard Woody talk so seriously about women before, about their views on sex, but he had never been involved in a case with him where it had been an issue, either.

"That has not always been the case, though, Herschel. Particularly with this woman." Woody shook his head without averting his eyes. "As far as I have been able to determine, Alice Marshallton has been well schooled in the art of sexual manipulation. She was introduced to the pleasures of the flesh at about the same age that other girls were playing with dolls and learning to ride a bicycle."

He waited a moment for Herschel's prudish convictions to grasp the direction they were taking before he picked up the top page. "Her father died when she was nine years old, and her mother remarried three years later."

Herschel snorted in disgust as he let the pen drop to the desk. He hadn't really considered how low buried snake shit could be.

"No, no." Woody frowned, shaking his head hurriedly in forbearance. "Her stepfather didn't rape her. He didn't abuse her, or force himself on her. It wasn't like that. In fact, I found nothing to indicate the man was anything other that a loving stepfather. Extremely loving."

Woody's nostrils flared as he leaned toward Herschel, his voice low. "The sumbitch seduced her."

"What difference does that make?" Herschel sullenly picked up the ballpoint and turned back to his pad. "It's still rape under the law."

"Oh, there's a world of difference." Woody replaced the page on the file and patiently clasped his hands together in front of him. "Forceable rape will usually traumatize a young girl, turn her against sex, sometimes for the rest of her life, but a girl's personality, and her perception of the male animal can be twisted all to hell when a man she knows, a man she has learned to love and trust, takes the time to wheedle his way into her confidence." Woody lowered his voice again. "Especially when the raunchy sumbitch has the patience to stalk her and talk her through the steps that will slip him right into her panties."

"Steps?" Herschel's face contorted. He wasn't aware of any legal, or even acceptable pattern of approach to something like that.

"Yes, Herschel. Steps." Woody's blood pressure rose as his tolerance began to dwindle. Discussing sex with a middle-aged bachelor could be as tedious as courting a jilted spinster. "Hugging, caressing, fondling. By the time the girl graduated from high school she was well versed in the art of sexual manipulation and its possibilities in the vast world waiting for her out there."

When Herschel just sat there, Woody sighed. He didn't want to alienate the man, just help him understand Alice Marshallton. Help him interpret the temperament of an enterprising woman of the world.

A twinge of compunction stirred Woody. "With what Alice Buchanan learned from her stepfather, and her years in the business of finagling and fornicating, she knows more about us egotistical bastards than any of us will probably ever know about ourselves."

Herschel stared solemnly down at his yellow pad. He didn't appreciate being categorized, especially in that vein. Promiscuous women, for whatever reason, had always been beyond his forgiveness. "I thought you said her name was Carson?"

Woody shrugged. "That was a trade name she used in Nevada. She's used other names."

Herschel wrote without looking up. "But Alice Buchanan was her maiden name?" He wasn't positive yet that he and Woody were talking about the same woman. Alice Marshallton might fool around some, but surely not big time, not like Woody was talking about.

"Her father's name was Buchanan." Woody turned the page over and picked up the next one, his eyes still of Herschel. "I couldn't find anything to show her stepfather ever made any effort to adopt her."

Herschel mumbled curtly to himself as he scribbled a couple of entries on his pad. "The spherical sonofabitch."

Woody's sober expression didn't change as he scanned down the top page of the file and continued. "She left home after high school and went to California, where she put herself through college."

Herschel continued to mumble general aspersions as he wrote.

"I couldn't find anything that would really indicate she accomplished that on her back." Woody shook his head. "But I couldn't find any evidence that she ever held a job, or lived with anyone, or even associated with anyone in particular during those years, either."

He paused to let Herschel catch up. "After graduation, with a liberal arts degree, she settled into an apartment in San Francisco, and was doing very well working the conventions and hotels, until a Governor running for reelection mounted a crusade against prostitution. She left California about a jump and a half ahead of the man's pussy posse."

Herschel continued to write stolidly, with no show of emotion except his eyebrows. They lifted slightly as he wrote the last two words.

"That's when she moved to Nevada and became Candy Carson." Woody turned the page and placed it to the left. "She was associated with an escort service until she left Nevada to marry Jake Marshallton."

Herschel had begun to grumble again as he wrote. The idea of a man knowingly marrying a prostitute still rankled him even though he couldn't generate any kind of animosity toward Alice

Marshallton. The woman just didn't strike him as being that kind of person.

"During her years with the escort service she became even more refined." Woody watched Herschel wrestle with his emotions. "She became an Occidental geisha, learned all the tricks of the trade. How to pamper the high-muck-a-mucks, how to dress."

Herschel's voice was coarse, devoid of any humor, as he spoke without looking up. "I thought women like that only had to know how to *un*dress?"

"We're not talking streetwalkers, Herschel." Woody sighed at the sullen attorney's apparent level of understanding on the subject. "We're talking class ass here. These women exude dignity and refinement when they walk through a posh hotel lobby to deliver a nooner, then pass right by security and the front desk on their way out, just as fresh and charming as they were going in."

The confusion on Herschel's face caused Woody to realize the man's horizons were even more limited on the subject than he had suspected. He was aware of the possibility that Herschel had never partaken of a nooner, but surely the man was familiar with the term.

"Today's call girls dress very conservatively, Herschel. Alice Marshallton wears two-piece suits, hose, heels and very little makeup. And she carries her supplies, all of her paraphernalia in a leather briefcase."

When Herschel stopped writing and looked up, Woody chortled to himself. The man's concept of prostitution had apparently never advanced beyond the street-corner or truck stop level. "These women carry spermicidal lubrication, tissues, douches, extra panties, and of course, an assortment of rubbers."

Herschel just sat there, staring at nothing in particular. Woody had described Alice Marshallton very well, even to the dark brown briefcase she was carrying the day Ned Ashcroft pointed her out crossing the lobby of the Ben Franklin Hotel. And the items she probably carried in the briefcase hadn't really been all that personal until Woody got to the condoms. That *was* personal, and an assortment could only be interpreted that she anticipated having intercourse with a variety of men. Like the corny joke someone had told him once about the secretary getting ready to go to the company picnic.

"But don't let that mislead you, Herschel." Woody's voice softened. "This woman has maneuvered her way into a position to service an exclusive clientele for reasons other than money, so she is not a vindictive woman anymore. All her demons have been, ah.., vanquished." He took out his pen and made a correction. *Surmounted* might sound too facetious for Ned Ashcroft. "Alice Marshallton's heart is considerably warmer now than her sausage grinder ever was."

Herschel let his eyes fall back to the legal pad as he drew in a breath. He didn't give a damn how warm her heart or anything else was, indiscrimate sex had always sounded so cold to him, so indecent.

Woody was aware of Herschel's inner turmoil and kept his voice low. "Promiscuousness doesn't necessarily make a woman heartless, Herschel. Not this one, anyway."

The strength of Herschel's exhale attested to his utter disgust. Why did women have to be so goddamned complicated.

"As far as I could determine, Alice Marshallton has never compromised her principles." Woody leaned closer, his voice solemn. "The woman will fuck you but she won't screw you."

Herschel's brow furrowed as he turned. "She won't.., screw you?"

Woody's austerity faded with a chuckle as he began tidying the file again. "Not literally, no. The pricks she crawls into bed with are the ones who are screwing the Postal Service, not her. It's strictly business with this woman." He grew serious again as he began tapping the file. "That sumbitching Jake sent her over to the motel that night to put a nose ring in another transportation wimp, and your boy wouldn't play. He turned her down."

"That's what Ron told me." Herschel nodded adamantly. "And I don't have any reason to doubt him."

"Think, Hershel." Woody began tapping the file again. "This case, these very goddamned charges, tell me that's exactly what happened. The woman went back home and told that silly shithead the young man wasn't going to play the game. Said thanks, but no thanks."

Woody hesitated, caught up in the fervor of his own rationale. "And I'd bet almost anything I own that the woman was impressed with your boy's refusal. Surprised to meet a man who still had a few scruples."

The likelihood of Woody's take on the incident shot through Herschel like a tonic as he turned to his desk, pulling his pad into position.

"But I wouldn't look for any kind of deliverance from the woman, Herschel." Woody's head shook. "The mere fact that she's involved in the charges tells me she is just as underhanded as Jake or that sumbitching Hardesty, and won't hesitate to follow whatever instructions they give her."

Herschel stopped with his pen poised above the yellow legal pad. He realized he didn't actually know the woman, had nothing to base his opinion of her on, and it still bothered him to think she had allowed herself to become involved in such a situation.

"From what I could find out about her," Woody nodded to the file, "she still has her principles, but she's also latched onto an easy lifestyle, one that has excellent retirement benefits, and that, I'm fairly certain, will override any pressure this case might be putting on her conscience."

The thought of Alice Marshallton being badgered by her husband and that overbearing shyster irritated Herschel, but he could understand Woody's reasoning. "I suppose she'll have to go along with their story."

"She already has, Herschel." Woody shrugged. "When they included her in their letter. But it doesn't mean the woman dwells on their level. Doesn't mean she's malicious."

When Herschel frowned and looked down at his pad, Woody began leafing through his file for a certain page. "Let me show you what I mean."

Woody found the page and moved it to the top of his file. "Two years ago, on August 7th at 6:45 p.m., Alice Marshallton was smuggled into the emergency room of the Sherbourne Memorial Hospital there in Cape Girardeau by their family doctor."

Herschel's frown grew more severe as he stopped writing and turned to study the back of the page Woody was holding.

"The records show the doctor had her x-rayed, wired her jaws together and took her back home. She claimed she had suffered the hairline fracture of her lower left jaw when she tripped on a throw rug in the family room and struck her chin on the arm of a leather recliner."

Woody turned the page and held it out, as though offering it as proof. "There's no mention of any other injuries. No bruises, sprains or contusions."

While Herschel stared, appalled by the insinuation, Woody placed the page on the pile to the left and picked up the next one.

"And on October 12th of last year, some fourteen months after *that* little fantasia, the same doctor smuggled her into the same emergency room of the same hospital with three cracked ribs. This time she had supposedly slipped in the bathtub, and again," he flipped the page in surrender, "there was no mention of any further injuries. No bruises, sprains or contusions."

Woody turned the page over and placed it to the left. "And the odd part of it is, in both instances," his voice rose with comtempt as he spit the name out, "*Mr. Marshallton* was indisposed longer than his wife was. Strange, wouldn't you say?"

Herschel just sat there, frowning, his voice low. "What do you mean, *indisposed?*"

"The man was out of it, Herschel." Woody's voice was low but his tone was snippish, on the verge of even being rude. "Away from the fold."

"The funny farm again?"

"No." Woody shook his head. "I couldn't find any record that Jake has been to either place, New Mexico or Arizona, since he married this woman. He just wasn't seen for some time after each of her trips to the emergency room."

Herschel glanced around, pondering the idea for a moment. "You're saying something set the bastard off, the sonofabitch went berserk and hurt her, and then she took care of him at home?"

"It would appear that way."

"What makes you think that?"

"Well." Woody nodded toward the page he was holding. "The doctor stopped by the house just about everyday, in both instances."

"Couldn't it have been to see her?"

"I doubt it. A wired jaw or taped ribs wouldn't require that much attention." Woody hesitated a moment. "Then when the doctor's visits began to taper off, people started seeing him riding along with her in the car as she went about her business. The guy at the drive-up cleaners where she takes their clothes said Jake was in his own little world the first couple of times she came in to drop off or pick up something, but gradually began to act like he knew where he was, to loosen up and speak. Began to pass the time of day."

Herschel fumed as he turned, mumbling to himself and began to write. "Took care of the sonofabitch after he beat the hell out of her."

Woody's head began to shake as he leaned closer. "People like Jake Marshallton don't *beat the hell* out of anybody, Herschel. They just explode, suddenly lash out, then crumble when they have vented their spleen. They curl up and start crying and cussing, desecrating everybody from God and the government on down."

"Lash out?" The thought of Jake throwing the phone and the cat through a glass sliding door was still bothering Herschel. "Maybe we should ask for some security at the hearing."

"Naw." Woody turned the page over, squaring the pile as he spoke. "I can't imagine anything happening at the hearing that would set the man off, and besides, people like that have never been known to lash out where there's a possibility that someone might lash back."

"I don't know." Herschel settled back in his chair. The thought of facing Jake Marshallton, of opposing an unstable person was frightening. "I'd feel a lot better if we could have a guard, someone from security in the room."

Woody smiled, clasping his hands together on top of the file. "Walter Hardesty is not going to let anybody cramp his style. I'm sure the man realizes one of Jake's temper tantrums would not only flush the hearing, but also deprive him of a trial, of the opportunity to put on one of his spectaculars."

Herschel turned back to his desk, his eyes wide at the thought of this thing not only getting out of hand, but the possibility of it getting ugly, too. He didn't want to see anybody hurt, especially himself.

"Don't let it worry you, Herschel." Woody closed his file as he talked. "It's only a hearing. The letter of charges, and Walter Hardesty's performance before the judge, will probably be sufficient to bring the matter to trial. Unless, of course, you can catch them in a lie, and that's very unlikely with Walter Hardesty."

"What?" Herschel whirled around, indignation raising his voice. "Lying?"

"No, no." Woody chuckled as he moved the rubber band from his wrist to the folder. "Catching him at it, Herschel."

Herschel slumped back, twiddling his pen over the yellow pad. The thing with the office car was really the only sure thing he had, and he intended to see that it was abundantly clear in the transcript. That, in itself, would show the judge the bastard's story had been fabricated, that part of it anyway.

"This hearing will probably be nothing more than a formality, Herschel." Woody turned and slid the folder into his shopping bag, sorry he hadn't discovered something that would contradict the allegations. In his experience, when there were specific charges and the plaintiffs had a couple of witnesses to attest to them, the case usually went right to trial. "Unless you can find something that will trip them up, something that will dispute their story."

"I'll find something, Woody." Herschel nodded as he reached for his pen, breathing noisily through his nose. "Ned insists there's a weak spot in every case, a flaw in every fabrication, and, by God, I intend to find it."

"I hope you do, Herschel, but that sumbitching Hardesty is a real stickler for detail." Woody picked up his shopping bag and stood, resting it in the seat of the chair. "He even had Jake to personally withdraw ten thousand dollars in cash on the day before they claimed your boy came by to pick it up."

Herschel reached for the letter on top of his file. "September 22nd?"

Woody nodded. "And I can just imagine Walter Hardesty managing to work that little fact in while he has his highly incensed client on the stand."

Herschel frowned, wilting into his chair as he dropped the letter back on the file. That sonofabitching Hardesty had apparently put some thought into this thing.

Woody lifted his tattered bag from the chair as he turned toward the door. "Jake even had the Vice President of the bank, a Mr.

Ferguson, handle the transaction himself. The withdrawal is on record for whenever they need it."

A chilliness began to move in on Herschel. He had been so intent on trying to figure out what Walter Hardesty would do that he had ignored the fact that he was also dealing with a demented multimillionaire with his own private hooker. A woman who wouldn't hesitate to stand behind the sonofabitch.

"But I'll stay on it, Herschel. And when they appoint a judge I'll get what I can on him. In the meantime I'll stay on all of them, including the bartender that night, if anybody ever remembers who he was." Woody didn't look back as he stepped through the door. "See you."

Herschel just nodded as he pulled the pages of the legal pad back into position and settled down to review his notes. There had to be a goddamn wrinkle somewhere in all of this mess. Walter Hardesty may be impeccable and a maestro in the courtroom, and Alice Marshallton feverishly protective of her retirement plan, but that goddamn Jake was as flaky as the cereal section in a supermarket.

CHAPTER TEN

Judge Franklin W. Chandler continued to hold the letter firmly before him as his eyes turned away, looking at nothing in particular. It would appear that all of the problems in transportation contracting were not related to the actual transportation of mail or the terms of the contract itself. After a moment he turned and read the letter again, much slower and deliberate the second time, then lowered it back to the meager file on the desk in front of him. He just sat there, his measured breathing the only sound in the solitude of his office. The tips of his fingers almost felt soiled by the contents of the letter. He loathed greed and abusiveness, in any shape or form, and at any level.

When he had been appointed to the Twelfth Circuit Court of Appeals almost three years ago, he was elated to finally be in a position to correct some of the inequities of the present-day judicial system. Overly exploited juries and their benevolent verdicts, and the ballyhoo of televised trials were tipping the scales of justice away from the letter of the law. There had even been instances where the same attorneys had been involved in representing both sides of an issue.

In the Twelfth Circuit Court, his area of responsibility, the majority of the verdicts had been just, seldom left any grounds for appeal, yet overall, appeals were on the increase. He realized, of course, that the media's glut of courtroom dramas had turned a lot of people into recliner authorities on jurisprudence, couch attorneys who insisted a second opinion was their legal right, but he couldn't overlook the unscrupulous attorneys, either. There were far too many members of the legal profession who were deceiving their clients into filing a futile appeal merely for the fee. It was the appeals with merit, the ones for a procedural error or tainted jury that concerned Frank, that made his efforts on the Twelfth Circuit Court of Appeals worthwhile.

The first appeal he had handled, however, had been a real fiasco. A young man had been convicted of not only participating in the burglary of an auto parts store, but also of stealing, then burning the panel truck he and his accomplices had used to haul away the appropriated merchandise.

Frank had followed the case close enough to be familiar with what it was all about, and had just happened to see the interviews in the paper with two of the jurors during the week following the verdict. The one woman stated that the battery had been stolen from her car a year or so before, and felt the time was long overdue for something to be done about those prowling hoodlums. The other woman had made it abundantly clear that she harbored no sympathy for the *street trash* who slept all day and caroused all night, preying on honest working people just because they could hire some glib lawyer who knew how to manipulate the system and keep them out of jail.

The two women's prejudicial attitudes should have been discovered during voir dire, and been excused for cause, and then, on top of that, the defense attorney, who also handled the appeal, hadn't even mentioned the two jurors published statements. Frank couldn't help but wonder if the omissions had been due to carelessness, incompetence or possibly even collusion. The shenanigans of some of his fellow members of the legal profession infuriated him.

That's why his first hearing on the Postal Service Board of Contract Appeals had been so gratifying. When both parties had presented their case, the contractor asked for a moment to confer with his attorney, then rose and withdrew his complaint.

The participants respect for the court, as well as the thoroughness and candor of each of their presentations had impressed Frank.

The contractor, as the plaintiff, had taken the stand first. He and his attorney had presented their case, with documentation to substantiate their claim that the mileage in the contract he had been awarded for the transportation of mail between the Kansas City and Atlanta Bulk Mail Centers had been understated by 32 miles per round trip. Through a copy of the contract, driver logs, and a copy of the cost breakdown submitted with his bid, the contractor itemized the additional daily operational costs he was incurring due to the mileage deficiency in the solicitation.

Frank had thanked the contractor and his attorney as they gathered their paperwork and returned to their seats, then watched the Postal Transportation Officer as he took the stand. The young man, as well as the Postal Service attorney, were both courteous and confident, and apparently not intimidated by the contractor's documented argument.

The Postal Service attorney began by having the Transportation Officer introduce a copy of the solicitation, drawing particular attention to the paragraph that stated the mileage shown was believed to be accurate, but cautioned bidders to check their own proposed line of travel for the round trip mileage on which they would base their bid.

Frank was aware that he was not too familiar with Postal Service transportation contracts, but he felt the fog index of that particular paragraph was high enough to make it questionable.

The Postal Service attorney and the Transportation Officer then proceeded with their rebuttal. On receipt of the contractor's complaint, the odometer on the Transportation Office car had been calibrated for accuracy, and the Transportation Officer, accompanied by one of the Highway Specialists in his office, had inconspicuously followed the contractor's vehicle when it left the Kansas City Bulk Mail Center on a scheduled run. They had kept the contractor's vehicle in sight the entire trip, logging mileage as well as the line of travel, all the way to the Atlanta BMC. The actual mileage recorded on that trip had been two miles *less* than the one-way mileage shown in the schedule plate of the solicitation, which became the contract on award.

Then, on the return trip, the driver had left I-24 at Metropolis, IL, and went cross-country on State Routes 45 and 169 to the small town of Cascade, just off I-57, still in Illinois. The driver had stopped at a small white house for about two hours, then returned to I-57, heading north, where he was again on his regular line of travel after he passed the junction where I-24 ended at I-57. This unscheduled routing added 36 miles to the return trip, making the round trip mileage exactly 32 miles farther than the mileage shown in the contract.

Frank was as amazed by the scope of the Transportation Officer's response to the allegation, and the revelation of the driver's unauthorized detour, as the contractor and his attorney had been. The two men had just sat there, frowns furrowing their brows, then began to confer quietly. When they had whispered and nodded for a moment, the contractor pushed himself up from his chair, and not only asked to withdraw his claim, but apologized for filing a complaint without conducting his own investigation first.

It was heartwarming to Frank to be working with such honorable people. Especially after the brazen approach he had experienced on one of his Twelfth Circuit Court of Appeals cases. A carmaker had appealed the jury's award to a woman whose van had suddenly burst into flame while parked in her driveway.

Frank had wondered what it was all about the day one of the State Representatives had dropped by to see him. The man said he *just happened* to be in town. Frank had never met the Congressman, or had the slightest inkling the carmaker's appeal was being assigned to him, when the man casually worked the conversation around to the case. Nor had Frank been aware that the particular carmaker was still undecided on the location of a regional warehouse they were planning to build for the distribution of its car parts.

Whether the State Congressman was operating on his own, or had been sent by someone, made no difference. When Frank received the appeal he had reviewed it on its merits, as impartially as he did all the other cases, and then prepared himself for the backlash. It had never come, not a word, but less than two months after he handed down his decision he was notified that he had been *loaned* to the Postal Service Board of Contract Appeals for a two year term.

Frank sighed as he thought about it. The whole thing had been so absurd. Had someone actually thought he would jeopardize his career, or even chance tarnishing his own reputation for the benefit of some greedy politician. It didn't happen on the Twelfth Circuit

Court of Appeals, and it wouldn't happen where he was serving now.

But these postal people, and contractors, too, had been quite honorable so far, and besides, he wasn't really into appeals here on the Board of Appeals. He was more in the position of a one-man Grand Jury. He conducted the hearing, then, based on the contents of the transcript, determined if there was sufficient cause to warrant a trial.

He picked up the letter of charges and looked at it again. This one was going to be different from anything he had handled before. There was no contract involved, or prior decision to question. And there is hardly ever any way to really prove extortion unless the money had been marked in some way, and later recovered. That was something, however, that would come out at the trial if the matter should get that far.

And then there was the thing with the contractor's wife. Frank scanned the letter slowly to see just how the accusation had been worded. He didn't recall that the word *rape* had been used, but that had been the insinuation. He began to nod as he approached that part, *forced himself on.*

Frank drew in a breath and let it out as he thought. Surely they wouldn't subject the contractor's wife to an appearance at the hearing. The extortion charge in itself would appear to be enough to bring the matter to trial.

Most women were reluctant to discuss something like that in an open courtroom, anyway. They always became so emotional on the witness stand, especially when it was they, themselves, who had supposedly been violated, abused, or even mistreated. Sometimes they became so distraught that it was virtually impossible to determine exactly what *had* happened.

Judge Chandler drew in a breath as he placed the contractor's letter to one side and began examining the list of participants. The only preliminary information ever furnished on these hearings was the plaintiff and the defendant, and who was representing them. Each of the attorneys would furnish the names of their witnesses at the opening of the hearing.

Frank went over the roster carefully, but none of the people involved were familiar to him. Jacob R. Marshallton, the contractor/plaintiff, Ronald E. Hamilton, the accused Transprotation Officer, or Herschel W. Birdwell, the Postal Service Attorney here in St. Louis who had been assigned to defend Mr. Hamilton. Frank looked away for a moment, blinking as he thought back over the indoctrination he had received on his appointment to the Contract Board of Appeals. He couldn't recall that the Postal Service had any trial attorneys stationed in field offices. As far as he could remember they all worked out of the Law Department of Postal Service Headquarters in Washington.

The judge had heard of Walter H. Hardesty, though, the attorney retained by Mr. Marshallton, the contractor. Walter Hardesty had never argued a case before Judge Chandler, but he *was* one of the more prominent trial attorneys in the midwest. A bit flamboyant, perhaps, and quite controversial, as Frank remembered, but usually most effective.

Frank shrugged as he pulled his legal pad into position and reached for the gold pen in the polished walnut stand at the front of his desk. He noted the date, then began studying the small calendar across the top of his desk blotter.

The first step was to set a tentative date for the hearing, and notify the two attorneys so any conflict in schedules could be resolved. He intended to handle this hearing strictly by the book.

Extortion was a very serious charge, as far as Frank was concerned, and the violation of a man's wife in her own home, however they were going to address it, was truly despicable.

He frowned as the thought crossed his mind. Apparently Mr. Marshallton thought so, too. It could be why the man had gone to the expense of retaining an attorney of Mr. Hardesty's distinction.

CHAPTER ELEVEN

Walter Hardesty lowered himself into the chair at the mahogany conference table in Jake's study, the same one he had occupied at their last meeting, and placed his elbows on the table. He clasped his hands together and brought them up in front of him to gaze into the sparkle of the pinky rings and reflect on their progress so far, while he waited for Jake to bring his wife.

With Frank Chandler assigned to conduct their hearing, things were shaping up considerably better than he had anticipated. It was much easier to play to an impartial judge, and Alice Marshallton was proving to be a woman with enough principle to make her a compelling witness, even more so than he had expected.

He turned at the sound of the door and watched Jake come in and push it shut behind him, then cross to the armchair at the head of the table.

"Alice will be along in a minute." Jake pulled the chair out and slouched into it with a smug grin. "She's been doing some shopping, so I thought she might as well give you a dress rehearsal for the hearing."

"That will be fine." The attorney dipped his head. "One of the first rules of practice is to properly impress the court. To prepare your participants, both mentally and physically, for the part they will be playing."

Jake smiled at the thought of his wife's comments regarding the clothes she had bought. "Have you heard anything on who the judge is going to be?"

Walter Hardesty nodded. "They gave our case to Frank Chandler."

"Aw, for Christ's sake, Walt." Jake sobered suddenly, slapping his open hand down on the table. "Do you know who that simple son of a bitch is?"

"I have never met Judge Chandler, or appeared before him." Walter Hardesty began to nod, "but I know *of* him, know who he is. A very prudent gentleman from the Twelfth Circuit Court of Appeals."

"You're goddamn right." Jake's voice rose as he slumped back in his chair. "That's the arrogant son of a bitch who screwed the state out of that big automotive parts warehouse last year."

Walter Hardesty drew in a resentful breath as he glanced down at his hands, then turned to Jake again, managing to keep his voice calm. "Judge Chandler's record has nothing to do with us. What he has or hasn't done in the past will have no bearing on this hearing. None whatsoever."

"What do you mean, *have no bearing.*" Jake lunged against the table, his words harsh. "We don't need a sanctimonious bastard like that deciding whether we have a chance to get rid of this goddamn Shadrach they've saddled us with."

Walter Hardesty looked down at his hands, waiting for Jake to finish, managing to keep his voice calm. "Frank Chandler is an honest man, Jake, and honesty *does* have its merits."

Jake was still glaring when his wife came in and quietly closed the door behind her. She hesitated at the heavy silence for a moment, then turned self-consciously to face them before she crossed the room, passing behind Jake to take the same chair as before, across the table from Walter Hardesty.

She watched defiantly as the attorney looked her over, as though daring him to criticize the straight print dress and flat shoes. The ecru pantyhose weren't too bad, they were a little lighter than they appeared in the box, but she hadn't worn a skirt below her knees, or buttoned a collar around her throat since she was in grade school.

Walter Hardesty finally nodded. "That will be quite appropriate. Between now and the day of the hearing, though, you might do something with your hair. Have it trimmed, or comb it out and tie it back with a modest ribbon. It doesn't fit in with the rest of the ensemble."

Alice sighed and nodded as she looked down. This was becoming so preposterous. If she had known she was going to have to play charades for Jake's attorney and some judge she would never have agreed to let them involve her.

Jake was still fuming over the judge they had drawn. "They've given our case to a damned bible thumper, Alice." Jake drew back angrily, still breathing noisily through his nose. "Even looks like a goddamn preacher in his tinted glasses and cheap suit."

Walter Hardesty raised his hand, solemnly turning to face Jake. "You will not disparage the judge or the court at any time." He lowered his hand back to the table without looking away, or even blinking. "It's true that Judge Chandler is a deacon in his church, and apparently not addicted to fashion, but that doesn't concern our business with him. We are only interested in the man's mind."

Jake's voice was gruff as he leaned forward on the table, still scowling. "You can't expect anything from a self-righteous son of a bitch like that. They all live in their own little world, with their goddamned minds closed."

"That's true." Walter Hardesty nodded without breaking eye contact. "And closed minds are highly desirable in a courtroom. They're uncontaminated, and quite easily influenced when you understand their demeanor. Aware of their preferences and their prejudices."

Alice Marshallton sat quietly, becoming even more uncomfortable as she listened. Her distress had very little to do with her clothes or the flat shoes that made the backs of her legs ache. This man, this overbearing ass, made her husband look like an amateur when it came to manipulating people.

"Do you think you can handle this stupid prick?" Jake's eyebrows lifted. "Are you sure you can interpret this righteous bastard's narrow little mind?"

"I have no doubts whatsoever, Jake." Walter Hardesty nodded politely. "I will have all the information on the judge that I could possibly need long before the hearing. And we will henceforth refer to the judge as The Honorable Franklin W. Chandler." His face became grim as he dipped his head and waited. "Is that understood?"

Jake threw his hands up in surrender. "Whatever you say, Walt. You just get the man's attention and we'll have Alice tell him a fuck story. The simple son of a..," Jake hesitated when the attorney raised his hand sternly, then continued in a more condescending tone. "*The Honorable* Franklin W. Chandler probably thinks sex perversion is when the woman gets on top, anyway."

Alice's words were coarse. "I will do no such thing." They both turned at the sound of her voice. "I have no intention of being used to embarrass anybody, or being drug any further into this than I already am."

"You will be involved in this as far as Walt tells you to be." Jake's eyes beaded as he stared at her. "You'll get up on that stand and describe whatever Walt tells you happened that day."

Alice frowned as she began shaking her head. "Jake, I know absolutely nothing about this young man. I have only met him that one time."

"That doesn't have a goddamn thing to do with it. Walt will tell you what you know about the son of a bitch, even to describing how the bastard made you go down on him, if that's what it will take."

Walter Hardesty raised his hand quickly. "Hold it, stop right there." His words were sharp. "Our goal is not to shock Judge Chandler or even embarrass him. We merely want to convince the man that your wife was violated, as we stated in our letter." The attorney's tone remained stern. "And someone like Judge Chandler, a man of some integrity, would most certainly not appreciate our being vulgar about it."

Jake continued to glare, merely enduring the lecture. "Where does it say we're supposed to give a fuck what *The Honorable* Franklin W. Chandler appreciates?"

"When you lose sight of your perspective, Jake, you're flirting with defeat." Walter Hardesty's voice remained stern, his eyes piercing. "Your quarrel is not with Judge Chandler, and you *are* asking the man for a favorable decision."

Jake scowled down at the table as he slumped back in his chair. "Gripes the shit out of me." He breathed heavily for a moment before he looked up, his tone still angry. "When the Postal Service started asking the Legal System to loan them judges for their Board of Contract Appeals, they should have known they wouldn't be getting any fireballs. That's how the courts get rid of their goddamn misfits. The Twelfth Circuit sure as hell did with this stupid cocksucker."

Walter Hardesty's words were curt. "Be that as it may, Judge Chandler is a respected jurist, and a man of some principle."

"You damn sure got that right." Jake laughed as he shifted in his chair. "When little Frankie boy fucked up that car parts warehouse deal the governor stuck the arrogant son of a bitch's principles up his ass and put him on the next bus coming through town."

"Our only concern is that he still has them." Walter Hardesty settled back in his chair, looking back and forth between Jake and his wife. "And we are going to approach the man accordingly."

Walter Hardesty clasped his hands together in front of him again, studying the two pinky rings as if they were a crystal ball.

"Mrs. Marshallton." He hesitated a moment before he looked over at her. "I have already covered the basic points of your husbands testimony with him, and now I need to do the same with you. Clarify the points we will need to make."

He paused but Alice just sat there, frowning her apprehension. "I am reasonably certain the extortion charge is enough for Judge Chandler to allow this to go to trial, but we also claimed you had been violated in our letter so we will be expected to address that also at the hearing."

"You're goddamn right we're going to address it." Jake shifted haughtily in his chair. "I want that fucking Hamilton transferred to a back dock somewhere, out of my face. I want the bastard's nose out of my business, away from my books."

The attorney's voice was firm. "Right now our only concern is bringing this to trial." He waited for Jake to nod. "And to do that we need to convince Judge Chandler that there is just cause."

Jake turned in his chair and crossed his legs, but Alice didn't move. She was more concerned with what kind of story Walter Hardesty had concocted for her while she was on the witness stand.

Walter Hardesty turned again to Alice. "In our letter we stated the young man had forced himself on you, but we made no mention of any abusiveness or injury. It would have been a futile effort. In the time it takes to schedule a hearing all signs of physical abuse would have been gone, anyway. So, to stay within the context of our letter we are going to use compelling fear. Jake and I have already discussed the setting we will use to explain to the court how the act was accomplished without causing you any physical injury, yet leave no doubt whatsoever in Judge Chandler's mind that there were certain liberties taken, and with an absence of consent."

Jake grinned as he uncrossed his legs and scooted up to the table, but Alice still hadn't moved. Her frown continued to draw tighter as she listened.

Walter Hardesty managed to suppress his enthusiasm as he watched her features. "In arguing a case before a jury, when there has been no claim of physical injury to the victim, there has to be circumstances presented that will establish beyond a reasonable doubt an absence of consent in twelve different minds. We will only have the judge to convince, but there is a general consensus in the legal profession that a lack of injury during a rape implies the victim was lubricated, and that, in itself, can also be interpreted as a form of willingness."

Alice's features didn't change as she spoke. "I think you're wrong about that. A woman can be lubricated by fear."

The attorney's eyes crinkled as he began to nod. "By a panic fear, yes. A fear of immediate danger or bodily harm, perhaps, but hardly ever by a compelling fear, which is more in the form of an angriness. That's why we will show the judge that you were highly indignant, infuriated at being accosted in your own home, yet you were uninjured because the young man used a lubricated condom. And, also, the presence of a condom will establish premeditation."

Jake Marshallton settled back in his chair, smiling at the thought of such an exchange taking place in the courtroom. He gloated at the thought of watching The *Most* Honorable Franklin W. Chandler try to look so goddamn prim and proper up there on his high and mighty bench while he listened to Walt and Alice run the gamut on the implications of a wet pussy.

Walter Hardesty looked back and forth between the two of them as he talked. "I'll fine tune that part of it before the hearing and get back to you." He hesitated, looking to the side for a moment, as though listening to an inner voice. "And both of you need to understand that any sign, or even a gesture of disrespect for the judge or the court will certainly not benefit our cause. And Mrs.

Marshallton, you are to avoid looking at the defendant, for any reason. You will sit quietly, showing no emotion even when the defendant is mentioned, or on the stand before the court. While Mr. Hamilton is testifying you are to look down all the while, as though embarrassed. But Jake, as the aggrieved husband, will be his usual self toward the defendant. And only the defendant. There will be no show of animosity toward the judge or the court. And certainly not toward the defense attorney. Mr. Birdwell, as counsel for the defense, will be an officer of the court, and your gripe is not with him, anyway. Understood?"

The attorney waited while Alice nodded and Jake smirked as he shifted in his chair to cross his legs. Jake and his wife were actually responding to his instructions much better than he had expected.

"Also, Jake, in using you as the basis for your wife's compelling fear, it will be necessary to introduce the court to your temper, and we will do that while you are on the stand. We will orchestrate your outbursts toward the defendant to introduce Judge Chandler to your violent nature, thereby establishing the background we will need for Mrs. Marshallton's testimony. I, of course, will reprimand you and apologize to the court each time."

Walter Hardesty quickly raised his forefinger for emphasis. "*And*, in the event Judge Chandler should choose to censure you personally, you are to just look away. I'm afraid that any remark from you could only be detrimental, and your apology would not fit the image we will be presenting to the court."

Jake's smile grew wider as his attorney talked, but Alice just nodded and continued to frown down at her lap.

"Then when you," Walter Hardesty nodded across the table at Alice, "get on the stand we will give the judge a plausible description of the defendant's visit that muggy September afternoon."

Alice began to shake her head, even before he quit talking. "I've told you. I don't know the young man. I know absolutely nothing about him."

Walter Hardesty leaned toward her on the table. "This is only a hearing, Mrs. Marshallton. And our presentation will certainly be sufficient to convince Judge Chandler of the need for a trial. The trial is where we will be required to prove our allegations, and by that time I will have all the personal information on Mr. Hamilton that we could possibly need."

"I still don't like it." Her voice was low as she shook her head.

"That don't have a damn thing to do with it." Her husbsnd's words were gruff. "You just listen to Walt."

"If it was any one of a dozen other guys, Jake, I wouldn't hesitate to tell what I know about them." She looked pleadingly at her husband. "I wouldn't hesitate for a second, but I don't know this young man. I don't know anything at all about him."

"You will when the time comes." Jake's frown was almost a smirk now. "Walt will make sure you know as much about the hardheaded son of a bitch as you would if he had actually mounted your frame at home that day, or managed to *lure* you into his room at the Holiday Inn that night."

Walter Hardesty held up his hand. "I'll have no more of this bickering. Not even *just* between us. Is that clear?" He pushed his chair back and stood while he waited for Jake's acknowledgement. "When the judge sets a date we'll get together to rehearse our testimony. We'll go over our questions and answers so each of you can respond immediately, get the points we want to make on record before Mr. Birdwell can object. And each of you will bear in mind to hesitate before answering Mr. Birdwell's questions so I can object to anything we would rather not have in the transcript."

Jake guffawed at the instructions. "I doubt that little son of a bitch will have..."

"*Mister* Birdwell." Walter Hardesty glared, his words sharp as he turned toward Jake. "You will address all members of the court with the utmost respect."

Jake continued to laugh coarsely as he hesitated, then started over. "I doubt that *Mister* Birdwell will have much of *anything*. For the transcript or not."

"I'll be the judge of that. You just hesitate before you respond to his questions, but we'll go over that again while we're fine tuning our own testimony. I don't intend to leave anything to chance."

CHAPTER TWELVE

Ron Hamilton got up from his seat and moved toward the front of the bus as its airbrakes began to hiss an approach to his stop. It was some consolation that the passengers he saw everyday had become as tired of his predicament as he was. Even the driver no longer gloried in ribbing him about it. It had been several weeks now since the man had asked him for a loan or a call if he needed a little help with the ladies.

When the bus rocked to a stop and the doors opened, Ron said good night, wished the driver a nice weekend and headed down the street. He had begun to feel that preparations for the hearing were taking much too long, but then today, when Herschel called to tell him a judge had finally been assigned, he felt things were suddenly moving too fast.

Herschel had sounded like he was satisfied with the judge that had been given their case, who was from one of the Circuit Courts somewhere in the state. Herschel said Ned Ashcroft had appeared before this judge, and had told him the man was a no-nonsense jurist who strictly adhered to the letter of the law.

Then when Herschel asked Ron to come to his office in Kirkwood tomorrow to discuss the judge and make further preparations, he felt he really should mention that Judy was insisting that she be allowed to attend the hearing. Herschel had taken it in stride, just told him to bring her along tomorrow. Said he would discuss her presence in the courtrooom with Ned Ashcroft, and would see them both in his office tomorrow around one o'clock.

Ron realized that Judy met with the other women in her Sunday School class on Saturdays, to prepare the Romper Room to handle the smaller children during worship services on Sunday. He also realized that Judy's friends would be glad to cover for her. Particularly Wanda. He smiled at the way Wanda and several of their friends, their true friends, had reacted to the contractor's charges against him. Several of them had even offered to take the day off to appear at the hearing for whatever good it might do, or even as a character witness, if his attorney thought their presence might help.

And then there was Herschel. Ron had considered Herschel more of a business associate than a friend, until this came up. And even though he still couldn't completely shake his misgivings about Herschel's ability to defend him, they were becoming closer, even good friends.

Herschel had dived right in when he was appointed to represent Ron, to handle the defense, never once snickering or even insinuating the charges were anything other than a farce, even though Ron had not hesitated to let Herschel know he felt he was in over his head. At least until he learned about Ned Ashcroft. Ron had never met Mr. Ashcroft, yet the man had volunteered to assist Herschel in his handling of Ron's defense, and even assigned one of his investigators to help Herschel with the case.

And there was Mrs. Hendley. She had gone out of her way to console Judy when she heard about the charges. A woman in her position taking an interest, taking the time to be concerned about one of the young couples in the church. Ron couldn't remember that either he or Judy had ever actually met Mrs. Hendley, or even her late husband, the doctor, but the woman had stepped forward anyway, offering to help.

Ron frowned at the thought of the matronly woman as he walked along the quiet street, headed home. She really didn't look her age, whatever it was. The first morning he was out for a run after she had approached Judy at the mall, Mrs. Hendely had come out on her porch as he came down the street. She had picked up her paper, nodded pleasantly as he passed, then turned and went back in the house. After that she was out there every morning for her paper, with a wave and a smile. Then she had started wiggling her fingers when she waved at him, and consequently came the morning she was waiting by her gate.

He had slowed to a walk, nodding a hello as he stopped. Mrs. Hendley congratulated him on the condition of his body and the effort he put into staying healthy. Her remarks didn't seem unusual, coming from a doctor's widow, but the way she had looked at him *was*. Her eyes had moved over his body as she inquired about Judy and how things were going with his work. Even though he had assured her that everything was fine, Mrs. Hendley reminded him to not hesitate to let her know if there was something she could do to help. She said she understood he traveled some in his work and mentioned that she, too, had business interests around the state. She said it was sometimes necessary that she be away from home for a day or two, and perhaps sometime when they were both going to be in Cape Girardeau or Jefferson City at the same time they might possibly be able to get together to *do lunch,* and discuss his problem and how she might possibly be able to help in some way.

The woman had sounded so concerned, had been most cordial, yet the way she kept glancing down at his body as they talked across the woven wire fence had flustered him.

Ron vaguely remembered nodding as he backed away, thanking her for her interest as he turned to finish his run. He had tried to think that his cut-off sweats had slipped and Mrs. Hendley had been looking at the scar on his stomach, but he knew it wasn't that. The scar was low enough that it didn't even show when he wore the new swim trunks Judy had given him for his birthday last year.

He hadn't mentioned the incident, or any of their conversation to Judy even though he had come to regret that he hadn't told her about the woman at the Holiday Inn at the time it happened.

Mrs. Hendley's attention was beginning to worry Ron. With Walter Hardesty getting ready to paint him as some kind of transportation Lothario, he certainly couldn't afford to be seen having lunch with her somewhere out of town, particularly in Cape Girardeau. In fact, he had made a point to stay away from Cape Girardeau altogether since the charges had been filed. Any business that might come up in Cape Girardeau that couldn't be handled by phone or mail would have to be tabled until this mess was cleared up. He had already told Herschel about Mrs. Hendley's interest and offer to help, but that was all. The rest was probably just his own imagination, anyway.

Ron was beginning to realize through all of this how little he really knew about women. Mrs. Marshallton at the Holiday Inn bar, if that's who the woman was that night, had been so friendly. She had invited him to go bar hopping with her, and hadn't seemed to be offended when he turned her down, but now she was accusing him of finagling things around to where he could force her to have sex with him in her own home.

And now there was Mrs. Hendley. Ron had been certain the talk of her alleged escapades were nothing more than rumors until she started being so nice, even offering to meet him somewhere out of town. Herschel would probably tell him he was overreacting to the woman's offer to meet him for lunch to discuss how she might possibly help him with his dilemma, but Herschel wasn't aware of how friendly Mrs. Hendley had become lately.

Even Judy, who he had known since they were just kids, could be so complicated at times. They had been married and living together for eight years now, yet there were times when he didn't even understand *her*. When he told her about the charges against him she had turned away, as though he were guilty, and when he had finally told her about the woman in the bar she had cried and questioned him as if she thought he actually had been intimate with the woman.

There had been other times, too. One night, not too long after they were married and set up housekeeping, he snuggled up behind Judy in bed, kissing her neck and nipping at her earlobe while he reached around and fondled her breasts. She had shrugged him away, gruffly telling him to go to sleep, yet several nights later he awoke in the middle of the night, in such an advanced state of erection that the skin on his body was stretched so tight his eyes had been pulled open. Judy had slipped out of her nightie, undone his pajamas and cuddled up so close to fondle him that he had almost lost it before he even knew what was going on.

And he would never forget that Friday evening after he had been promoted and began to travel. When he got home it was late, and looked like there was no one home until he realized the candles on the dining room table were burning. Judy had already had her bath and was in her black silk nightgown. She told him to shower and put on his pajamas, and they would have a glass of wine by candlelight before dinner. They had nestled down on the couch, with the wine helping to fan the flames of desire, until he leaned across to set his glass on the coffee table and kissed her throat as he whispered. "Let's make love." Judy had drawn back in astonishment, her eyebrow lifting. "Isn't that what we're doing now?"

Ron hurried across the small front yard. He knew Judy would arrange to go with him tomorrow, and he was glad she wanted to attend the hearing. It would do her good to know that Herschel felt it was a good idea, thought she might catch something that would help their case, and had even commented that when Judge Chandler saw her, the man would surely realize that her husband would have absolutely no reason to force himself on another woman.

Ron smiled to himself as he went up the front steps. Herschel had actually said *older* woman, but he hadn't met Judy yet, either.

CHAPTER THIRTEEN

Herschel examined the molded fiber glass chair he had borrowed from the small real estate office across the hall, then wiped the dust cloth over it and positioned it in front of his desk. He ran the cloth carefully over the other chair and the top of his desk before he placed it back on the shelf in the utility room. He seldom had more than one visitor at a time, and when he did they never had any reason to linger. They were only there to pick up their tax forms.

His tax customers were never there long enough to look around, but today was different. He was aware, though, that all the neatness in the world would not relieve his apprehension of impressing Ron's wife, would not compensate for his lack of experience, but it *did* make him feel a little better.

He had never met Ron's wife, but he felt sure that her attendance at the hearing wouldn't cause any problems, and Ned had agreed. Ned told him that too many supporters could be construed as overkill, but the presence of Mrs. Hamilton would go a long way in bringing her husband in out of the cold.

It would show Judge Chandler that Ron Hamilton was a husband, a respected member of his community, and not necessarily the greedy philanderer the plaintiffs were alleging. Especially if his wife understood her role, and didn't over react. Ned had suggested that Herschel could not only make her feel welcome by enlisting her assistance, but there was also the possibility she might catch some flaw in their story that only she would know about.

After Herschel had left Ned Ashcroft's office yesterday evening, the night seemed to go on forever. He had stopped for a quick bite to eat, then went directly home to work on his notes and put some kind of order to his case. It would be necessary for him to acquaint Ron and his wife with the impression they needed to make at the hearing, the importance of their personal deportment, and what they could expect from Walter Hardesty and the Marshalltons. The possible ramifications of Walter Hardesty's presentation became even more frightening every time he thought about it.

Herschel sighed as he rested his elbows on his desk. He had sometimes felt sure that trial attorneys exaggerated their place in the system, overstated what was really required to represent a client, but not any more. He was not only beginning to believe a lot of the stories he had heard, but felt that he might even come up with a few of his own after this was over.

The sound of voices in the hall brought Herschel back to the case at hand. He rose from his chair as the door opened and Ron entered, his hand at the waist of the attractive young woman with him. Her crisp white blouse and tan slacks, and bouncing pony tail pleased Herschel, but her simple beauty and radiant smile sent an exhilaration through him. He was glad *he* didn't have to try to convince some judge that this woman's husband had been out fooling around, out somewhere forcing himself on an older woman.

Ron kept his open hand lightly at the small of his wife's back, keeping her abreast of him as they approached the desk. "Herschel, this is Judy."

"Mr. Birdwell." Judy smiled pleasantly, nodding and extending her hand as she spoke.

Herschel took the hand gently and just held it, unwilling to give it a shake and subject such a superb example of femininity to what he considered a masculine ritual. "It's nice to meet you, Judy. Sorry it had to be under these circumstances." He patted her hand softly as he released it, then motioned to the molded chair in front of his desk. "Just call me Herschel. Let's save the formalities for the courtroom."

"Okay." She sidled over to the borrowed chair and placed her small purse on the corner of the desk as she sat down. When she was situated, Ron lowered himself into the other chair.

When they were settled Herschel moved back to his chair and sat down, scooting up to the desk as he pulled his notes into position.

Ned's advice drifted through his mind as he faced the young couple. A case can seem to be awesome if you look at it as a whole, like a forest, but if you approach it as merely a bunch of trees, and take them one at a time, you can handle the problem, each item in its turn.

He glanced at Ron, then turned to Judy. "I'm delighted that you want to attend the hearing." He hadn't really been sure about that until now, after he had met her, but she didn't need to know that. "Your presence in the courtroom can be a great help if you understand what this is all about, and willing to help."

Judy leaned forward solemnly. "Mr. Birdwell?" She stopped, as though flustered, and started again. "Herschel, I want you to know I don't appreciate what these people are trying to do to my husband, and I want *them* to know that, too. I will certainly do whatever I can to help."

Herschel nodded, touched by the anguish in her voice but satisfied with her determination. "First, you need to be aware of what this is all about. Have you and your husband talked about it? How much do you know about the case?"

Judy frowned as she thought about it. Mr. Birdwell looked so sinister, made it sound so bad. "Ron told me what they have accused him of, and I know it isn't true. My husband would never take money from anybody, or," she hesitated with a blush, "well, take advantage of that contractor's wife."

Ron shifted uncomfortably in his chair. "I told her about talking to the woman at the Holiday Inn that night, and how you think they might bring it up, try to use it at the hearing."

Herschel nodded, raising his ballpoint like a baton. "Okay. That's fine, and as of right now, I want you to understand, both of you, that everything we talk about is to remain between the three of us. I don't want either one of you to discuss anything about our case with anybody. Not your family, not your friends, not your co-workers. Nobody. Understood?"

Herschel watched the two of them turn to each other, becoming serious as they begin to nod, then turned his attention to Judy.

"Ron and I have been over this thing in depth. We have covered every angle, considered every possibility, and I am satisfied that Ron will be able to handle himself during the hearing, particularly on the witness stand." Herschel paused for a moment to get her reaction. "And we can certainly use your help at the hearing, but for you to give it your undivided attention, and not be distracted by a lot of gutter talk, bewildered by any surprises, you need to know what this is all about, understand where the allegations came from and what Jake Marshallton and his attorney are trying to accomplish."

Herschel glanced over at Ron, then back to Judy. "I don't know how much your husband has told you about these people, but you need to know who is involved and aware of how low they will stoop, even in a public courtroom. There will be some ugly accusations at the hearing, and probably some rather harsh insinuations concerning your husband's character."

As Herschel waited for her reaction he realized how tense she had become. "I don't mean to scare you, Judy, but there are things you need to be aware of, things you need to know. If you will just relax, settle back and make yourself comfortable, we'll explain the situation and bring you up to where we are on this thing."

Judy smiled wanly, nodding as she stiffly settled back in the molded chair and crossed her legs. She was frightened for her husband, and would be until this had all been resolved.

Herschel clicked the ballpoint in and out as he watched her. He needed to work on relieving her anxiety. "How familiar are you with your husband's job? What do you know about his work?"

She began to shake her head. "Just that he's responsible for a lot of contracts that haul mail. Ron never discusses his work with me. He told me right after he was promoted that contracting business is not public information, but Ron did tell me when all of this came up that Mr. Marshallton is one of the more difficult contractors he works with."

Herschel nodded. "Jake Marshallton isn't like anyone you've ever met before, Judy. He has no principles whatsoever. The man inherited a fortune from his father, as well as the business enterprise that holds a number of transportation contracts with the Postal Service, and Jake makes it a point to compromise the people he does business with so he can control any situation that may arise."

Judy continued to sit rigidly, a chill setting in between her shoulders as her frown became tighter. "What do you mean, *compromise?*"

"Buy, bribe, finagle. Whatever it takes to gain embarrassing personal information or other evidence that will give him an edge, that will render them virtually defenseless." Herschel paused for a moment. It pained him to see what anguish could do to such a pretty face. "That's why Jake Marshallton sent his wife to the Holiday Inn that night, to, ah," he glanced away briefly, "gain carnal knowledge of your husband."

She blanched as she turned slowly to her husband. "You didn't tell me the woman you talked to at the bar that night was the contractor's wife."

Judy's sudden chagrin brought Herschel forward in his chair. "Ron didn't know who she was at the time, and we still don't know for sure that the woman was Alice Marshallton. From Ron's description of the woman, though, and the way she went about approaching him, some of the things she mentioned, we can only surmise that's who she was."

She turned away and reached for her purse, keeping her back to them while she took out a tissue and dabbed at her eyes. Herschel continued, his voice soft, his tone becoming almost apologetic.

"Jake Marshallton has always been obstinate, and is being particularly so with Ron about some current contract business, and was probably just waiting for a chance like this. I have no doubt that when he found out Ron would be staying at the Holiday Inn that night, he sent his wife over there for a little salacious compromising, hanky-panky if you will, and Ron turned her down. He declined her invitation to go bar hopping, and whatever else they had in mind that would put your husband at a distinct disadvantage."

Herschel waited until Judy turned back, touching the tissue lightly to her nose. He held his hands out on each side of the file on the desk before him as he spoke, palms up, as though offering it as an example. "Your husband refused to play their little game, so Jake's trying to get rid of him?"

Judy's eyes began to moisten again as she wadded the tissue into her left hand and slid her right hand over to where her husband's left hand was resting on the edge of the desk. Their little fingers grasped each other as she spoke. "I've known my husband for a long time, Herschel, nearly all of my life, and I know he would never do the things they claim. Ron would never do either one of the things they have charged him with."

She still felt a twinge of shame at her reaction the night Ron had told her about the charges. "Ron explained how Mr. Marshallton's present marriage is no more than a business arrangement. I'm not concerned with what those people do or how they run their lives, until they start interfering in our life, mine and Ron's, trying to discredit my husband. Then I *am* concerned."

She released Ron's hand and brought the wrinkled tissue to her eyes. "I want to be there, Herschel. I want those people to know I don't appreciate what they're trying to do. I want to see that woman, I want look at her while she is saying what they have told her to say about my husband."

Herschel had never considered himself any kind of a fighter, but the cause for the emotion in her soft voice infuriated him, made him want to pull the big sword out of that rock and ride out to slaughter her dragons as he nodded and pulled his yellow pad over beside the file. "That's exactly what I had in mind. I want you to listen very carefully to every word, listen to everything they say at the hearing, and tell me what doesn't fit. Tell me what isn't right about anything they say, especially when they are talking about your husband."

He turned to Ron. "And I want you to listen like you've been doing at the other hearings we've been involved in, and tell me anything that anybody says that is wrong, or even questionable. Walter Hardesty will have to give the judge a believable account of your alleged actions. The sonofa..," he flushed suddenly at his blunder. "The man is a real pro at stuff like this, but in fabricating the complete story, and the testimony to verify what they claim, it would seem almost impossible to not slip up somewhere."

Herschel turned back to Judy. "I'll see that you're in the front row, where you can pass your notes to your husband at the defense table." He paused for a moment, scratching the side of his head. "Each of you will need to have something to take notes on. A small notebook should do fine. I don't want either of you to flaunt what you're doing, but don't try to hide it either. Just act natural, listening and making notes of whatever you think I should know. It might not hurt to write something every now and then anyway, just to keep them on their toes. If something important should come up while I'm questioning somebody, something that I should know immediately, Ron will place the note on the table in front of my chair, where I can step over and look at it. Otherwise he will just hold it until I get through with whatever I'm doing."

A resolve began to rise in Judy as she listened. She had watched Ron go over paperwork he had brought home on the nights before he was going to attend a hearing with Herschel. He had told her that Herschel was never familiar with the contract in question, the contractor's record of performance or even the reason for the hearing sometimes, and it was up to him to keep Herschel advised as the hearing progressed. It hadn't dawned on her at the time that her husband was preparing to appear in court as an adviser to an attorney. It gave her confidence that they apparently knew what they were doing as Herschel continued.

"And the image you give the judge, your personal appearance and behavior, is just as important as any testimony." He waited for them to nod. "I want you both to look nice, dressed as though you were going to church. That will show respect for the court, but I don't want to see anything that the judge could even remotely intrepret as a recent splurge. No new clothes or shoes, no jewelry other than a watch and wedding rings." Herschel smiled. "I don't mean for you to look like paupers, but I don't want there to be any signs of recent prosperity, either."

Herschel looked down at his file. He wished he could sound more optimistic, more confident, or even better organized, but the only thing he had so far, the only thing he could document, was the deal with the car. That in itself should be enough, but he would feel a whole lot better if Ron or his wife could come up with something to add to that, some additional item that Ron could contradict while he's on the stand.

He closed the file as he glanced at Ron. "I believe I told you the hearing is scheduled for a week from Friday, unless Walter Hardesty or the Marshalltons have a conflict. I sent my okay to Judge Chandler for that date after I talked to you yesterday."

Ron turned to his wife. "I told Herschel the date was fine with us. The hearing will probably be held in one of the smaller courtrooms downtown."

The casual mention of *downtown* bothered Judy. She had heard some real horror stories from people who had been called for jury duty. "You're talking about the Federal Building? At Twelfth and Market?"

"Yeah." Ron nodded. "That's where Herschel and I hold most of our hearings with contractors."

"Don't let the location frighten you, Judy." Herschel could understand her concern. He had often heard Ned Ashcroft refer to the ominous effect a federal courtroom had on someone who had never had to appear in one. "The judge we have is a respected jurist, and the hallowed halls and grandeur of the courtroom will have no bearing on our case."

Judy smiled wanly at Herschel as she stood, then reached over for her purse. "I'm not too happy about this whole thing, anyway, but we do appreciate your efforts on Ron's behalf."

Herschel pushed up from his chair as Judy took her husband's arm. It was such a shame that the law allowed the Jake Marshalltons and the Walter Hardestys of the world to prey on decent people. "Don't let it get to you, Judy. We need you to be alert, to help us catch the discrepancies in their story. I'll let you know about the date when it's firmed up, and in the meantime, call me if either of you think of something that sounds strange or doesn't precisely fit."

After they were gone, Herschel just stood there, listening until their footsteps had faded away down the hall. Ned's idea of giving Judy something to do at the hearing would take her mind away from her husband's troubles, and who knows, she just might come up with something. Sam Whitely had always insisted that truth would truimph in the end, but Sam had never heard of Walter Hardesty. Walter Hardesty had been at it so long that it was second nature to him. The man was a smooth sonofabitch, but then, Herschel shrugged, Jake Marshallton was a devout hothead, and people like that can sometimes be a loose cannon.

He still felt that it wouldn't be a bad idea to inquire about some security in the courtroom as he picked up the file and slid it into his briefcase, then reached for his coat. Ned would know about things like that.

CHAPTER FOURTEEN

Bill Warden was still fuming as he lifted his carry-on bag from the trunk of his car, slammed the lid down and turned toward the airport terminal. It had never occurred to him that he would be expected to attend the hearing tomorrow. The idea had never entered his mind when Hiram Jordan called this morning.

That shitass had snookered him into going to Cape Girardeau to talk to Jake Marshallton about the charges against Ron. Bill felt he had handled that fairly well, had managed to approach Jake and talk about the case without pissing him off, but he had no intention of pushing his luck any farther, no intention of going anywhere near that courtroom.

The thought of being called to the witness stand to face Walter Hardesty and Herschel Birdwell in front of Jake Marshallton and Ron, and particularly that judge, was out of the question. He wasn't about to jeopardize his position on Jake's guest list. It had taken too long to work his way into the upper echelons of management, and the perks that went with it. He readily admitted he had developed a certain affinity for Ron Hamilton, but that didn't mean he was going to be stupid about it. There were other transportation people around who were looking for a promotion.

He nodded agreement with his decision to put some distance between himself and the hearing as he hurried across the sprawling white-lined parking lot. He had learned a long time ago to maintain a standing *emergency* that could be used for his own emergencies anytime they came up.

Hiram Jordan and the rest of the so called *wheels* in the Region and the District offices might just as well realize that Bill Warden was nobody's patsy. He was beginning to understand the rules of the game, or the fact that there really weren't any. That goddamn Jordan and the rest of those conniving bastards might as well get it through their heads that Bill Warden was as quick on his feet as the rest of them.

Bill had countered Hiram's little ploy this morning by telling him that he was just getting ready to call when the phone ring. It tickled Bill to recall how the bastard had actually sounded concerned when Bill went into a gripping rendition of his aging mother being rushed to the hospital last night in Florida. The irritation in his voice had apparently been mistaken for anxiety because it had knocked the wind out of Hiram's sails, had left the man dead in the water. He had never heard Hiram so apologetic before. Then when Bill hung up, just on the chance that goddamn Jordan might decide to check his story, he had immediately called the airport and made a reservation on the evening flight to Tampa.

He slowed as he stepped up on the curb and approached the automatic doors, then headed across the main terminal to the concourse where the Tampa flight was already being called for boarding.

Bill had never been too close to his family, even before his father died. Then when the old man finally kicked the bucket, and his mother went to live with his sister in a trailer court near Lakeland, Bill had not bothered to keep in touch. When his sister *did* call or write it was always to ask for money or whine about something. She had finally given up on that, though, until last month when she wrote to tell him their mother's health had deteriorated to the point that she could no longer care for her, and had put the old woman in a nursing home.

His sister's letter had aggravated him. In fact, everything she did aggravated him. Besides a whiny vocabulary, she had the idea that money grew on the trees in his backyard, and was the answer to all her problems.

Bill shrugged off a twinge of remorse as he handed the flight attendant his boarding pass, then moved down the aisle in search of his seat. He guessed he really should go see his mother while he was in Florida, in case someone should get nosy. It *would* verify his story, validate his excuse for leaving town on such short notice. He wouldn't have to stay long at the Nursing Home even though he had no intention of returning home, and surely not going back to the office for several days, at least not until that damn hearing was over. He didn't want to be too obvious about it.

The thought of spending a few days in Florida excited Bill. It had been several years since he had allowed himself any kind of a decent holiday, and he shouldn't have too much trouble killing time. Cypress Gardens was just to the south of Lakeland, and he could drive across the state to Cape Canaveral, even take in Disney World while he was over there. A person could easily kill a day at each one of those places.

When his carry-on bag was stowed in the overhead compartment, Bill took off his suit coat, carefully folded it with the lining out and flattened it across the top of his bag, then snapped the door shut. As he settled into his seat he smiled at the thought of not only avoiding the hearing, and outwitting Hiram Jordan and those other bastards, but being free of the whole damn mess. He could call the office, act like he was at the hospital, and be sure the hearing was over and done with before he called the airline for a reservation to go back home.

He pulled the seat belt from under him and fastened it, then began fingering through the magazines in the seat pocket, frowning at the thought of going to Florida alone. It would have been much more enjoyable if he could have brought Helen along.

The thought of spending a few days in Florida with the spirited red-head from Rockmarsh Lodge quickened his pulse, then faded as the image of Alice Marshallton moved into his mind. Helen was a nice young lady, really knew how to treat a man, but Alice Marshallton was the ultimate prize. Bill had considered the woman as something he could only lust after for the time being, a kewpie doll on the next higher level of the transportation contracting carnival, until he read Jake's letter of charges that day.

The very idea of his transportation officer, he own damn subordinate, having the audacity to ignore the unwritten rules, to step the fuck around him and partake of the higher level spoils of the business world had just about blown his mind. While he had choked on his coffee, coughing up pieces of the powdered-sugar donut Maggie had brought him that morning, not only a vision of Ron

Hamilton humping Alice Marshallton had exploded through his system, but the boy had a five thousand dollar bouquet of greenbacks clutched in each hand. It had raised his blood pressure well into the stroke zone, and started a gut rumble that put an ungodly strain on his bowels.

Bill just sat there fuming, subconsciously watching the auburn-haired stewardess prepare her galley for the flight. The movement of a female body, even a fully clothed one, could keep him enraptured even when his thoughts were somewhere else. His eyes often worked independently of his mind, and sometimes, if the woman's body or her movements were provocative enough, his eyes could even operate independently of each other.

His expression gave no hint of his disgust with the Postal Service hierarchy, particularly the higher authority of transportation management, who apparently had no sense of propriety. Had no allegiance to anything other than their own crude ego. He couldn't help but feel the hearing had been staged more to appease Jake Marshallton than it was to defend his transportation officer, otherwise one of the trial attorneys from Headquarters would have been assigned to handle the case. Bill doubted that Hiram had even mentioned Jake's accusations to the Law Department in Washington.

His stomach churned at the thought of the outcome of the hearing. He hated to lose Ron, the boy was a good transportation officer, but it disturbed him more to think of being dropped from the roster for the week-end parties at Rockmarsh Lodge. His only consolation was that he was in the same boat with Hiram Jordan, and Hiram had managed to navigate that well known creek several times before, both with and without a paddle, and had never picked up any stain or stink.

Bill's eyes continued to follow the flight attendant as she turned and came down the aisle, stretching up to check the door latch on each overhead luggage compartment, then straightening her clothes as she looked down to make sure the passenger occupying that particular seat had their lap belt fastened. She leaned across Bill as she reached up to check the overhead compartment latch, then settled back with a warm smile and a pat on his shoulder as she moved on. The closeness of her body and the scent of her perfume activated the hair-trigger antenna on Bill's overactive libido.

His eyebrows raised as he turned to watch the woman work her way down the aisle, checking the baggage compartments, and seat belts where there was a passenger in the seat. He hadn't seen her smile at anyone else, or pat another shoulder either.

He would have to keep her in sight when they landed. Tampa was apparently the designated layover point for a lot of those women. He almost purred at the thought of so many lonely women in one place, a regular libido luau, and he had told no one he was coming, or even made motel reservations.

Bill smirked as he turned back and picked up the magazine again. He could visit the damn nursing home anytime.

CHAPTER FIFTEEN

Herschel glanced around the empty courtroom as he placed his briefcase on the defense counsel table. He and Ron had never used this particular courtroom for a contractor hearing, but he had been here several times with Ned Ashcroft. It wasn't as a second chair or anything like that. He had just tagged along as an interested party and helped with whatever he could.

There was always a smell of furniture polish and dust in these imposing rooms in spite of the janitor's best efforts. The furniture and varnished woodwork always glistened in spite of a few dust motes drifting lazily in the narrow ray of sunshine slanting down from the small windows high above the judges bench.

He had arrived early intentionally. The quiet before the others started arriving would give him a chance to get settled and go over his notes, to organize his thoughts and be ready to face the task he had been preparing for. He was aware that some trial attorneys labored under the illusion that the one who could attract the most attention, the one who came swirling in at the last minute with their client and a large entourage would make the best impression. That was fine with him because he was also aware that the judge never entered the courtroom until everyone else was in place, and the judge, and of course Ron and his wife, were the only ones he was concerned about today.

The door from the hall in the back of the building, the one that led to the conference rooms and the judges chambers, opened and a blonde woman, who looked to be in her forties, came in and closed the door behind her. She crossed to the small table between the jury box and the judge's bench, positioned to face the witness stand, and began setting up her recorder.

Herschel opened his briefcase and took out his file as John Bernstein, who had served as court clerk at a couple of his and Ron's hearings, stepped just inside the rear door to look around. He nodded to Herschel, turned to watch the woman setting up her recorder for a moment, then went back out and closed the door.

Herschel pulled the chair out and sat down. The butterflies in his stomach had settled down considerably since he had gotten up this morning and doused them with some orange juice and several cups of scalding black coffee, but it still bothered him that some obnoxious sonofabitch could cause so much trouble, could put a respectable young man's future in jeopardy by just writing a letter. There ought to be some kind of protection. He shrugged away his annoyance as he opened the file, conceding that was what these hearings were really all about, what he had been assigned to do. Convince the judge that the charges were a big glob of bullshit so the man could officially hand Jake Marshallton and Walter Hardesty their letter of charges back and tell them what they could do with it.

Herschel had managed to go all the way through the file, and organize the points in his mind that he wanted to concentrate on before he sensed another presence, and looked up. Ron stood just inside the gate in the railing, facing his wife who had stopped on the other side.

"Hello, Ron." Herschel nodded to Judy as he pushed himself up from his chair. "Mrs. Hamilton." He closed the file and moved over next to Ron. "I didn't hear you two come in." Herschel gave each of them a quick inspection, then glanced hurriedly around the room to see who else had arrived. There was still only the court reporter, and she was sitting sideways in her chair now, turned partially away from them, reading a paperback book.

Herschel kept his voice low as he turned to Judy, trying to sound more confident than he really was. "Ron will sit here at the table with me, like he always does, and I want you to sit here." He indicated the chair in the front row that was right across the rail from where Ron would be sitting. "I doubt there will be anyone over here on this side except us, but I want you close enough to be in touch with Ron. I would rather you two didn't try to talk to each other while the hearing is in session, just slip your notes through the railing. Ron will sit so he can keep his eye on you, so don't hesitate to mention anything you think we should know."

When she nodded tensely, he continued with a whimsical grin. "I'm aware that men would have women believe they are infallible, master of all they survey, but we'll have to forgo that little misconception for today. We will appreciate any help you can give us."

It pleased Herschel when she relaxed and smiled at her husband. "And don't let any of this," he gestured to the high bench with its seal and flags, "or any of these people scare you. Jake Marshallton is innately contemptible and Walter Hardesty has been known to manipulate a jury, but I don't believe either one of them will try to deceive or hassle a judge, not a judge with Frank Chandler's reputation, anyway."

The sound of footsteps and garbled voices interrupted them a moment before the tall doors at the back of the courtroom opened, the double doors from the front corridor. The three of them turned to watch Walter Hardesty, in all of his professional splendor, step inside the courtroom and turn. The attorney waited until the short woman with black hair, wearing a plain print dress and low heeled shoes had entered, then swung around and pompously proceeded down the aisle, a brown leather briefcase in his right hand and the woman on his left.

Walter Hardesty wasn't holding the somber woman's hand, or even touching her, but he gave the impression he was escorting her protectively until they reached the railing, then he stopped and turned, like a theater usher, and motioned her into the front row of seats to the left. She sidled along in front of the chairs until she was adjacent to the plaintiff's counsel table, then eased herself down and sat demurely with her feet together on the floor. Her dress was long enough to cover her knees, and the collar was buttoned loosely around her throat. She looked stolidly down at her hands clasped together in her lap.

Herschel was trying to place her, trying to imagine where she might fit in the production he was sure Walter Hardesty had prepared for today, when he turned and saw Jake Marshallton ambling down the aisle alone. The man was his usual self, ignoring everything and everybody as he pushed through the gate and turned toward the plaintiff's counsel table. He pushed Walter Hardesty's briefcase toward the end of the table, out of his way, then just stood there, haughtily surveying the courtroom and everyone in it.

Herschel had seen people enter a place as if they owned it, or at least wanted you to think they were a friend of the person who did, but Jake Marshallton gave the impression he wasn't particularly interested in who owned this courtroom, or had the slightest respect for a Federal Courthouse, and wanted everyone present to know it.

In the apparent absence of Mrs. Marshallton, Herschel turned back to the woman, who was still sitting quietly, just across the railing from where Walter Hardesty and Jake Marshallton had seated themselves at their counsel table. As he studied her downcast face, she glanced up at Jake and his attorney, across the railing from her, and the small mole above her eyebrow caused a strange sensation to creep up on him. He had heard of someone making a silk purse out of a sow's ear, but damned if Walter Hardesty hadn't accomplished the exact opposite. The bastard had managed to reverse the procedure.

Herschel turned to Ron, keeping his voice to a whisper as he leaned close. "That woman over there, the one that came in with Walter Hardesty. Have you seen her before?"

Ron frowned as he moved to his left to look past Herschel. He began to shake his head as he studied her. There was nothing familiar about her, nothing that he could see from where he stood.

Herschel's voice was still low. "There won't be a chance in hell that the judge will see anything about her that could possibly have instigated the alleged violation of her body."

Herschel moved closer to the rail, next to Judy, with his back to the plaintiff's side of the courtroom. He still spoke in a whisper. "Don't look now, but the woman sitting over there behind the railing is Mrs. Marshallton. In all fairness, though, I must tell you that she is a much more attractive woman than they would have the judge see today."

Judy frowned as she glanced over Herschel's shoulder, then brought her attention back to him. "I noticed her as she came in. She appeared to be embarrassed. I felt that it was probably due to the way she's dressed, with her hair pulled back on the sides with a ribbon like that."

Ron moved closer to them. "Are you sure, Herschel? She doesn't look anything like the woman I talked to in the bar that night."

Herschel's eyebrows lifted as he whispered. "I told you Walter Hardesty never leaves anything to chance. The man has made sure she won't be doing any flashing here today, even if it's unintentional. He doesn't intend for there to be the least doubt in the judge's mind about who took who into that bedroom."

Judy turned cautiously to look at the woman again for a moment, then she turned to study Jake Marshallton and Walter Hardesty, busily huddled together. It frightened her as she watched them, to think that a businessman and an attorney, a member of the legal profession, were conspiring, actually concocting a story to get Ron fired, or at least demoted, and the courts apparently had provisions for handling something like that. It was all so wrong.

Herschel kept his eye on Judy as they waited, concerned with her apparent discomfort. He had done his best to impart a confidence to both Ron and his wife that he really didn't have himself. He watched them both until the blonde woman, the court recorder, glanced up from her book and looked around, then put it away and turned to position herself in front of her machine. Heschel slowly checked the rest of the room then reluctantly took his seat at the defense table.

Judy nodded when Ron asked if she was okay, even though she wasn't sure. She had never been involved in anything like this before. She couldn't imagine a married woman, even at the direction of her husband, attempting to seduce another woman's husband. Then she remembered Herschel had said there would be *ugly accusations* here in court today, and the anguish of it all began to gnaw at her again. Some of the words Ron said Herschel had used were bad enough, so there was no telling what kind of language these other people were going to use.

She tried to smile as she whispered and stepped back from the railing. "I'll be just fine, honey. You concentrate on what you and Mr. Birdwell have to do. I'll be right here, listening to everything they say."

Ron waited until she was seated, watched her take a pen and small spiral notebook from her purse, then pulled his chair out and sat down sideways to the counsel table. Herschel had already placed a yellow legal pad and ballpoint in front of his chair. He still didn't like the idea of his wife being here, being exposed to the vulgarities these people were sure to bring up, but he had to admit that Judy's presence *did* make him feel a lot better.

CHAPTER SIXTEEN

Frank Chandler quietly entered the courtroom and pulled the door shut behind him. He wasn't wearing a robe, just a dark brown suit and white shirt, with a diagonally stripped multicolored tie. Frank was aware that some judges insisted on wearing their robe anytime they presided in a courtroom, but these contract appeal hearings were conducted in more of an informal manner. He felt a business suit would suffice, and without the robe, the court clerk's ritualistic introduction and call to order could also be dispensed with.

He made his way across the room, nodding to the court reporter as he passed, and mounted the narrow steps to the small platform behind the bench. Frank placed the manila folder he was carrying on the desk while the sweep of his eyes took in the people at both counsel tables, as well as the lone woman sitting behind the railing on each side. The young woman on the defense side held a small notebook and ballpoint at the ready, as though she couldn't wait to get started, but the somber woman on the plaintiff side sat with her hands folded in her lap, looking down as if she would rather be anywhere other than here. After a moment he stepped over and lowered himself into the high-backed leather chair and scooted up to the desk.

Walter Hardesty calmly reached out and put his hand on Jake's arm when he saw the judge wasn't wearing a robe. The bombastic attorney was aware that Jake Marshallton would be offended by the judge's casualness. When Jake brought someone into court, especially when he had failed to influence the choice of the judge, he insisted on the full sacraments of the judiciary. Without the robe and the *hear ye, hear ye, all rise* intonation of the clerk, Walter Hardesty couldn't be sure that his client would just sit there. Jake might very well decide to take it on himself to let the judge know who he was, and that he certainly didn't appreciate the man belittling his case by relinquishing the legal system's pomp and ceremonial grandeur.

When Herschel noticed Walter Hardesty's show of concern for his client at the plaintiff's table, his stomach cringed as the butterflies began to throw off the overdose of caffeine and respond to the Vitamin C in the orange juice as they started flitting about. He glanced around to make sure he knew exactly where Ron's wife was sitting. Surely Jake wouldn't throw one of his tantrums right here in the courtroom, but Herschel couldn't be certain. He had no experience at all in dealing with devout dementia.

After Walter Hardesty withdrew his hand from Jake's arm with a few whispered words, Jake nodded sullenly as he shifted in his chair and pulled a handkerchief from his back pocket. He slowly wrapped a corner of it around the eraser end of a yellow lead pencil, then began cleaning his left ear while everyone else in the room concentrated on the judge.

Frank Chandler studied the small group of people in the courtroom, those at each counsel table, and particularly the two women sitting outside the railing. He could understand the difference in their apparent attitudes, but the difference in their appearances just didn't fit the charges. Not if they were who he could only presume they were. He looked down at the file in front of him, pondering the problem for a moment before he turned to glance at the clock on the wall. He compared the clock's time with his wristwatch, then looked over at the court reporter poised in front of her machine. "Are you ready, Ms. Compton?"

"Yes, Your Honor." The woman nodded as she waited, her fingers resting lightly on the keys. "I'm ready when you are."

The judge drew himself up, keeping his attention on the two tables before him, particularly the plaintiff's table, where things seemed to be much more tense. "I am Judge Franklin Chandler, from the Twelfth Circuit Court of Appeals, currently serving a term on the United States Postal Service Board of Contract Appeals.

Even though the hearing today will be informal, we will abide by all rules of procedure and protocol of the Court."

He frowned toward the plaintiff's table, at the apparent indifference of the man in the tan suit as he switched the pencil and handkerchief to the other ear, then gave the defense table a quick glance and nodded toward the court reporter. "Ms. Marlene Compton will record the hearing in its entirety, and all testimony will be given under oath. Are there any questions?"

Walter Hardesty seemed to give the matter some thought for a moment before he started shaking his head. "No, Your Honor."

Herschel sat hunched over the legal pad and open file in front of him on the table. In his discussions with Ned Ashcroft, he had asked about the possibility of filing a motion to dismiss, but Ned had explained that at the present time there was only the letter of accusation, that nothing had actually been recognized by the court. The hearing would determine if there was enough evidence to warrant a trial, and if the judge felt there was, then a motion to dismiss the charges would be in order at that time. However, Ned had cautioned, that if the same judge were handling the trial, Herschel should bear in mind that he would be asking the judge to reverse his own decision.

Herschel felt as though he were sitting on the down side of a teeter-totter, trying to operate the contraption by himself as he raised his eyes to the bench without moving his head. "I have no questions, Your Honor."

Judge Chandler glanced over at the recorder as she paused, keeping her fingers in position on the keys, then opened the file before him and moved a legal pad into position.

"Is counsel for the plaintiff present?"

Walter Hardesty rose solemnly from his chair. "I am Walter H. Hardesty, Your Honor, representing the plaintiff, Jacob R. Marshallton."

The judge waited for him to finish, then nodded and entered the names on his pad. "How many witnesses do you plan to call today, Mr. Hardesty?"

"Two, Your Honor." The attorney nodded politely as he gave his vest a tug. "The plaintiff, Jacob R. Marshallton, and his wife, Alice Marshallton."

Herschel's eyebrows lifted at the information. He had been warned about that sonofabitching Hardesty. The absence of a bartender today, and probably someone who *just happened* to see Ron cozying up to the woman in a booth at the roadhouse that night, didn't mean they weren't going to use a twisted version of the attempted deflowering of Ron that he had walked out on at the Holiday Inn that night. The bastard was apparently harboring his collection of so-called *eye*witnesses for the trial.

When the judge finished writing, he thanked Walter Hardesty and turned his attention to the defense table. "Is counsel for the defense present?"

Herschel pushed himself to his feet, the judge's bench seemingly even higher than when he was sitting. "Herschel Birdwell, Your Honor. I am counsel for the defendant, Ronald Hamilton."

The judge nodded as he wrote. "And how many witnesses do you plan to call today, Mr. Birdwell?"

"Just one, Your Honor." Herschel took a deep breath to quell the swirling butterflies and the apprehension their wings were fanning within him. "I will call the defendant, Ronald Hamilton."

Judge Chandler nodded slightly, hesitating a moment before he started writing. The whole thing was beginning to appear a little lopsided. Walter Hardesty, a prominent trial lawyer, being opposed by Herschel Birdwell, who was listed in the Postal Service Legal Department as Assistant Counsel for Transportation Contracts at the Regional level. And he was only going to call the accused as a witness.

The judge finished writing and stopped, going back over the contractor's letter in his mind. With the nature of the charges against the young man, there really weren't any other witnesses to call.

Frank shrugged as he realized that nothing other than the testimony given here today could have any bearing on his decision. The court reporter would have no way of entering the attitudes or descriptions of the witnesses, or the vast difference between the attorneys into the transcription. But there was nothing to keep him from making notes for his own information.

He looked up from his yellow pad and thanked Herschel Birdwell, then sighed as he turned toward the plaintiff's table. "Mr. Hardesty, you may call your first witness."

CHAPTER SEVENTEEN

Walter Hardesty scooted his chair back quietly and stood. He reached up and fingered his floppy bow tie, gave his red broadcloth vest a sharp tug, then began fastening the top button of his dark blue suit coat as he stepped away from his chair at the end of the counsel table. "I call the plaintiff, Your Honor. Jacob R. Marshallton."

Jake slowly withdrew the yellow pencil from his handkerchief and placed it by the legal pad on the table in front of him, then began refolding the handkerchief along its original creases. He rose from the table, pushing his tan gabardine suit coat back to replace the handkerchief in his hip pocket as he crossed to the witness stand. The cuff of his right pant leg was caught on the pull strap at the top of his blue ostrich skin western boot.

When he stepped up on the low platform in front of the heavy chair and turned, John Bernstein, who had come from where he had been sitting in the empty jury box, moved to the front of the chair and raised his right hand.

"Do you, Jacob R. Marshallton, promise to tell the truth, the whole truth and nothing but the truth, so help you God?"

When Jake just nodded and sat down, Judge Chandler quickly leaned to one side to look around the court clerk, and make eye contact with the plaintiff's attorney. "Mr. Hardesty, will you remind your witness that this hearing is being recorded, and a verbal response will be necessary?"

Before Walter Hardesty could respond, Jake pushed himself up from the witness chair, raised his right hand higher than required as he drew himself up, and began to recite the oath in a tone verging on mockery. "I, Jacob R. Marshallton, do hereby solemnly swear by

God to tell the truth, the whole truth and nothing but the truth in this courtroom."

John Bernstein scowled his distaste as he turned and headed toward his seat in the empty jury box. "A simple *I do* would have been sufficient."

Jake chortled as he leaned forward, raising his voice to reach the court clerk where he was turning by now to take his seat. "Too many *I do's* can put a man in the poorhouse."

"We will have order in this courtroom." Judge Chandler's words were sharp as he rapped his gavel. "Mr. Hardesty, remind your witness that he is in a court of law, then have him take his seat and let's get started."

"Your Honor?" The attorney made a point of glaring at Jake for a moment before he turned to the judge. "I respectfully request that the court clerk's remark, and my client's response be stricken from the record."

"On what grounds?"

"It isn't relevant to the hearing, Your Honor."

Judge Chandler placed his elbows on the desk and steepled his fingers in front of his chin without taking his eyes from Walter Hardesty. It irritated him for someone, especially an insolent attorney, to attempt to manipulate the proceedings in his courtroom.

"In my earlier instructions I believe I stated that the hearing would be recorded in its entirety." The judge paused, still not taking his eyes from the presumptuous attorney. "I will be quite capable of determining what is and what is not relevant when I review the transcript. Is that clear, Mr. Hardesty?"

"Yes, Your Honor."

"For the record, your request is denied." The judge turned his chair toward the witness and settled back. "Now, let's quit wasting time and get on with the business at hand."

Walter Hardesty turned boldly to the witness chair, where Jake was now seated again, gloating up at him as if they had just won a point on arrogance.

Jake Marshallton's bluster frightened Ron, especially his disrespect for the judge as well as the court, and Ron could only shrug when Herschel glanced at him quizzically. He had never actually had any dealings, personal or otherwise, with Jake

Marshallton, but the contractor was certainly living up to his reputation.

"You Honor?" Walter Hardesty rubbed his palms together as he looked up at the judge. "If it pleases the court, I would like to enter some information into the record, an opening statement of sorts, to provide background for Mr. Marshallton's problems with the Transportation Office, and clarify his testimony here today."

"Very well." The judge nodded. "As long as it pertains to the subject matter of this hearing."

"It does, Your Honor." The attorney unbuttoned his suit coat as he stepped back over to the witness stand and nodded toward Jake. "Mr. Marshallton has eight contracts with the Postal Service for the transportation of mail. These contracts were awarded to him as the lowest responsible bidder through the competitive bid process, and four of them have been renewed for an additional term by good-faith negotiation. The combined annual rate of these eight contracts, at the present time, is slightly in excess of two million dollars, and the contracts are administered by the Transportation Office here in St. Louis. Due to the ever increasing cost of fuel, and the fact that particular item in transportation contracts is adjustable, is therefore the crux of our being here today."

Herschel glanced at Ron's pad. He turned his head slightly to read the five words written there. *Fluctuating fuel costs, not increasing.* He nodded knowlingly, glad to see that Ron was paying such close attention, and his expression indicating that he wasn't exactly overjoyed with Walter Hardesty's attempt to mislead the judge on the actual *crux* of this tour de farce.

"Now." Walter Hardesty nodded to the judge and turned to face his witness, indicating he was finished with the lecture. "When did the Transportation Office start badgering you about your fuel costs, Mr. Marshallton?"

Herschel pushed his chair back and started to rise. The word *badgering* didn't exactly fit the situation, but Jake Marshallton had already started answering the question before he had time to object.

"It started about a year ago." Jake leaned forward angrily, his eyes glaring as he waved his hand toward the defense table. "Right after they brought in what's-his-face. The hard charger over there."

Judge Chandler's voice was calm as he placed his elbows on the desk and leaned forward. "Mr. Hardesty, everyone involved here today has been introduced. Surely your witness can identify the person he is referring by name, in a civil tone, and without pointing."

Before Walter Hardesty could reply, Jake raised his finger again and waggled it toward the defense table. "I'm talking about Ace over there, the wonder boy. Knows more about my business than I do."

The attorney glared at Jake for a moment, then turned, looking up at the judge. "The witness was indicating the defendant, Your Honor. May we have the record show the witness was pointing to Mr. Hamilton at the defense table?"

The judge's voice was still calm in spite of his rising annoyance. "The only thing the record shows so far, Mr. Hardesty, is the fact that Mr. Marshallton is referring to someone that he apparently doesn't know."

Jake Marshallton came out of his chair, sputtering as he angrily jabbed his finger toward the defense table again. "I'm talking about Hamilton over there, the boy wonder who started all this bullshit about fuel costs."

Walter Hardesty pointed angrily to the witness chair, crowding in on Jake Marshallton until he was seated again, then turned to the judge. "May we have a moment, Your Honor?"

Judge Chandler slumped back into his chair with a nod. "I think that would be an excellent idea, Counselor."

A faint smile crossed Herschel's face. In his discussions with Ned Ashcroft concerning his first appearance before the bench, Ned had told him that judges often used the word *counselor* when they were upset with an attorney. A tingle ran up his spine as he watched Walter Hardesty turn his back to the judge and lean down into Jake's face, his head bobbing as he whispered harshly.

Herschel got up and moved over to crouch between Ron and the railing, motioning Judy to lean forward for a conference. He kept his voice low. "Don't let these guys fool you. It's all part of the act. Walter Hardesty is merely setting the stage for one of his dramas, for something he apparently intends to use later."

Herschel returned to his chair at the sound of Walter Hardesty's voice. "Thank you, Your Honor. We're ready to continue."

"I hope so, Mr. Hardesty." The judge glanced at the court reporter, then the defense table. "You have wasted enough of the court's time."

"Sorry, Your Honor." Walter Hardesty stepped back from the witness chair. "Mr. Marshallton, explain briefly how Mr. Hamilton's obsession with transportation contract fuel costs has involved you."

Jake scowled toward the defense table as he placed his elbows on the chair arms. "Right after Hamilton came into the Transportation Office he started a program of contractors certifying their fuel costs on a monthly basis."

"And did you comply with that program?"

"I did." Jake nodded testily. "And I was informed that my fuel costs were higher than the average price of fuel in the areas where my contracts operate."

"What was your response?"

Jake got louder as he talked. "I told them my drivers don't buy fuel on the road. My trucks are equipped with extra saddle tanks, and carry more than enough fuel to complete their run when they leave any of my service facilities."

Walter Hardesty nodded, as though prompting his witness. "Then you have your own fuel pumps?"

"Yes." The word was sharp as Jake began to nod. "I have my own tanks, and buy all my fuel in bulk."

"And the bulk cost per gallon isn't cheaper than the average price per gallon on the street?" Walter Hardesty stepped back with a smugness.

"The price of the fuel itself is," Jake nodded hastily, "but I have to pay a delivery charge, insurance on the tanks, wages for an employee to maintain the tanks and fuel the trucks. All that adds up, but I don't have any problems with inferior fuel."

Walter Hardesty stayed where he was, glancing complacently up at the judge as he spoke. "Does the Transportation Office accept the explanation of your fuel costs?"

Jake shook his head tiredly. "Apparently not. They keep insisting on a new set of certification forms every month."

"And do you furnish a new set of forms each month?"

"When there's a change I do, otherwise I just tell them it's the same as the last one." Jake scowled as he turned and looked up at the judge. "If they keep it up I'm going to have to start charging them for the clerk time spent on completing all those certification forms."

Walter Hardesty's voice rose slightly as he stepped closer to the witness chair. "Is the *price* of fuel your only problem with the Transportation Office?"

Jake began to shake his head woefully. "No. Now *Mister* Hamilton has started dictating fuel *consumption*."

The attorney looked up at the judge, his eyebrows lifting as though he had been caught unaware. "Fuel consumption?"

Herschel rose from the table while Walter Hardesty was putting on his little act. "Your Honor, the Transportation Office doesn't dictate fuel usage *or* cost to its contractors. They merely monitor it."

Judge Chandler glanced at Herschel as though surprised, then turned his attention back to the witness stand. "Be patient, Mr. Birdwell. You can cover that when you cross-examine the witness."

Herschel lowered himself back into the chair as Jake Marshallton turned and guffawed loudly.

"Mr. Marshallton?" Walter Hardesty's sharp tone sounded more like a reprimand, but he quickly composed himself and went right into his next question. "Tell us about Mr. Hamilton's theory on fuel consumption."

"Well." Jake squinted at the ceiling for a moment. "I don't recall offhand when the boy wonder, *Mister* Hamilton, started talking about air deflectors, radial tires, smooth sides and bubble noses. All kind of good stuff that's supposed to reduce the wind resistance on a vehicle and do wonders for your gas mileage."

"Did you find any merit in Mr. Hamilton's hypothesis?"

Jake shook his head slowly. "I don't care how many smooth sides and bubble noses and radial tires and wind deflectors you put on an eighteen wheeler, the motor is still going to need fuel, a lot of fuel, to move eighty thousand pounds of mail, or anything else down the highway."

"So you don't subscribe..?"

"Mr. Hardesty?" Judge Chandler's voice was curt as he held up his copy of the letter of charges. "How does all of this pertain to the *crux* of our being here today." His voice rose slightly to emphasize the attorney's word.

"I'm coming to that, Your Honor."

"Let's hope so." The judge slumped back in his chair and let the letter fall back onto the file.

Walter Hardesty stepped back, thoughtfully rubbing his chin for a moment before he approached his witness again. "Mr. Marshallton, have you been able to realize any savings at all during this fuel blitz, in either reduced cost or usage."

Herschel didn't feel that Ron's program should be described as a *fuel blitz* in the transcript of the hearing, but Jake had already started talking.

"Nobody has offered to reimburse me to make any alterations on my vehicles, or even convinced me all that stuff would do any good, would be cost effective, so I'm still using the same amount of fuel, and incurring the same costs for that fuel."

"Then you haven't agreed to share any fuel savings with the Transportation Office here in St. Louis?"

Jake shook his head woefully again. "I can't share something I don't have."

Walter Hardesty fingered his bow tie as he watched the judge out of the corner of his eye. "Has the Transportation Office ever mentioned what kind of fuel savings might be involved, the dollar amount they are talking about?"

Jake Marshallton shrugged, raising his eyebrows in an air of innocence as he looked up at his attorney. "I had no idea until the night *Mister* Hamilton, over there at the defense table, called me at home. He said the total savings on my eight contracts could very easily be in excess of a hundred large."

A quick frown took Judge Chandler as he leaned toward the witness. "Excuse me. Be in excess of what?"

Jake Marshallton slouched back in his chair and looked away with a satisfied grin as his attorney stepped over in front of the high bench.

"Mr. Marshallton said a hundred large, Your Honor." Walter Hardesty paused but the judge still appeared to be confused. "Mr.

Hamilton, the defendant, suggested to Mr. Marshallton that the combined annual fuel savings on his eight contracts could easily be in excess of a hundred thousand dollars."

Judge Chandler blanched, his eyebrows arching, as though Walter Hardesty had just mentioned the national debt.

Herschel glanced at Ron, to get his reaction to the testimony, and saw he was writing hurriedly. Herschel's eyes went to the pad.

I have never talked to Jake Marshallton on the phone. I have never called him anywhere, especially at home. In fact, I don't even have his home number. I talk to his bookkeeper in Cape Girardeau about costs and his terminal managers on operational matters.

Herschel made a few notes and nodded as Ron stopped writing and looked up. Herschel leaned close to whisper. "And you said your negotiations had never progressed far enough to reach a total." Herschel drew back quizzically. "Remember? I asked you about that the first time we met to discuss this."

Ron nodded. "I've never progressed far enough with Jake's bookkeeper on cost *or* usage to have a total on anything, but that's a pretty good guess."

Herschel nodded as he scribbled, then stopped and looked up sternly at Walter Hardesty's next question.

"Did the defendant suggest anything else during that phone call?"

When Jake began to nod, Walter Hardesty spoke tiredly. "The court needs a verbal response, Jake."

"He did." Jake raised his voice, continuing to nod. "*Mister* Hamilton said he would be willing to bury the matter in the files if I made it worth his while."

Walter Hardesty glanced up at the judge, then back to Jake. "Did the defendant, by any chance, explain what he meant by *worth his while*?"

"He did." Jake's voice was becoming gruff. "When I told the bastard he was out of his cotton-picking mind, he said he thought ten thousand dollars was reasonable for the amount of money that could possibly be involved."

"Were you coerced," Walter Hardesty raised his hand as though prompting a response, "threatened in any way by the defendant concerning the matter during that phone call?"

"I guess you could call it that." Jake glared over at the defense table. "The son of a bitch said it wouldn't be any problem to make the paperwork show that my two routes expiring next year were no longer competitive, and they could both be readvertised."

"What did you say to that?"

"What could I say?" Jake raised his hands and let them fall back to the chair arms in surrender. "I've got drivers and mechanics, people in my terminals who need the work. I've got good people working for me, and I take care of them."

Walter Hardesty drew himself up, and glanced toward the judge to make sure he was paying attention. "So you agreed?"

"No, I didn't *agree*." Jake growled, shaking his head angrily. "But I've been in business long enough to know there are occasional *under the table* costs. I just asked him where he wanted me to send the money."

"What did he tell you?"

"He said he would get back to me, and hung up."

"And did he?"

"He did." Jake turned away for a moment, as if in thought. "It was less than a week. I was in St. Louis on some other business and stopped by the Transportation Office to drop off some fuel certification forms that were due."

"Do you remember when that was."

Jake nodded. "It was in September, last year. Hamilton caught me in the hall and told me he would be in Cape Girardeau on other business the following Wednesday, and would pick the money up then."

Judge Chandler had leaned farther over the bench, becoming deeply engrossed in the testimony with the mention of the proposed amount of the fuel savings, and was now apparently more intrigued by the amount of hush money and how it was to be delivered.

Walter Hardesty kept his witness talking. "Yes. Go on."

"I told him I would be out inspecting routes most of the following week, but I would leave the money with my secretary, and he could pick it up."

"And he agreed?"

"No." Jake frowned as he shook his head. "He said this was just between the two of us, and said he would rather pick the money up at my house. If I would have had any idea at the time of what the son of a bitch had in mind, I would have knocked him on his ass right there, and flushed the whole thing down the toilet."

Judge Chandler settled back in his chair. He didn't appreciate rough language in his courtroom, but he could see Mr. Marshallton's position, could certainly understand the man's feelings.

Walter Hardesty's voice had become low, sympathetic. "So, when you told Mr. Hamilton that you would be out of town the day he would be in Cape Girardeau, it was *his*, Mr. Hamilton's, idea to come to your home to pick the money up from your wife."

When Jake began to nod slowly, the judge turned toward the court reporter, his tone overly polite. "Ms. Compton, let the record show that Mr. Marshallton responded in the affirmative."

Walter Hardesty stepped back from the witness chair and waited solemnly while Judge Chandler instructed the court reporter, then began buttoning his suit coat as he turned and nodded graciously to the defense table. His impudent smirk was not visible to the judge. "Your witness, Mr. Birdwell."

CHAPTER EIGHTEEN

Herschel checked his notes while Walter Hardesty returned to his seat at the plaintiff's table, then, in a whisper, turned to Ron. "You're sure of what you've told me? About the fuel savings program? About Jake? Everything?"

"Yes, Herschel." Ron leaned closer, keeping his voice down. "Jake is very uncooperative, and he doesn't lower himself to talk to the working class. When he comes into the office he never talks to anyone below Mr. Warden."

"Then you've never talked to Jake in the office?"

"I told you, Herschel. Just the one time trying to set up a meeting to discuss a contract renewal. I've never talked to the man anywhere else."

While Judge Chandler waited for Walter Hardesty to reach the plaintiff table and take his seat, he folded the page over on his yellow pad in preparation for the cross-examination. He waited another moment before he looked toward the defense table. "Mr. Birdwell, do you have any questions for this witness?"

"Yes, Your Honor." Herschel rose, positioning his legal pad on the table so he could readily refer to his notes as he went along. "There are a few things I need to clarify for the record."

He stepped over in front of the bench and looked up at the judge. "Your Honor, Mr. Hardesty referred to the ever increasing cost of fuel as being the crux of our being here today, but I believe the key word here is *fluctuating*, not increasing. There are no provisions in a transportation contract for the contractor to realize a profit on operating costs, nor is the contractor expected to absorb unforeseen increases in those costs, either. On proper application to the transportation office, a contracter is allowed increases in operating costs, and are also expected to notify the transporation office when there has been a decrease in their operation costs, and *that* I believe is the crux of our little get together here today."

Judge Chandler lifted a glass of water and took a sip as Herschel finished, then nodded and set the glass back on the small tray at the corner of his desk. "I believe you have made your point, Mr. Birdwell, now let's move along."

"Thank you, Your Honor." Herschel realized he wasn't as suave as Walter Hardesty, and made no attempt to be as he turned and approached the witness. That wasn't what he was here for. He took a couple of deep breaths to ease his apprehension and settle his butterflies, then looked directly at Jake. Ned Ashcroft had told him to maintain eye contact with the witness at all times. He said a witness is usually telling the truth when they will look you in the eye, but seldom have the courage to look at you while they are perjuring themselves.

He hadn't thought to ask Ned how that rule applied to people who dwell on the fringe, people who probably didn't know the difference as he drew himself up. "Mr. Marshallton, when you bring fuel forms to the Transportation Office here in St. Louis, who do you usually give them to?"

"The secretary." Jake turned away to keep from grinning at the frumpy attorney's awkwardness. He had almost laughed out loud that day when Hiram Jordan agreed to assign the little son of a bitch to defend that goddamn Hamilton.

"You don't give them to the person who handles your contracts?"

"Mr. Birdwell." Jake settled back, looking down as he adjusted the crease in his trousers, and trying to sound acquiescent. "When anyone comes into my office, or the manager's office at any of my facilities, I don't want them interrupting my employees. I expect them to approach the secretary and state their business." Jake glanced toward the plaintiff's table as he shifted uncomfortably in the chair. The scrubby bastard was looking at him as though he were waiting for the punch line. "I follow that same policy at other offices. When I come to the Transportation Office here in St. Louis,

I approach the secretary and give whatever I've brought to her, state my business, then take a seat and wait."

Herschel's eyebrows lifted as he watched Jake fidget. The man's composure was apparently all on the surface. He had seen the way Jake blustered and stalked around when he entered an office, or any other place of business. Herschel had always felt that people who were continually on the offensive were terribly insecure, anyway. "Who do you usually talk to in the Transportation Office about an adjustment in the rate on one of your contracts?"

Jake drew himself up haughtily. "I have a full-time CPA on my office staff in Cape Girardeau to handle financial matters on all my contracts, and a manager at each of my service facilities to handle operational matters."

"Your Honor?" Walter Hardesty rose from the table. He wasn't comfortable with the direction Herschel Birdwell was headed. The man evidently wasn't the neophyte that Jake had thought he was. "Could we get back to the gist of the matter? I see no relevance in these questions."

"I tend to agree, Mr. Birdwell." Judge Chandler frowned. "Mr. Hardesty very adequately covered contract adjustments on direct. Let's move on."

Herschel began scratching the side of his head as he nodded, but it wasn't due wholly to his agreement with the judge. The thought crossed his mind that it might carry more weight to bring out the fact that Ron's position wasn't considered at a level to personally talk to Jake while he had Ron on the stand.

Herschel stepped over and leaned down to scribble a note on his legal pad, studied it a second, then approached the witness stand again. "You stated earlier in your testimony, Mr. Marshallton, that no one has offered to reimburse you for altering your equipment to comply with the fuel savings program."

Jake just sat there, scowling. The scruffy son of a bitch's eyes were too eager, like a goddamn terrier waiting for you to throw the ball.

When Jake failed to respond, Herschel leaned forward quizzically. "Isn't it a fact, Mr. Marshallton, that major equipment changes are usually negotiated into a contract at renewal?"

Walter Hardesty was on his feet again. "Your Honor, I fail to see any relevance in these questions, either".

"Where exactly are you headed with this, Mr. Birdwell?" The judge managed to suppress a smile as he waited. The novice was certainly keeping the old pro on his toes.

"Well, Your Honor," Herschel scratched the side of his head again while he stepped over to study his notes. "Mr. Marshallton stated on direct that no one had offered to reimburse him for any equipment alterations in conjunction with the fuel savings program that was instigated by my client." He turned from his pad and looked up at the judge. "I just want to clarify that equipment changes are usually negotiated into contracts at renewal, and that Mr. Marshallton hasn't had a contract renewed since Mr. Hamilton started the fuel savings program."

When Judge Chandler glanced at Walter Hardesty and then back at him, Herschel continued. "The only thing Mr. Marshallton has been requested to do is document his actual fuel costs on a monthly basis."

"I see." The judge scribbled for a moment on his legal pad and looked up. "And you say equipment changes are made at renewal, are negotiated into a transportation contract at that time?"

"Yes, Your Honor. The major changes that Mr. Hardesty and Mr. Marshallton were referring to. The transportation people haven't discussed any equipment alterations with Mr. Marshallton because there haven't been any renewals of any of his contracts yet."

"Very well." The judge dipped his head as he finished writing. "You may continue, Mr. Birdwell.

"Thank you, Your Honor." Herschel turned back to Jake. "In your direct testimony I believe you stated your fuel costs included pumping the fuel into the truck." Herschel paused, but the only response was the coarse sound of Jake Marshallton's breathing. "It wasn't clear, to me at least, who exactly does the pumping."

Herschel continued when he saw Jake cut his eyes toward his attorney. "If the driver is pumping his own fuel, it could be included in the driver wages item, or if a mechanic does it while servicing the vehicle, preparing the truck for a trip, the cost could be in the operational costs item, but in any event, the cost of pumping the fuel could hardly be claimed in all three of the items mentioned."

"Your Honor." Walter Hardesty rose from his chair, his tone almost pleading now. "I fail to see how Mr. Birdwell's question could be considered relevant to the case at hand."

Judge Chandler studied his legal pad for a moment before he looked up at Herschel. "I'm afraid I will have to agree with Mr. Hardesty on that point. Where Mr. Marshallton chooses to claim his cost of pumping fuel into his trucks would have no bearing on this hearing. I think that would be something for the Transportation Office to determine."

"Yes, Your Honor." Herschel stepped over in front of the high bench. "I realize that. I just wanted to get it in the record that the transportation people are trying, that Mr. Hamilton and his office staff have been doing just that." Herschel turned and nodded toward the plaintiff's table. "That's what Mr. Hardesty was referring to when he asked Mr. Marshallton how long the Transportation Office had been *badgering* him about his fuel costs."

The judge continued to write without looking up. "I believe you've made your point, Mr. Birdwell. Do you have any further questions for this witness?"

"Yes, Your Honor." Herschel moved over in front of Jake again. "Do you recall what night it was that Mr. Hamilton allegedly called you at your home?"

Jake began to shake his head as he glanced toward his attorney, then back at Herschel. He was going to have to get serious because this little son of a bitch apparently had a goddamn guru somewhere. "Not exactly. It was a couple of weeks before the day he came by the house to pick up the money."

Herschel leaned closer. "I didn't find your home phone number listed in the Cape Girardeau directory, and the only phone numbers, and addresses for that matter, shown in your contracts are for your business office, and the terminal facilities applicable to that particular contract."

"That's right." Jake grinned as he drew himself up. Walt had mentioned the possibility of that point being brought up. "My home phone number *is* unlisted."

Herschel hesitated at Jake's sudden change in attitude. The man's disposition was so capricious, so flighty. Sulking one minute and so belligerent and bullying the next.

"When I got my first contract, Mr. Birdwell, and that was long before *Mister* Hamilton ever came on the scene, I gave my home phone number to the manager of the Transportation Office." Jake relaxed smugly into his chair, and the explanation he and Walt had discussed. "That was a Mr. Hanford at that time. George Hanford. I told him that my contract listed all my operational people, and their phone numbers, and if the Transportation Office ever failed to get satisfaction from any of my people, he should call me at home and I would see that the problem was taken care of."

Herschel stepped back as if he had been slapped. Ned had cautioned him about asking a witness a question that he didn't already have an answer for.

"And furthermore, *Mister* Birdwell," Jake's voice rose several decibels as he leaned forward. Walt had told him not to push it but the little son of a bitch needed something to take back to his godfather, something to let the son of a bitch, whoever he was, know that you don't fuck with Big Jake. "I make sure all of my contract employees are aware of the fact that the Transportation Office has my number at home, and know why that office has it, and I make it perfectly clear to every one of them that they had better hope to hell the Transportation Office never has any reason to use it."

Herschel nodded as he stepped back and turned toward the defense table. He would have to check with Ron on the home phone number, and if Jake had lied about it he could bring it up while he had Ron on the stand. The explanation had sounded good, about what could be expected from Walter Hardesty, but Jake Marshallton had never been that gracious about anything before. It was surprising to know the man even knew how to smile.

At least, Herschel thought, he had managed to get Jake Marshallton to admit he didn't personally handle transactions with Ron or any of his Transportation Specialists. He scratched the side of his head for a moment before he picked up the pad and moved around the table to his chair. He still had a couple of items, but maybe it would be better for Jake's wife to clarify them. "I have nothing further for Mr. Marshallton, Your Honor."

"Mr. Hardesty?" The judge turned. "Do you have anything else for this witness?"

Walter Hardesty looked up from his legal pad, studying Herschel for a moment, then Jake before he started shaking his head. "No, Your Honor."

"Very well." Judge Chandler leaned politely toward the witness stand. "That will be all, Mr. Marshallton. You may step down."

Jake pushed up from the chair, chuckling coarsely to himself as he left the witness stand. He glanced toward the defense table, still smirking while he pulled out his chair at the plaintiff's table and sat down.

Judge Chandler watched Jake walk away, frowning as he folded the page over on his yellow pad. Sometimes it was a real chore to remain objective. "Call your next witness, Mr. Hardesty."

Walter Hardesty rose from his chair, buttoning his suit jacket as he turned toward the gate in the railing. "I call Mrs. Alice Marshallton, Your Honor."

CHAPTER NINETEEN

    Walter Hardesty held the small gate open while Alice Marshallton sidled her way across from her seat, then let it close when she had passed through. He walked to her left, and a pace behind, until they reached the witness stand, then stopped while she stepped up on the small platform and turned to face John Bernstein. The court clerk quickly swore her in and returned to his seat.
    Herschel had watched from the moment Mrs. Marshallton rose from her chair until she was seated on the witness stand. An air of restiveness surrounded the woman, and he couldn't believe it was due entirely to the way she was dressed. Walter Hardesty had tried to give the impression he was escorting her, but he made no attempt to take her arm or touch her, and there had been no eye contact or sign of recognition between them. Herschel wasn't sure if Alice Marshallton could be considered a hostile witness, but he could plainly see that the woman wasn't too happy about being here.
    Judge Chandler, too, had watched Alice Marshallton as she came forward. He had never been involved in a rape case before, and had not really anticipated seeing the woman the defendant had supposedly violated. She was sullen and withdrawn, and had undoubtedly been instructed to dress down for her appearance, but there could hardly be any comparison between her and the young man's wife sitting over there on the defense side. Judge Chandler was aware the legal system insisted that rape was not about sex, but power, the control over another body. They could explain it any way they wanted, but he couldn't recall ever seeing a totally unappealing rape victim.

Walter Hardesty glanced toward the judge and court recorder, then turned to the witness stand. His words were curt. "State your name for the record, and your relationship to the plaintiff."

The witness raised her eyes from her lap and looked straight ahead, at nothing in particular. "I am Alice Marshallton, Mrs. Jake Marshallton."

Walter Hardesty checked his bow tie, then unbuttoned his suit coat as he stepped back, out of her glowering line of vision. "Do you hold any kind of position in your husband's business enterprises?"

She continued to look straight ahead, still sitting rigidly. "No, I'm just a housewife, a homemaker."

Herschel's eyebrows lifted at the remark. From what Woody Schoffner had told him, a home was about the only thing Alice Marshallton *hadn't* made.

Walter Hardesty didn't hesitate, never taking his eyes from the woman as he shot his cuffs so the gaudy diamond studs would show, and moved closer. "But you do sometimes assist your husband in the operation of his transportation contracts, or other business enterprises?"

"I have, on occasion." Alice Marshallton nodded slightly, her body beginning to relax but her eyes were still fixed as she turned to avoid looking at the pompous attorney.

"In what way?" Walter Hardesty tried to appear surprised as he glanced at the judge, then the defense table and back to his witness for her answer.

Alice Marshallton shrugged, pausing briefly as if in thought. "There have been times when I was coming to St. Louis to shop that Jake has asked me to drop off an envelope at the Transportation Office, or deliver something to one of his maintenance facilities."

"Did your husband ask for your help, ask you to deliver an envelope for him on September 23rd of last year?"

She glanced quickly at the plaintiff's table where her husband was now looking down, casually cleaning his fingernails with a small pocket knife, and turned her stare to the far wall again. "In a way, yes."

Walter Hardesty raised his chin to look down at her with a smirk. "Explain what you mean by *in a way*."

Alice Marshallton clasped her hands together in her lap, drew in a breath to ponder the instructions a moment, then looked down, her voice coarse. "While my husband was getting ready to leave the house that morning, he handed me a brown business envelope. He said a young man from the Transportation Office in St. Louis would be in town that day, and would come by the house to pick it up."

Walter Hardesty glanced quickly to make sure the judge was paying attention. "Was there any particular reason why your husband couldn't hand the envelope to the young man himself?"

She nodded, continuing to look down. "Jake was going to ride one of his mail routes to St. Louis that morning, and another one to Chicago that night. He wouldn't get home, wouldn't be back in town until late the next afternoon."

The attorney smiled sweetly, nodding as he spoke. "And what was the reason for your husband riding these routes?"

Alice Marshallton drew in another breath, God, how she hated charades. She spoke in the same sullen tone. "My husband rides all of his routes periodically to assure that the drivers are operating on schedule, and taking care of the equipment."

Walter Hardesy leaned toward his witness, speaking quickly, as though he had just remembered. "And did the young man from the Transportation Office come by for the envelope?"

When Alice Marshallton began to nod the judge leaned forward but she remembered and spoke before he could say anything.

"Yes. The young man came to the house for the envelope."

Walter Hardesty made a show of stepping back out of her way, waving his arm to include the entire room, everyone there. "Do you see that young man here in the courtroom today?"

"Yes." Alice Marshallton nodded again without turning her head. "He's sitting over there at the table with his attorney."

"Which table? What Attorney?"

"The defense table, with Mr. Birdwell." Her words were snippish.

Walter Hardesty turned graciously to the judge. "Let the record show, Your Honor, that Mrs. Marshallton has identified Mr. Hamilton as the young man who came to her house on September 23rd of last year."

The man's presumptuous instructions caused Herschel to push his chair back and start to rise, but the judge had already started talking. Walter Hardesty's insolence was apparently beginning to irritate him, too.

"Mr. Hardesty," the judge's words were condescending. "I've already reminded you that the only ones who will see the transcript of this hearing other than myself are you and Mr. Birdwell, and I believe the three of us understand that the proper wording should be *the young man who allegedly came to her house* until it has been proven otherwise." Judge Chandler scribbled hurriedly for a moment. "Now, let's move on."

Herschel settled back in his chair with a grin, satisfied that the judge apparently wasn't being impressed by all the grandiose posturing, wasn't being dazzled by Walter Hardesty's verbal tap dancing.

The judge's rebuke hadn't seemed to faze Walter Hardesty as he turned back to the witness. "Had you met the defendant, Mr. Hamilton, before then? Before September 23rd?"

Alice looked down at her hands again, raising her eyebrows as she said the word, scarecly above a whisper. "Yes."

Herschel turned to get Ron's reaction and noticed that Ron's wife had been somewhat shaken by the timid response. Even though he and Ron had both made sure Judy knew about the incident, and he had warned her that unfounded, possibly even salacious accusations would be made, it still bothered him to see the young lady so distressed.

As Herschel turned back to the front, Walter Hardesty seemed to be hitting his stride. "Please tell the court, Mrs. Marshallton, how you came to know Mr. Hamilton before the day he came to your house to pick up the money."

Alice looked up, shaking her head sternly. "I didn't say I *knew* him. You asked if I had met him before and I said yes."

Herschel's apprehension of Alice Marshallton was beginning to dissolve with her honesty and apparent distaste for Walter Hardesty.

"Whatever." The attorney sobered as he shrugged it away, his words now becoming sharp. "Just tell the court how you met the defendant."

"Well." Alice studied her hands for a moment, as though assembling her thoughts, and possibly choosing a starting point. "I had been to St. Louis that day to shop, and attend to a couple of other things. It had been a long day and I was exhausted as I came down the highway. When I saw the Holiday Inn's lights, and the lounge sign, I thought a glass of wine might relax me."

"Had you ever been in the Holiday Inn Lounge before?"

Herschel shifted testily in his chair. The man's grandiloquence nauseated him, but he could appreciate the idea of casting a veil of innocence over Alice Marshallton, even though the judge probably wasn't that familiar with her.

Alice nodded slowly. "I had stopped in there for a drink several years ago with the women from the Library Guild. Two of them were celebrating a birthday."

"I see." The presumptuous attorney was in full swing now, prancing back and forth as he talked. "Do you recall the date you went to St. Louis, what night it was that you stopped in the Holiday Inn Lounge for a glass of wine?"

"Not really." She shook her head absently. "Just that it was in late Spring of last year. I try to do my shopping before the weather gets too hot."

"We can certainly understand that." Walter Hardesty smiled as he glanced up at the judge. "Please go on."

Herschel watched in awe. Ned had cautioned him about Walter Hardesty. Said the man was an accomplished chameleon, had the ability to be whatever he needed to be, even to the point of giving the impression at times that he might even be capable of showing compassion.

Alice Marshallton drew in a slow breath. "The bartender was working at something behind the bar at one end, and Mr. Hamilton was sitting at the other, so I took a stool near the bartender. I didn't want to inconvenience the man any more than I had to."

Walter Hardesty drew back as though confused. "You said Mr. Hamilton was setting at the other end of the bar. Had you met the young man before?"

Herschel turned to get Ron's reaction and noticed Ron's wife had turned away, dabbing at her eyes with a tissue, and it didn't seem to help any when Alice Marshallton said that she hadn't.

Maybe they should have talked Judy out of attending the hearing after all. He felt so helpless as he turned back in time to catch that sonofabitching Hardesty's smirk fade as he continued.

"And there was no one else there?"

Alice shook her head. "No. It was a weeknight."

Walter Hardesty nodded knowingly. "Do you remember what time it was?"

"It was late." She glanced around as though trying to remember. "It was a little after six when I left St. Louis, so it was probably close to nine."

The attorney nodded. "Go on."

"When I asked the bartender for a glass of white wine, the young man picked up his drink and moved down the bar to the stool next to me."

"Did he act like he knew you?"

She continued as if she hadn't heard the question. "When the bartender brought my wine, the young man placed some money on the bar and told the man to bring him another drink, too, then pushed one of the bills across the bar."

"So you let Mr. Hamilton buy you a drink?"

Alice Marshallton just shrugged. "I was tired, and I guess I didn't think it was worth making a scene over."

"Did he give you any reason to believe he knew you?"

She nodded, looking down at her hands as she talked. "He asked about Jake, and made a point of telling me that he was from the Transportation Office in St. Louis and administered all of my husband's contracts."

Herschel glanced warily around to see how the Hamiltons were taking the woman's testimony. Ron had written *LIES* on his pad and underlined it twice, and Judy was looking away grimly, the tissue wadded up in one hand and the other pensively twiddling her ballpoint over the small notebook in her lap.

Walter Hardesty had been keeping his eye on the defense side of the room since he had started, and was pleased with their reactions, particularly the young man's wife. "What else did you talk about?"

Alice Marshallton splayed her hand at the base of her throat as she shook her head. "*I* didn't talk about anything. I just listened."

"What else did *Mr. Hamilton* talk about?"

She looked down thoughtfully. "He mentioned going to Sikeston and Poplar Bluff, and how pretty the country was in southeast Missouri. I believe he said he had been conducting some contractor seminars."

"And that was all?"

She hesitated a moment, as though reluctant to continue, until Walter Hardesty leaned closer, his smile gone. "Did he say anything else?"

"Well." Alice Marshallton leaned back, looking away from him. "When I finished my drink he said he knew of a small club that had live music, and suggested we go there for another drink. He said the place had a dance floor."

"Did you agree?"

"No, I did not agree." She shook her head adamantly.

"Did he try to pressure you?"

"Not really. I just told him I wasn't interested."

"And he accepted that?"

"Yes. He was very nice about it."

"And that was the end of it?"

"Yes. I thanked him for the drink, and when I turned to leave he said he had enjoyed talking to me and told me to drive careful."

Judy had listened to every word, searching for a flaw, anything that didn't fit, and had managed to keep an open mind until the woman started sounding like she might actually have met her husband, but Ron would never approach a woman that way at a bar, especially an older woman. And he wasn't much of a dancer or that casual about money. But then the woman said he had told her to drive careful. Judy's lips began to tremble as a tear spilled over and made its way down her cheek. That's what Ron always told *her* when she was getting ready to go somewhere in the car by herself.

CHAPTER TWENTY

Walter Hardesty had learned years ago that human emotions and personal mannerisms would tell a jury, or a judge, much more than dispassionate testimony ever could. He was delighted with the way the defendant's young wife had reacted to the testimony that her husband had been flirting with a woman in a motel bar. It was amazing the damage an obscure phrase or innocent word could effectuate when programmed to be casually mentioned in the proper setting.

"Now." Walter Hardesty chortled softly to himself and clasped his hands together, dispersing the sparkle of the two pinky rings as he studied his witness again. "Let's get back to September 23rd. What time of day was it when Mr. Hamilton arrived at your house?"

"Early afternoon." Alice Marshallton frowned at the thought of the ordeal ahead. "I'd say in the neighborhood of two o'clock."

"And you answered the door yourself?"

"Yes." She nodded hastily, her words becoming sharp. "I said I was the only one there."

"Was Mr. Hamilton impudent?" The attorney almost smiled at the way she glared up at him. "Did he give you any reason to believe he expected you to know who he was, expected you to remember him?"

Alice's shoulders lifted as she shook her head. "No." The young man's quiet manner at the bar that night had impressed her. "He just said hello, and that he had come to pick up an envelope from Jake."

Walter Hardesty was keeping the judge in the corner of his eye. "Go on."

"Well. The envelope was still on the kitchen cabinet where Jake had left it, so I invited the young man to step into the foyer while I went to get it."

The attorney's eyebrows lifted as though surprised. "You invited the defendant into your home?"

"I said I did." Alice nodded sternly. "It was terribly hot and muggy that day. I couldn't just leave him standing out there on the porch."

Walter Hardesty's tone became incredulous. "You had no qualms about inviting a barroom casanova into your home?"

Herschel pushed his chair back and rose as Alice Marshallton shook her head, explaining that she had no reason to believe the young man intended anything other that picking up the envelope.

"Your Honor?" Herschel had stood quietly until Alice finished. "The record identifies my client by name, and also as the defendant. I would think that either one would suffice when Mr. Hardesty finds it necessary to refer to Mr. Hamilton."

Judge Chandler hesitated a moment to quell his annoyance with both attorneys. "I have already stated my position on the use of petty aspersions, Mr. Birdwell, and reminded you both that this is only a hearing. You will each have a chance to enter your suggestions and objections when you review your copy of the hearing transcript."

"Thank you, Your Honor." Herschel nodded at the idea that had just crossed his mind with the judge's remarks, and eased himself back into his chair. While he had Ron on the stand he would make sure to get the fact into the record that Alice Marshallton was the aggressor that night, the one who had been *on the make* at the motel bar. Then when he got his copy of the transcript, if it wasn't properly worded to show that, he would make damn sure that it was, make damn sure that it was abundantly clear just who in the hell was propositioning who before he mailed the transcript back.

When Judge Chandler turned his attention back to the witness, Walter Hardesty continued as though there had been no interruption. "What was the defendant's reaction, Mrs. Marshallton, when you handed him the money?"

Alice's voice was gruff, her eyes showing disgust as they met Walter Hardesty's. "I handed the young man an envelope. I had no knowledge of what was in the envelope."

"What did the defendant do then?"

"Nothing." She waved it away with her hand. " He just thanked me and put the envelope in his briefcase."

"He didn't open it?" The attorney stepped back in apparent disbelief. "The defendant didn't make any effort to check the envelope's contents?"

"I would have told you if he had opened it." Alice glared at the attorney as they approached the part of the testimony she had objected to, the part she wasn't comfortable with. "He just closed his briefcase, then said he wanted us to go into the bedroom and finish what we had started at the motel bar that night."

Judy Hamilton began to shake her head at the woman's accusation. She couldn't remember Ron ever coming right out and asking *her* to go into the bedroom. Her husband wasn't like that. When he wanted to have sex he started fooling around. Touching, kissing, fondling. There were times when they never even made it to the bedroom.

Walter Hardesty glanced around as though composing his thoughts, making sure Judge Chandler had noticed Mrs. Hamilton's apparent discomfort, then turned back to his witness.

"Did you agree?"

Alice Marshallton continued to glare at him, as though offended by the question. "I most certainly did not."

"What happened then?"

Alice Marshallton drew herself up, her voice firm as she had been instructed. "I stepped over to the door and told him I thought he had better leave."

Walter Hardesty nodded sternly and just stood there, his arms crossed in front of him as though daring her to deviate from the story he had concocted.

The attorney's methods as well as his arrogance made it easy for Alice to sound irritated. "The young man said he hoped he wouldn't have to call my husband and tell him there had only been five thousand dollars in the envelope, and that he couldn't finish their deal until he received the other half of the money."

"And you didn't know for sure whether the envelope contained the full ten thousand dollars?"

"I told you I had no knowledge of the envelope's contents, and besides it was sealed." Alice sounded tired, her words laden with disgust. "If Jake had thought it was necessary for me to know what was in it, he would have told me."

Walter Hardesty hadn't missed Judge Chandler's growing concern over the apparent importance of the contents of the envelope. The attorney managed to keep a straight face as he leaned closer, his voice becoming sympathetic. "Tell the court, Mrs. Marshallton, how Mr. Hamilton's claiming a shortage in the money in that envelope might concern you."

As Alice drew in a breath and reached up to run her fingertips under each eye, Walter Hardesty pulled a folded white handkerchief from his coat pocket and handed it to her. "Would you like a short recess?"

"No." Her voice was husky as she dabbed at her eyes and quietly blew her nose. "I'm okay."

Judge Chandler frowned as he cast a confused glance toward the defense table, to Jake Marshallton at the plaintiff's table, then back to the witness.

When Alice had finally composed herself and wadded the handkerchief in her hands, she drew in a breath but didn't look up. "My husband has a dreadful temper and becomes violent when someone crosses him, especially where money is concerned."

Walter Hardesty gave his vest a tug and checked his bow tie as he appeared to be in thought, giving the judge time to finish writing. "Did you have any reason to believe Mr. Hamilton's threat would provoke your husband?"

The word was low as she opened the handkerchief and raised it to cover her eyes. "Yes."

"Afraid it might bring you husband's wrath down on you?"

The word was muffled this time, barely above a whisper. "Yes."

Judge Chandler, taken somewhat aback by the nature of the testimony, looked sternly over at the plaintiff's table. Jake Marshallton sat there grinning, listening attentively, much like a man watching his small granddaughter perform a piano recital.

Walter Hardesty was all innocence as he moved closer again. "Mrs. Marshallton, had your husband ever physically harmed you before that day?"

When Alice Marshallton covered her eyes with the handkerchief again and began to nod, Judge Chandler turned toward the court reporter, his words compassionately soft. "Ms. Compton, let the record show that Mrs. Marshallton responded in the affirmative."

Walter Hardesty's voice was still low, dripping with tenderness as he leaned down. "Was it over money?"

As Alice began nodding again, Judge Chandler turned and dipped his head to the court recorder, then made a point of glaring at her husband.

Judy Hamilton just sat there, staring toward the witness stand in disbelief. Marital abuse was so far removed from her world that it was shocking, not only that it happened, but that the woman would admit it, would accuse Ron of taking advantage of something like that. How could Ron have even known?

Herschel fumed, twiddling the ballpoint over his legal pad. The whole putrid mess made him want to puke. To some people marriage was nothing more than a piece of goddamn paper. It pissed him off to think a woman like Alice Marshallton would subject herself to such treatment, but deep in his mind he had to agree with Woody Schoffner. She was only protecting the lifestyle she had chosen, protecting the retirement plan she had managed to latch on to.

Walter Hardesty stepped over to the plaintiff table, pretending to ignore Jake as he referred to his notes until Alice had composed herself, then approached the witness stand again.

"When was the first time your husband injured you over money?"

Alice was sitting quietly, looking straight ahead. "My husband is a good man. Jake provides employment for a lot of people, and he pays them well. He's a caring person. He just can't control his temper at times."

Walter Hardesty's voice rose slightly. "Mrs. Marshallton, when was the first time your husband confronted you over money?"

"It was really my fault." She hesitated as she looked away, kneading the handkerchief in her hands. "I had donated some money to the church, and Jake found out about it before I had a chance to tell him."

"How much money?"

Alice Marshallton shrugged, raising one hand to brush it away. "I really don't recall. A few hundred dollars."

"Did your husband strike you when he found out about it?"

Alice slumped back in the chair. "Jake was upset."

Walter Hardesty's voice rose. "Did your husband strike you?"

Alice hesitated a moment, bringing herself forward in the chair again. "When I got home from shopping that day, and came in from the garage, Jake was waiting for me in the family room. It startled me when he began to shout and wave the bank statement around, and I tripped over a throw rug."

The attorney had stepped back from the witness chair, keeping an eye on the judge's reactions as he proceeded. "Were you hurt?"

Alice spoke softly, looking down at her hands. "I fell with an armful of packages and struck my chin on the arm of a recliner."

"Were you physically injured?"

Alice began to nod, still looking down. "I suffered a hairline fracture of my lower jaw."

Herschel gripped the ballpoint as he scowled down at the table. Motion Picture Oscars had been handed out for a lot worse performances than this one. Ned had warned him about that sonofabitching Hardesty. The way that prick was wringing the story out of her, the judge would damn sure hang the mantle on Ron.

Walter Hardesty had maneuvered himself around now to where he could keep his eye on the defense side of the room as well as the judge. "Was that the only time your husband assaulted you over money?"

Alice began to shake her head, looking down again. "There was another time when my mother needed help."

"How much money are we talking about this time?"

Alice just shrugged as she flipped her hand to wave it away, then let it fall back to her lap.

"Was it more than a few hundred?"

Alice nodded solemnly. " My mother is in a nursing home, and needed to have her dentures replaced." She glanced above the handkerchief to see that everyone was watching her. Alice had never had trouble handling attention, but not like this. "I was just finishing my bath that afternoon when Jake stormed into the house and confronted me about it." She hesitated again without looking up. All she could hear was breathing. "I fell in the tub and fractured some ribs."

Judy Hamilton hadn't taken her eyes from the attorney or Mrs. Marshallton, and was aware that Mr. Hardesty and Judge Chandler were both glancing at her occasionally. She wanted the judge to know that any anxiety he saw in her expressions or reactions was for the woman on the witness stand, and how all this might concern Ron's case. She also wanted the man to know she was confident that her husband would never take advantage of something like that, even if he knew about it. Judy was sure the judge would realize Ron wasn't that kind of person before this was all over.

Walter Hardesty was extremely pleased with the tension in the air, and let it build for a moment longer. He even made a point of glaring at the defendant before he turned back to the witness. "And now Mr. Hamilton was threatening to tell your husband that you had skimmed *five thousand dollars*," his eyebrows and voice both lifted to emphasize the gravity of her predicament, "from a business transaction he had entrusted you to handle."

Herschel half rose from his chair. "Is that a question, Your Honor?"

Judge Chandler stopped writing and looked up. "Mr. Hardesty?"

Walter Hardesty smirked at Herschel, then turned and looked innocently up at the judge. "I was merely establishing for the record, Your Honor, that Mrs. Marshallton did not voluntarily take Mr. Hamilton into her bedroom that day. She was forced to choose between the lesser of two evils."

Judy Hamilton's brow furrowed in frustration as she looked down at her notepad. She was satisfied that Ron had turned the woman down that night at the motel bar, and believed him when he told her he had never been to the contractor's house, but her composure slipped at the insinuation the woman had taken Ron into the bedroom as a second choice. It rankled her to think another woman had considered her husband to be nothing more than a consolation prize.

CHAPTER TWENTY ONE

Herschel sank slowly back into his chair. The sonofabitch was putting the stain on Ron and there didn't seem to be anything he could do about it. He hadn't noticed Ron or his wife writing anything so far, and *he* sure as hell hadn't heard anything he could actually dispute. The malfunction of the office car that day was still the only thing he had that might trip them up.

He felt so small, so insignificant as he sat there watching that pompous asshole crucify Ron.

Walter Hardesty glanced around arrogantly as he adjusted his coat, shot his cuffs to bring out the flashy studs again, and turned to the witness. "And now, Mrs. Marshallton, please tell the court what happened when you and Mr. Hamilton arrived in your bedroom."

Nausea gripped Herschel at the thought of the judge allowing this mockery to drag on any farther. Woody had said this judge was big in the church, but the sicko priests and television preachers had already shown that religion doesn't necessarily run intereference between a man's conscience and his libido.

Herschel had never felt the sex act was something to be discussed in mixed company, and certainly not in a public courtroom. He had never considered sex to be a spectator sport, anyway. To continue this charade would serve no purpose that he could see, except to stroke that sonofabitching Hardesty's voracious ego, and appease the meager mentality of that deranged prick sitting over there at the plaintiff's table.

The idea of Ron's wife being subjected to this.., this figment of a degenerate imagination, caused Herschel to push himself up from his chair again before he really knew what he was going to say.

"Your Honor, is it really necessary to delve any farther into this," he hesitated with a shrug, "this part of it?"

Jake Marshallton jumped up, his chair scraping back as his voice boomed. "You're damn right it's necessary."

Walter Hardesty turned to glare at Jake, then stepped over to the plaintiff's table with a sigh of disgust when Judge Chandler began hammering his gavel in rapid succession. "Mr. Hardesty, you will control your client or I will have him removed from this courtroom."

"Sorry, Your Honor." The attorney looked back as he reached Jake and forcibly turned him away from the judge. "If we could have a moment?"

The judge leaned forward sternly, holding the gavel at the ready. "A moment is about all that is left of my patience, Counselor. I will not tolerate such disrespect, such brazen outbursts in my courtroom."

Walter Hardesty hustled Jake unceremoniously toward the far corner of the room, his whispering rapid and sharp. As they stopped, Jake turned partially to glower at the defense table, nodding as his attorney continued to scold him even though he didn't appear to be losing any of his indignation. After several moments the attorney stopped talking and just stood there, huffing until Jake nodded, then escorted him back to his chair.

"I apologize, Your Honor." Walter Hardesty stepped over to the witness stand where Mrs. Marshallton sat rigidly, staring straight ahead. "I beg the court's indulgence and understanding of my client's animosity toward the loathsome violation of his dear wife."

Herschel made no attempt to get up as he spoke, just cradled the side of his head wearily in the palm of his hand. "Alleged loathsome violation, Your Honor."

Judge Chandler nodded tediously. "Alleged loathsome violation, Mr. Birdwell. Now can we get on with it?"

Judy Hamilton had watched the hostilities with increasing trepidation, particularly Walter Hardesty's sudden reaction and reprimand of Jake Marshallton, then her frown became even tighter. Now they were accusing her husband of violently abusing the woman, and even though Mr. Birdwell had managed to get the judge to qualify it, he hadn't objected to it being included in the record. She was sure Mr. Birdwell knew Ron better than that.

"Now, Mrs. Marshallton." The attorney stepped closer. "Tell the court what happened after Mr. Hamilton had left you no choice but to accompany him into your own bedroom to finish the seduction he had started when he bought you a drink that night at the motel."

Walter Hardesty's audacity brought Herschel out of his chair before he could phrase an objection to the slick sonofabitch's reference to the drink, but he would make a note and clarify that while he had Ron on the stand, and also clarify it in his copy of the transcript. He was fed up with the insinuations and snide innuendoes that were apparently a common courtroom practice. He stared at the arrogant attorney for a moment before he sat back down and reached for his pad.

Judge Chandler could understand the man's frustration as he watched him slump back into the chair. "Patience, Mr. Birdwell. You will have your turn."

Walter Hardesty made no attempt to suppress his smirk as he turned to his witness, prompting her to continue.

"Well." Alice hesitated, not comfortable with where she had been instructed to go with the story. "When I thought about it, considered how that would provoke my husband, I felt I really had no choice and headed down the hall toward the bedroom."

"And Mr. Hamilton followed you?"

"Yes." Alice nodded as she touched her eyes with the handkerchief, remembering the way Walter Hardesty had insisted she tell it. "The young man," she nodded toward the defense table, "left his briefcase in the foyer and followed me into the bedroom."

"The defendant made no attempt to touch you?"

"No". She shook her head. "He just followed me into the bedroom."

"What happened then?"

"He told me to undress and sit on the bed."

"Did you try to reason with him, try to talk him out of it?"

"Yes." Her voice was low. "But he just ignored me."

"And he still hadn't touched you?"

"No." She shook her head again. "He just started undressing and throwing his clothes over a chair."

Judy Hamilton looked down at her small notepad and began to write. Ron would never be so casual about his briefcase, especially if he had just put ten thousand dollars in it like the woman claimed. And Judy was sure her husband would never, under any circumstances, *just throw* his clothes over a chair. It also hovered in the back of her mind that the woman hadn't said anything about closing the bedroom door.

Judy paused with a frown. She wasn't sure if Ron closed the door for his own benefit or hers, but he always did during the day, even though there was no one else there. He surely would have made a point of closing the bedroom door in a strange house.

She turned at the sound of Walter Hardesty's voice.

"Did the defendant take off all of his clothes? Strip down all the way?"

"Yes." Alice nodded, looking modestly down at her hands now. "Everything but his socks."

The young man's *over the calf* dark blue hose had impressed her that night in the bar. They complimented his gray plaid suit very well. She had always thought it so tacky for a man's bare leg to show above his socks, especially when the man was wearing a suit and tie.

"Can you describe his socks?"

She nodded, remembering the attorney's instructions that giving the color might sound too contrived. "They were a dark color, knee length, I believe what is commonly known as *over the calf*."

"And you had finished undressing by now." The attorney's eyebrows lifted quizzically. "You were completely nude?"

"Yes." The word was hasty.

"And sitting on the bed?"

"Yes." Her voice rose testily.

"What did Mr. Hamilton do then?"

Herschel didn't bother to get up, his voice as tired as he looked. "Do we need to go into such detail, Your Honor?"

"Patience, Mr. Birdwell." Judge Chandler glanced toward Jake and turned back to Walter Hardesty. "Get to the point, Counselor."

"Your Honor." Walter Hardesty stepped back petulantly. "We have shown the court how the defendant went about establishing a compelling fear, and now we are merely explaining why there were no indications of physical force. Why Mrs. Marshallton suffered no abrasions, contusions or other signs of forcible submission."

"Very well, Mr. Hardesty."

Walter Hardesty turned back to his witness. "Tell us what Mr. Hamilton did then, Mrs. Marshallton?"

Alice drew in a breath, trying to keep a straight face at the thought of Hiram Jordan's quirky little ritual with a rubber.

"Mr. Hamilton had taken something from his coat pocket when he finished undressing, and when he stepped over in front of me I could see it was a condom in a foil packet." She drew in a breath as she looked down. "He told me to open it and put it on him."

"An individually sealed condom?"

"Yes." She nodded without looking up.

"What kind of condom was it?"

"I didn't pay any attention to the brand name."

Walter Hardesty lifted his eyebrows, feigning annoyance. "Was the condom dry, *lubricated* or what?"

"It was lubricated."

"And was he erect?"

"Yes." Alice Marshallton concentrated on dabbing at her eyes to suppress a smirk at the thought of how flaccid Hiram Jordan's penis usually was, and the effort it sometimes took for her to stimulate him enough to have something to put the rubber on.

Judy Hamilton had been watching Mrs. Marshallton's face, and listening very closely. The socks didn't matter because men with any sense at all about dressing properly wore long socks like that, but she was sure Mrs. Marshallton wasn't making it up about the condom. The woman didn't appear to be too upset, or give the impression she was recalling an unpleasant experience. Mrs. Marshallton had apparently performed the act before for someone, but Judy was certain it hadn't been *her* husband.

Judy knew how bashful her husband was about personal things, and how independent he had always been about everything, especially that. Ron wouldn't even let her trim his fingernails, or comb his hair.

"Mr. Hardesty?" Judge Chandler leaned forward over the bench. "I believe you've made your point. Is there a reason for us to go into..", he stopped and cleared his throat, " ah, pursue this particular matter any farther?"

Walter Hardesty's ebullience faded as he turned and looked up at the judge. "No, Your Honor. But I do have a couple of more items, some points to clarify if it pleases the court."

"Very well." Judge Chandler nodded. "Get on with it."

Walter Hardesty stepped over to the plaintiff's table and consulted his notes for a moment, then turned to face his witness again. "Did you report the incident to the authorities?"

"No." Alice shook her head. "After the young man left, I just took a shower and got dressed."

"Did you tell your husband about it?"

"Yes."

"When?"

Alice looked toward the plaintiff's table, but Jake had turned away, stretching his leg out to return something to his trouser pocket. "The next day when he got home."

"What was his reaction?"

Alice could still see Jake sitting in his recliner that night when she got home from the Holiday Inn. She had almost been afraid to tell him the truth, tell him the young man wasn't interested. She certainly didn't have to improvise *that* reaction, which Walter Hardesty had insisted she recall today. "He became terribly upset."

"Did he blame you, assault you in any way."

"No." She shook her head. "His anger was at the young man."

"Did *he* report it to the authorities?"

"No." Alice shook her head again. Everyone knew Jake Marshallton handled his own affairs. "My husband just said he would take care of it."

Walter Hardesty stood there, contemplating the situation for a moment, then turned and headed for his chair at the plaintiff's table. "I have no further questions, Your Honor."

Judge Chandler appeared to be relieved as he watched the attorney turn and walk away. He looked down, writing hurriedly for a moment, then folded the page over and looked toward the defense table. "Your witness, Mr. Birdwell."

CHAPTER TWENTY TWO

Judge Chandler's words gave Herschel a start even though he had watched Walter Hardesty turn and walk away, and was aware that it was now his turn. He had felt he would do much better questioning Jake's wife than he would Jake, but that was before she started talking about her injuries. Herschel hadn't forgotten Woody Schoffner mentioning the two times the woman had been injured by her husband, but the gravity of it hadn't really registered with him until she got on the witness stand today and so docilely defended the ornery sonofabitch.

The mere thought of the woman being manhandled, being slapped around like that rankled Herschel. He drew in a breath as he flipped the pages of his pad to the notes he had prepared, then turned the tablet toward the end of the table and pushed himself up. To him an uncontrollable temper was an indication of more than just a sick mind.

Herschel's thoughts turned to the transportation office car. He felt sure Walter Hardesty and Jake Marshallton were not aware Ron had used his own car that day. He was confident they had briefed Mrs. Marshallton on the color and make of the white Oldsmobile, so all he had to do was to get her to describe it, then have Ron testify as to what car he actually drove to Cape Girardeau that day, and enter a copy of his travel voucher as evidence.

And Ned's suggestions on approaching a witness, about how to avoid broadcasting an important item made a lot of sense, too. Herschel had decided to question Mrs. Marshallton on Ron's appearance, chitchat about that for a minute, and work his way around to casually asking her about the car Ron had supposedly been driving that day, as though it had just come to mind.

He was sure, from Mrs. Marshallton's previous testimony, that she remembered talking to Ron in the Holiday Inn Lounge that night, and shouldn't have any problem with giving a reasonable description of what Ron could have been wearing. Herschel really had no desire to humiliate the woman, or even try to embarrass her.

"Mrs. Marshallton?" Herschel felt a sudden impulse to stand up straight, button his coat and smooth his hair. Even with the way they had her dressed, he was still aware that she was an attractive woman. "I believe you testified earlier that you were alone at home the day Mr. Hamilton supposedly came to your house to pick up the money?"

Alice Marshallton raised the handkerchief to touch the corner of her mouth before she started nodding. "Yes."

"And I believe you said you answered the door yourself?"

"Your Honor?" Walter Hardesty's tone was imploring as he rose from his chair. This neophyte was apparently getting help from someone, and he had no idea of where this line of questions might be headed. "Is it necessary for Mrs. Marshallton to have to repeat her direct testimony? Defense counsel can review what was said when he gets his copy of the transcription."

Judge Chandler sighed, settling slowly back into his chair. He could understand Mr. Hardesty's tactics if they were at trial, but they didn't need that kind of aggravation here today. And the defense attorney certainly didn't either, even though it was a legitimate objection. "Is there a point to your questions, Mr. Birdwell?"

"Yes, Your Honor." Herschel nodded politely. He was elated that Walter Hardesty apparently didn't realize he was bringing Mrs. Marshallton to the front door so he could chitchat her for a moment before he asked about the car.

"Very well." The judge waited for Walter Hardesty to sit back down before he turned to the witness. "You may answer the question, Mrs. Marshallton."

Alice Marshallton nodded as she glanced down at her lap, then looked straight ahead, aware of Walter Hardesty's labored breathing. "Yes. I answered the door myself."

Herschel glanced toward the plaintiff's table as he moved closer. "Would you describe him for us?"

"Your Honor?" Walter Hardesty pushed himself up again. "The defendant is sitting..."

"Sit down, Mr. Hardesty." The judge made no effort to conceal his disgust. "I'm quite sure Mrs. Marshallton understands the context of the question."

Walter Hardesty made a show of settling grudgingly back into his chair.

Herschel looked up at the judge, frowning at his own self-reproach. "Sorry, Your Honor. Let me clarify the question for the record."

He turned to the witness with a renewed determination. He should have known that sonofabitching Hardesty would make a point of nitpicking every goddamn thing he said. "Tell us what Mr. Hamilton was wearing the day he supposedly came to your house, Mrs. Marshallton."

Alice nodded, suppressing a smile at the man's sincerity as her mind flashed back to the night in the bar. "As I remember, Mr. Hamilton was wearing a light gray suit. It was sort of a muted plaid."

When Herschel just stood there, waiting, she tried to remember the color of his tie but could only be sure that his socks were dark blue. "I really don't remember his tie, but he was wearing a white shirt."

Herschel nodded. He suddenly realized that he and Ron hadn't discussed what Ron wore the day he went to Cape Girardeau, but he remembered Ron did have a gray plaid suit, and usually wore a white shirt and solid tie. He managed to suppress a smile as he decided to forgo the shoes, even though it would be reasonable to assume that a woman should be able to describe a pair of shoes that she had just testified to have been placed under her bed.

"I believe you testified earlier that when you handed Mr. Hamilton the money, excuse me, the envelope, he made no effort to open it or check it, but merely placed it in his briefcase."

The object of his statement brought an uneasiness, causing her mind to begin to swirl. She was almost sure the young man didn't have his briefcase with him in the bar that night.

Herschel caught the slight change in her features at the mention of the briefcase. "Can you describe that briefcase for us, Mrs. Marshallton?"

Alice frowned as she dropped her eyes to her lap. Walter Hardesty had admonished her to not look at him, or even glance in his direction for any reason during cross examination. Especially on a difficult question. He said he would be listening and would take care of it.

"Your Honor?" Walter Hardesty rose from his chair when Alice looked down. "I fail to see the relevance of the description of a government issue briefcase."

Judge Chandler dropped his head in tolerance, blinking down at his desk. He hadn't really seen the relevance of it either until the attorney came to her rescue. "Sit down, counselor. You can address that when you get your copy of the hearing transcription."

He raised his head slowly, waiting for the man to be seated, then leaned toward the witness chair. "You may answer the question, Mrs. Marshallton."

When Walter Hardesty mentioned a government issue briefcase she recalled Hiram Jordan's briefcase was identical to the one's carried by a couple of the other men she had met in both St. Louis and Washington.

She began to relax, still clasping the handkerchief between her hands. "I really didn't pay that much attention to it, but as I recall it was something like a hard black vinyl, with sort of a pebbly finish, and the handle, or maybe it was the catches, were chrome. Shiny chrome."

Herschel nodded his approval of her description of a government issue briefcase, whosoever it was. If Ron's was different, in the least, he would bring it up while he had him on the stand. "And I believe you said the defendant set it by the front door before he followed you down the hall."

Walter Hardesty didn't bother to get up this time. "Is that a question, Your Honor?"

Judge Chandler's expression didn't change. "Mr. Birdwell?"

"Just an observation, I guess, Your Honor. It's beyond me to even try to imagine anyone being so casual about a briefcase they had just put that much cash money in."

The judge's eyebrows lifted momentarily at the remark. "I believe you've made your point, Mr. Birdwell. Let's move on."

"Thank you, You Honor." Herschel nodded and turned back to the witness.

"Mrs. Marshallton?" He stepped to the side, as though they were on her porch and he was giving her room to see, a faint smile tugging at his features. "Can you describe the car Mr. Hamilton was driving that day?" Let that sonofabitching Hardesty bail her out on that one.

Alice sighed and began to shake her head. "I didn't see his car."

Herschel stepped in close again, his voice becoming higher. "You can't describe the car he was driving?"

"No, sir."

"You didn't notice the car, or just don't remember?"

Walter Hardesty appeared to be concerned with some papers he was going through, but Jake Marshallton was openly amused.

Alice twisted the handkerchief between her hands in her lap as she looked at Herschel. "I didn't see the car he was driving. Our house is on a corner lot, at Stapleton Avenue and Eighth Street."

Herschel just stood there, as though he had been kicked in the stomach, looking at the woman in disbelief as she continued.

"The house faces Stapleton, with our driveway coming in from Eighth. You can't see our driveway from the front door."

When Jake began to guffaw, Judge Chandler rapped his gavel sharply. "Mr. Hardesty, I've warned you. I will not tolerate these interruptions."

Walter Hardesty had immediately reached across the table to Jake, whispering in an air of censure even before the judge started banging his gavel. "Sorry, Your Honor. It won't happen again."

Herschel was oblivious to the harsh exchange as he moved back to the defense table and picked up his pad, mentally reprimanding himself for not going to Cape Girardeau, and at least circling the block. Ned had told him to be sure to look at everything, to familiarize himself with each detail, study every phase of the case. He said when you are preparing for a trial you never assume anything. Herschel had even thought it kind of corny when Ned brought in the old saw about breaking down the word *ass-u-me* to show how it could sometimes make an ass of everyone concerned.

His mind was frantically trying to rationalize his blunder when he suddenly realized Judge Chandler was talking.

"I had hoped to complete this hearing in one session, but it is now a quarter past noon and the defense has yet to be heard. Mr. Birdwell, you can continue you cross examination of Mrs. Marshallton when we reconvene after lunch."

The judge hesitated for effect, then rapped his gavel one time and continued when Herschel began to nod. "This hearing is recessed until one-thirty. I will expect each of you to be here and ready to proceed at that time."

CHAPTER TWENTY THREE

Herschel leafed slowly through his legal pad, studying the notes, his mind in a state of confusion. He waited until nearly everyone except Ron and his wife had headed for the doors, then, like a second thought, got up and hurried over to catch John Bernstein before he got away. The two of them talked low for a moment, until the court clerk nodded, then Herschel thanked him and came back to the defense table.

Judy had come through the gate and waited by her husband at the counsel table. They were not really sure of what Herschel had in mind, but they knew it certainly wasn't lunch. They waited while he hurriedly stuffed his briefcase, then followed him toward the back, to the door where John Bernstein had just left.

Herschel looked down as he crossed the room, seemingly preoccupied until they caught up with him at the door. "There's a conference room back here we're going to use. We've got a little over an hour to figure out where we're going with this thing."

He pulled the door open and waited for Judy and Ron to pass through, then stepped into the narrow hallway and closed it behind him.

Judy whispered quietly to Ron as they came into the hall, and he turned to Herschel. "Is there a rest room back here?"

"Yeah." Herschel nodded toward the door at the end of the short hall. "There's one in the conference room we're going to use. John Bernstein said he would unlock it for us."

Judy glanced around as they entered the room, then handed her notebook and pen to Ron and went across to the rest room.

Herschel placed his briefcase on the table and pulled out the chair at the end, motioning for Ron to have a seat to his right. "Did you pick up on anything they said that we can contradict, anything we can even question?"

Ron began to shake his head. "I'm sorry the thing with the car didn't work out. I can't argue about where the driveway is or which way their house faces because I've never been there, and I intend to make that abundantly clear when I testify. I want the judge to understand that I have never been to Jake Marshallton's house, or have any reason to even know where it is."

"Now, don't get upset." Herschel patted the air above the table. "We've got to get our heads together and find something in her testimony, something in their story that we can definitely refute. We have to find something that will convince the judge this whole thing has been contrived."

Herschel pulled a couple of pages back into place and studied them for a moment. "You know anything about that home phone number story Jake went into so much detail about? It struck me as just a little too convenient. I guess because it doesn't fit Jake Marshallton's character worth a damn."

"No." Ron shook his head. "And I've never heard Mr. Warden mention it, either. If this goes to trial you could put him on the stand."

"I kind of doubt that." Herschel's head began to shake even before Ron had finished talking. "I'd have to talk to him first. I'd have to feel him out about it, and even then I doubt I could trust him on the stand."

"You don't think he would make a good witness?"

"Ron." Herschel's voice was low as he leaned in. "I realize Bill Warden is your boss, and you get along very well with him, but the man has a reputation for being a shirt-chaser, a wimp. A man like that doesn't really know himself where his memory of the last conquest turns into anticipation of the next one."

"You think there's a possibility that he might lie under oath?"

"No." Herschel frowned. "I didn't say that. I'm just not sure Bill Warden even knows what the truth is, or cares. I couldn't put him on the stand until I was damn sure about him, and I don't believe that's possible."

They both looked up as Judy crossed the room, placed her purse on the table and slid into the chair opposite Ron. She finished massaging a dab of lotion into her hands and pulled her notebook and pen across the table from where Ron had put them. "Mr. Birdwell, I wrote down some things Mrs. Marshallton said about Ron that are simply not true. You need to ask her about them."

"Oh?" Herschel quickly folded back the pages on his legal pad, took a ballpoint from his shirt pocket and looked at her. "What kind of things?"

"Well, to start with." Judy scooted closer to the table, looking down at her notebook. "Ron's briefcase is not a government issue. I gave it to him on his promotion to the Transprotation Office last year, and he isn't that casual about it. He would never walk off and leave it setting in a foyer by the door like that. Not even at home."

Herschel smiled as he scribbled for a moment and looked up. "That's something I was going to bring up when I have Ron on the stand. It will be interesting to see the look on her face when she realizes the benevolent Mr. Hardesty is not quite as astute as he would have us believe. I'll make a note so we'll be sure and get that little contradiction in the transcript."

Judy glanced at her husband, then turned to Herschel. "You could put me on the stand, Mr. Birdwell. I could describe my husband's briefcase and tell the judge how he feels about the stuff in it, particularly if he had just put ten thousand dollars in it like Mrs. Marshallton claimed. Ron is just not that casual about his work papers, or money, either. Certainly not that much *cash* money."

Herschel's eyebrows lifted for a moment, then he nodded and leaned down, writing hurriedly.

"You can forget that, Herschel." Ron's voice was gruff as he pushed his chair back. "There's no way I'm going to let them drag Judy into this mess."

"But Honey, I could explain why a lot of the things Mrs. Marshallton said about you are simply not true."

"You wouldn't have a chance." He reached across the table and patted her hand. "I'm not about to let that attorney of theirs make a fool of you. I don't even want the man talking to you." Ron pushed himself up from his chair and headed across the room. "I'll be right back."

Herschel stopped writing and looked at her. "I'm afraid your husband's right. You have no idea how Walter Hardesty could browbeat you on the witness stand. How the man would twist everything you said."

"Mr. Birdwell." Judy's tone was imploring. "There were so many things Mrs. Marshallton said under oath that are simply not true."

"Like what?" Herschel frowned at the urgency in her voice, and her apparent anguish, her discomfort with the whole thing.

"Well." Judy drew in a breath as she looked down at her notebook. "Like Ron expecting her to go to bed with him just because he bought her a drink."

Herschel's frown grew tighter. "Ron insists that he didn't buy her a drink."

"That's what I mean." Her voice was becoming higher. "Ron just isn't like that. But even if he *did* buy her a drink it would have been merely because he wanted to, not that he expected her to.., well, you know, go to *bed* with him."

When Herschel just sat there looking at her, trying to extract something, anything at all from what she was saying, Judy continued.

"And that part about Ron walking around her bedroom in nothing but his socks." She fumbled in her purse for a tissue and raised it to dab at her eyes. "My husband would never be that brazen. Ron and I have been married for eight years, Mr. Birdwell, and he has never done that at home. He just doesn't do things like that."

Herschel wanted to reach out to her, to put his arm around her, at least take her hand, but he just sat there, struggling under a yoke of helplessness. A woman's tears went through him like a firebrand. They had a way of inciting him toward whatever caused them, whether he knew what it was or not.

Her delicate voice began to tremble. "And what she said about Ron handing her that condom." She turned the damp tissue and pressed it to her eyes again. "My husband has never asked *me* to do that for him, and even if he *had* told the woman to do that, and stood in front of her in nothing but his socks..." She pulled a corner of the tissue out and dabbed at her nose.

Herschel nodded as though he understood, but his confused expression gave her reason to believe he really didn't.

Judy raised a corner of the tissue and quietly blew her nose, then wadded the damp tissue into her hand and sat back, averting her eyes as she raised her chin defiantly. "If Mrs. Marshallton had actually done that, taken the time to do what she claims she did, she would surely have noticed Ron's scar, and would be able to describe it for you."

Herschel come up out of his slump like an erupting volcano, reaching for his pad. "Say that again."

Judy drew in a breath, placed her elbows on the table and timidly turned to him. "Ron has a scar on his stomach."

"What kind of scar?"

She hesitated as she glanced about, anxiously kneading the tissue in her hands. "It's on his lower right side. Ron doesn't like to talk about it, but he was injured while he was in the service."

Herschel became more resolved as his blood surged. "Ron told me he gets a small disability pension from the Veterans Administration when we were discussing finances, but I don't recall that he mentioned anything about what the money was for."

Judy looked down, her hands clasped together in her lap while she talked. "Ron hardly ever mentions it. He feels that a disabled veteran is someone who was wounded in battle, hurt while actually in combat with the enemy. He doesn't consider himself in that category because his injury was due to an accident, not an act of war."

"What kind of accident?"

Judy began to shake her head. "Ron wouldn't let me visit him while he was in the hospital, and from what little he has told me about it since then, a scaffolding of some sort on an obstacle course collapsed and Ron was impaled on a piece of broken timber."

Herschel had been writing as he listened. "And this happened while he was in the Army?"

Judy nodded. "Yes. He spent some time in the hospital, and had surgery to repair a couple of his intestines. I had hoped they would discharge him when he got well, but they didn't. They returned him to duty when he got out of the hospital and he served out his enlistment.

"What does the scar look like?"

She glanced across the room when she heard the toilet flush. "I'm not really sure I could describe it for you. Ron is so self-conscious about it." Judy hesitated when the rest room door opened. "It would probably be better for him to tell you about it."

Ron glanced back and forth between them as he approached the table. "Be better for me to tell him about what?"

Judy looked up at her husband. "I told Mr. Birdwell that if you had approached Mrs. Marshallton in nothing but your socks, the way she claimed you did, and stood there in front of her while she..," she shrugged, " well, did what she said you told her to do, I just thought maybe Mr. Birdwell should ask her to describe the scar on your stomach."

Herschel twiddled his ballpoint as he watched them. "Is there any chance Alice Marshallton might know what that scar looks like?"

Ron exhaled loudly as he slumped into the chair. "You still don't believe me, do you Herschel?"

Herschel leaned closer, his voice stern. "There's no reason for you to take the RA, Ron. I simply meant that if there is a chance that sonofa.., any chance Walter Hardesty could have found out about it, the slightest chance that Mrs. Marshallton could have been briefed on what that scar looks like, then we had damn sure better not bring it up."

In the sudden hush, Judy frowned quizzically as she turned to Herschel, her voice low. "What's the RA?"

Herschel blanched at the sudden realization he had let himself get carried away, had allowed her innocence to slip his mind. He hadn't meant to be vulgar, and surely had no intention to embarrass her. "Ah, wrong attitude."

Ron slumped forward on the table, all animosity gone as he reached across and patted his wife's hand. "Herschel means the red ass, Honey. And he's right, but I can't help it sometimes."

Herschel cleared his throat to remind them they weren't alone. "We can understand your position, Ron, but you've got to control yourself, and bear in mind that Walter Hardesty has access to a stable of very thorough investigators. If there is the slightest chance that the man has managed to find out about your scar, you can damn sure bet he has given Alice Marshallton a crash course on it. Briefed her to the point that she can convince the judge she at least noticed some kind of blemish on your stomach."

Judy began to shake her head, talking low, almost to herself. "I don't see how anyone could. Ron never lets that part of his body be seen, and never talks about his injury, not even at home."

Herschel twiddled the ballpoint while he watched her, then looked away, at nothing in particular. "Your husband wouldn't necessarily have to, Judy. Walter Hardesty's snoops could have been anywhere, talking to the people Ron works with, questioning anyone who uses the same rest room, or, who knows, one of them could have even observed Ron in the rest room theirself."

Ron began to shake his head. "I don't take my clothes down at a urinal, Herschel, and when I do take them down in a public rest room I'm always in a stall with the door closed."

Herschel considered that for a moment "And you've never mentioned your injury to anyone you work with, or anybody you might have come in contact with in some other capacity?"

"No." Ron looked across the table at his wife. "I've never had any reason to talk about it. I doubt that *Judy* could even describe it for you."

Herschel looked at his watch and pushed his chair back. "We're running out of time. Come on, Ron. Let's go over there to the rest room so I can look at your scar. I need to see it, need to know exactly what the damn thing looks like."

Ron made no effort to get up. "I'll tell you if the woman starts sounding like she might know what she's talking about."

"Ron." Herschel's tone dripped with aggravation. "I've already been caught short by not following up on that thing with the car, and I don't intend for it to happen again. If Alice Marshallton tries to improvise when I ask her about your scar, I need to know that. I need to know whether she's telling the truth or trying to fake it so I can question her accordingly."

Herschel looked at his watch again as he turned toward the rest room. "Come on, Ron. Our time is about up, and we can't afford to be late. And we certainly can't afford to incur the wrath of Judge Chandler. "

Judy watched Ron reluctantly get up and follow Herschel across the room. She had thought it was a good idea, but after Mr. Birdwell's doubts she just couldn't seem to work up any enthusiasm for even bringing it up. How many times had she been intimate with Ron in their eight years of marriage, and she would have to agree with Ron's remark to Mr. Birdwell. She doubted if she could describe her husband's scar with any degree of accuracy. She had never had the opportunity to scrutinize it, or the curiosity to really see what it looked like.

She suddenly cringed at the thought of professional investigators. She had never really had any reason to actually *see* the scar, but then she had never been paid to find out what it looks like, either.

CHAPTER TWENTY FOUR

Walter Hardesty and Jake Marshallton were standing casually at the end of the plaintiff's table, the attorney leaning close and talking solemnly, keeping his voice low as Herschel ushered Ron and Judy back into the courtroom. Alice Marshallton had lowered herself rigidly into the chair next to where her husband stood and just sat there, looking down at her lap.

When Jake grinned and raised his hand in greeting toward the rear of the courtroom, Herschel turned to look. Hiram Jordan had stepped through the tall double doors. He nodded to Jake but his attention was more on Alice as he pulled the door closed, then ambled down the aisle and took a seat on the defense side, several rows from the back of the room.

It surprised Herschel to see the man. He would have thought Bill Warden would be more concerned, but he really hadn't expected to see either one. Bill Warden considered himself sort of a free spirit since being promoted, free to pursue what he considered to be the spoils of his position, and Hiram Jordan hardly ever descended below the ramparts of his ivory tower, except by telephone.

Herschel watched Hiram out of the corner of his eye but the man never looked toward the defense table as he busied himself with getting settled. It really didn't matter because Ron, and Judy in her seat outside the railing, were both sitting with their backs to the man. Judy wouldn't know who Hiram Jordan was, and Judge Chandler, who had not yet taken the bench, probably wouldn't either, at least not by sight.

Hiram Jordan's presence didn't bother Herschel. He wasn't even surprised at the man's subtle lusting for Alice Marshallton from the defense side of the room. The sonofabitch would probably get a nose bleed if his mind ever rose above his goddamn waist, anyway. It nauseated Herschel to think of a womanizing bastard like that being in such a position of authority.

Walter Hardesty and Jake Marshallton took their seats when Judge Chandler entered the courtroom quietly and mounted the steps to the small platform behind the bench. He placed his folder on the desk and stood there a moment, surveying the courtroom. A frown crossed his brow at the sight of the newcomer sitting on the defense side, toward the back of the room. He calmly checked the remainder of the courtroom, then shrugged and took his seat.

He took a pen from his shirt pocket and opened the folder on the desk, looking down as he orally surveyed the court.

"Ms. Compton, are you ready to proceed?"

"Yes, Your Honor." She nodded and placed her fingers lightly on the keys of her machine. "I'm ready."

"Mr. Hardesty?"

The attorney glanced toward the defense table with a smugness, then looked up at the judge. "Yes, Your Honor. We're ready."

"Mr. Birdwell?"

"Yes, Your Honor. We're ready." Herschel moved his legal pad to the end of the table and turned it into position, not sure he really was, but aware that had nothing to do with it.

The judge looked up, checked the room again and turned toward the plaintiff's table, where Alice sat with her back to him. "Mrs. Marshallton, you may resume your place on the witness stand."

Walter Hardesty got up and stepped around the table to pull Mrs. Marshallton's chair out as she stood, then scooted it back to the table as she turned and walked away without acknowledging the courtesy.

Judge Chandler noticed her apparent sullenness as she approached the stand, but waited until she was seated. "You *are* aware, I believe, that you are still under oath?"

"Yes, sir. I understand that." She raised her hands to unfold a fresh white handkerchief and dab at her upper lip.

Judge Chandler hadn't missed the newcomer's interest in the witness. He watched the man's expression for a moment, then glanced at Jake and pulled his yellow tablet into position on the desk in front of him and turned to the defense table. "You may continue your cross-examination, Mr. Birdwell."

"Thank you, Your Honor." Herschel drew himself up and squared his shoulders, buttoning his coat as he crossed in front of the bench to approach the witness, then unbuttoned it and pushed one side back to place his hand on his hip. He wasn't sure if there was a prudent method, a discreet way to openly question a woman about something like this.

"Mrs. Marshallton, you testified this morning that the defendant, Mr. Hamilton.., ah, compelled you to go into your bedroom with him?"

She raised the handkerchief and touched each corner of her mouth, then returned her hands to her lap. "Yes, sir."

"And you said, as I recall, that Mr. Hamilton told you to take off your clothes and sit on the bed, and then began to undress himself?"

Alice appeared to consider the question a moment before she began to nod. "Yes, sir."

"And, I believe you testified that after Mr. Hamilton had taken off his clothes, everything but his socks, he approached you where you were sitting on the side of the bed?"

Walter Hardesty's tone was imploring as he rose solemnly from his chair. "Your Honor." He wasn't sure where the neophyte was headed now, but the lunch break seemed to have done wonders for the man's confidence. "Mrs. Marshallton was kind enough on direct examination this morning to relive her ordeal in the bedroom for the court. Is it necessary for her to have to go through the trauma of that experience again?"

Judge Chandler was learning to tolerate Walter Hardesty's impassioned pleadings, but the newcomer's apparent approval of the objection, and from the defense side of the room, caused him to hesitate a moment before he turned to Herschel. "Mr. Birdwell?"

"Your Honor?" Herschel stepped over in front of the bench and looked up at the judge. "I am merely recreating the scene that Mr. Hardesty set this morning. I intend to introduce an incident from my client's service in the armed forces of his country that could possibly have a bearing on this case."

Walter Hardesty's voice became gruff as he moved a step away from the plaintiff's table. "I must object most strenuously to this, Your Honor, to defense counsel's attempt to play on the sympathy of the court. I see absolutely no relevance in this line of questions. Peacetime military service could hardly be considered a thing of valor."

Judge Chandler dropped his pen on the legal pad, placed his elbows on the desk and raised his hands to support his head. "Your original objection, as I recall Mr. Hardesty, was to Mrs. Marshallton being asked to repeat previous testimony.

Let us dispense with that objection before we entertain another." The judge's eyes beaded as he leaned forward. "If that meets with your approval, Counselor."

"Yes, Your Honor." The attorney gave his lapels a tug and shot his cuffs as he nodded to the judge. "Sorry."

"Now." Judge Chandler picked up his pen and turned slowly toward Herschel. "If you will be kind enough, Mr. Birdwell, to enlighten the court as to why you feel it is necessary for the witness to go back into this particular part of her previous testimony, and how an incident in your clients military service might possibly be considered relevant to that testimony."

Herschel looked at the floor for a moment to bring his thoughts back to where they were before that sonofabitching Hardesty started trying to be cute. "I was merely bringing Mrs. Marshallton's attention, and the court's, if you please, back to the point where she testified this morning that she was sitting on the edge of her bed with Mr. Hamilton standing before her in nothing but his socks."

"Thank you, Mr. Birdwell." The judge nodded politely and turned toward the plaintiff's table.

"Are you with us, Mr. Hardesty?"

"Yes, Your Honor, and my objection still stands."

"That has been noted in the hearing transcript, Counselor, and you will have the opportunity to address that, as well as your other objections when you receive your copy."

The judge drew in a breath, then glanced at the newcomer as if it were a second thought. The man had him thoroughly confused by sitting on the defense side of the room even though he was apparently more concerned with the plaintiff's case, particularly this witness.

He shrugged it away and looked down at the woman. "Are you following this, Mrs. Marshallton?"

"Yes." Alice nodded as she spoke sharply.

Judge Chandler's eyebrows lifted at her surliness. "You understand that Mr. Birdwell is taking us back to where we were this morning, back to where you testified that you were sitting on your bed with Mr. Hamilton standing before you?"

"Yes, sir. I said I was listening." Her voice rose several decibels and her words were curt as she glared at her husband.

The judge watched her for a moment, then shot a glance at both Jake Marshallton and the newcomer before he made an entry on his pad.

Judge Chandler cut his eyes toward Walter Hardesty again to see the man had finally decided to lower himself back into his chair. "And now, Mr. Birdwell, tell the court how your client's military service might possibly have a bearing on the bedroom scene where we are all mentally gathered together again."

"Thank you, Your Honor." Herschel, still standing in front of the judge's bench, drew himself up as he buttoned his suit coat. "I wasn't referring to Mr. Hamilton's *military service*, per se, but merely that he was injured while serving in the military, and the fact that the wound was serious enough for the Veterans Administration to recognize its existence."

Herschel stepped back and nodded toward Ron at the defense table, encouraged by the judge's sudden interest. "If Mr. Hamilton had stood in front of Mrs. Marshallton in nothing but his socks while she installed..," Herschel's mind tried to balk, until he remembered the way Walter Hardesty had sneered when *he* mentioned it, "a condom, a lubricated condom, I would think she would be able to describe Mr. Hamilton's..." Herschel hesitated again. Ned Ashcroft's advice about phrasing questions to make the witness supply any pertinent details flashed before him when he started to say *scar*. "Shall we say, abnormality?"

"A high, piercing shriek, like fingernails on slate, split the courtroom, causing Herschel and the judge to both cringe as they turned. Alice Marshallton had raised her hands to cover her face with the handkerchief, her voice becoming shrill as she slumped forward in the witness chair. "I'm sorry, Jake. I told you it wasn't going to work."

Herschel turned farther at the sound of a loud guttural growl, like an enraged animal would make, then a chair scraping back and upending as it clattered across the floor. Jake Marshallton had lunged away from the plaintiff's table, the veins in his neck becoming engorged as his face reddened and contorted with a furor. His hands reached out savagely, hurling another chair aside as he charged toward the witness stand.

The very sight of Jake Marshallton sent a tremor through Herschel. The man's eyes were shooting fire and his mouth spewing spittle as his voice reached a fevered pitch. "You goddamned stupid-assed bitch."

All sense of fear left Herschel, though, at the thought of Woody Schoffner's report on Alice Marshallton's broken jaw and fractured ribs, and her attempt here in court today to vindicate the obnoxious bastard. He had been appalled at the stories, and was horrified now by the thought that it was going to happen again.

Herschel quickly stepped over in front of the witness chair and turned, squarely in the path of the onrushing maniac, and hunched forward to brace himself. He had never had anyone to roughhouse with as he grew up, or found time for sports in school, but he had watched enough football to have some idea of how to go about stopping the crazy sonofabitch from hurting this defenseless woman again.

As Jake charged, becoming louder and more profane, Herschel's patience with the repulsive sonofabitch gave out and he lunged forward to divert the attack by ramming his shoulder into the man's midsection.

Jake Marshallton's momentum, as well as his size and weight advantage, overwhelmed Herschel and slammed him backward into the side of the witness stand, but the impact also threw Jake off balance and sent him crashing headlong into the solid front of the judge's bench. As Jake fell back and crumpled to the floor he slowly pulled himself into a fetal position and began to sob, sniveling his animosity toward women, lawyers, the courts and his own stupidity for allowing himself to become involved with them.

CHAPTER TWENTY FIVE

Judge Chandler had recoiled at the sudden eruption, furious over such complete disrespect for the court and the apparent attempt to circumvent the law. A moment after a stillness had settled over the courtroom he rose slowly from his chair, still seething, scowlng his indignation as he placed his hands flat on the desk and leaned forward to survey the chaos in front of the bench. The judiciary was like a religion with him, and any violation of its sanctity was even worse than a sin. It was an abomination

He considered blatant deceit and an uncontrollable temper to be the work of the devil, a form of mental illness, and felt a degree of guilt for not recognizing it from the plaintiff's flagrant disrespect for the court. Or at least from the way the man had smirked while his wife was talking about her injuries. A rational person would never find delight in a loved one's humiliation.

The moment the ruckus ended, even before Judge Chandler rose out of his chair to assess the situation, Alice Marshallton slipped quietly out of the witness chair, leaned down to see that the defense attorney was not badly hurt, then stepped carefully around him and hurried over to her sobbing husband. She knelt down in front of him to loosen his tie and unbutton his shirt collar, talking softly, reassuring him, then grasped his hand and began to fan at his face with her handkerchief.

Herschel rolled over and pushed himself up onto one knee, and had just noticed that the witness chair was empty when he felt a hand slip firmly under his arm. A fear that he had failed to protect the woman plagued him as John Bernstein helped him up. "Are you okay, Mr. Birdwell?"

"I think so." Herschel staggered to his feet, touching his fingertips to the angry abrasion above his eyebrow as he looked over to where Jake had landed. He wasn't really surprised at Alice Marshallton's concern for the offensive sonofabitch. The woman was truly a marvel. He guessed he just wasn't meant to understand women, but at least she didn't appear to be hurt.

John Bernstein kept his hand under Herschel's elbow as they moved over to where Jake had landed. They managed to get the disoriented man on his feet, steadying him while his wife loosened his tie and collar a bit more, then brushed at his clothes with her handkerchief, softly reassuring him all the while that everything would be okay.

As John and Herschel walked Jake toward the plaintiff's table she hurried ahead to right his chair, and hold it while they lowered her husband into it. When Jake was seated, she stepped around in front to wipe saliva from his mouth and chin, then fold his hands in his lap and make sure he was sitting solidly.

Herschel couldn't help feeling sorry for the poor bastard. The man had let his arrogance soar, taking him to even greater heights here in the courtroom, and like Icarus, Jake had ignored the heat of the sun of reality, and allowed it to melt the paraffin anchoring the feathers of his fragile ego, plummeting him back into the world of truth, and the bottomless chasm of defeat and shame.

"Your Honor." Walter Hardesty rose slowly from his chair, where he had witnessed the disruption of his case, and watched the physical efforts to restore order. His manner was subdued, his voice benignly soft. "If we could have a break here, or possibly even continue the hearing at a later..."

"We'll finish it now." Alice Marshallton's words reflected her impatience with the entire mess as she turned and looked up at the judge. "Just give me a couple of minutes."

"You don't feel you need a recess?" Judge Chandler ignored Walter Hardesty as he turned to the woman, watching her settle her still blubbering husband into the chair. He was concerned for her now, afraid of what her refusal to support this travesty any farther might entail.

"No, sir. My husband will be okay for no longer than it will take for us to finish this.., this..." She raised a hand and waved it away.

"Very well, then." The judge lowered himself back into his chair, watching the woman, amazed at her devotion, at the way she continued to fuss over her husband. "You may return to the witness stand when you are ready, and bear in mind that you are still under oath."

"Yes, sir." She nodded testily. " I'll be right there."

"Ms. Compton?" The judge raised his eyebrows toward the court reporter. "Have you kept us on the record?"

"Yes, Your Honor." She nodded assuredly. "I have included everything that has been said so far."

"Thank you. I trust you will see that all conversation here today will appear in the transcript. Including the admission of the witness and the plaintiff's outburst as he.., ah, approached the witness stand"

"Yes, Your Honor." She nodded again. "I will make sure it has all been included."

When Alice Marshallton finally had her husband quieted, and turned toward the witness stand, Judge Chandler scooted up to his desk and pulled his pad into position. While he waited for her to be seated he glanced toward the plaintiff's side, where Walter Hardesty continued to stand in front of his chair, then to the defense side where Herschel Birdwell stood, his hip resting against the corner of the table. The defendant and his wife were both now seated at the defense table, glancing around, as though in awe of what had happened. The newcomer had never left his seat during the outburst, but seemed to be more interested in the defense table now, and Mr. Birdwell's condition.

The judge cleared his throat softly. "Are you ready, Mrs. Marshallton?"

"Yes, sir." She drew herself up, ignoring Walter Hardesty's eyes and his feigned show of concern.

Judge Chandler's tone was polite as he leaned toward her. "You will recall that Mr. Birdwell introduced the fact that the defendant is recognized as being disabled by the Veterans Administration, and referred to the reason for that disability as an *abnormality*. Can you describe that for the court?"

Alice Marshallton sighed heavily as she looked down, touched the handkerchief to each eye and began to shake her head. "No, sir."

Judge Chandler began to write as he spoke, his words low, his mind still on the bedroom scene the defense attorney had been so insistent on recreating. "Then you have no knowledge of the defendant's.., you have no personal knowledge of Mr. Hamilton's anatomy?"

Her words were barely audible even though the courtroom had become deathly quiet. "No, sir. I don't."

"None at all?"

"No sir."

The judge finished writing and looked up, hesitating thoughtfully for a moment before he turned toward the plaintiff's table. "Do you have any further questions for this witness, Mr. Hardesty?"

"No, Your Honor."

The judge let his eyes drift to the plaintiff, still slumped dejectedly in the chair, drooling and quietly mumbling as he stared off into space, then turned his attention to the defense table. "Mr. Birdwell?"

"No, Your Honor." Herschel's words were politely soft. He had just seen the mighty Jake Marshallton crumble, had witnessed the illustrious attorney prostitute himself, then watched all the insolence, all the pomp and arrogance go out of the poor sonofabitch, but he no desire to gloat. He couldn't generate any sensation of victory. "I don't have any more questions."

"Very well." The judge leaned toward the witness chair. "That will be all, Mrs. Marshallton. You may step down."

Judge Chandler watched as Alice Marshallton left the witness chair, stopped to speak briefly with John Bernstein, then the two of them raise her husband to his feet and walk the doddering man through the gate in the railing and down the aisle to the double doors at the back of the courtroom. And the newcomer had the judge even more confused now. The man had turned away as they passed, as though making a point of dissociating himself with the plaintiff and his wife.

The judge waited until the doors to the front hall had closed behind them before he returned to the business at hand.

"Mr. Hardesty, Mr. Birdwell, if you will approach the bench."

Walter Hardesty had busied himself with his files, and looked up with an indifference at the judge's words. He gave his vest a tug, checked his bow tie and glanced contemptuously toward the defense table as he moved forward.

Herschel attempted to button his coat as he nodded and headed toward the bench, and, on discovering the button gone, glanced hurriedly around the floor. As he approached the judge, Herschel straightened his coat and drew himself up sternly, despite the missing button, a torn lapel and the blood that had trickled down into his eyebrow from the angry abrasion on his forehead.

Walter Hardesty shifted haughtily as he waited, as though merely enduring the judge's instructions. He had composed himself graciously and was staring beyond the bench as though the whole thing was beneath him now.

The judge had closed the legal pad and placed it in his folder, then returned his pen to his shirt pocket as he waited for the two attorneys. "Do either of you have any reason for continuing this hearing? Do either of you have anything further to add?"

Walter Hardesty stiffened at the question, but Herschel Birdwell just reached up self-consciously to check the blood on his forehead and pull his torn coat together.

"Mr. Hardesty?"

The attorney's words were sharp as he continued to look beyond the bench. "No, Your Honor."

"Mr. Birdwell?"

"No, Your Honor." Herschel's head began to shake as he looked up at the judge. "The defense sees no reason to continue."

"Very well, then. I will give you your instructions."

Judge Chandler clasped his hands together on the desk in front of him and raised his eyes to the ceiling for a moment to gather his thoughts. The sudden turn of events had unsettled him.

"Each of you will be furnished a typed copy of the transcript of this hearing within thirty days from today. You will then, in turn, have thirty days from the date of your receipt to review the transcription and enter any corrections or objections you may have. There will be nothing new entered." The judge paused, eyeing the attorneys until they had both responded.

"All correspondence pertaining to this hearing will be by certified mail, and there are no provisions for extensions or delays. You will return the transcript to me, properly signed and dated, within thirty days from the date of your receipt. There will be a return address, and a repeat of these instructions included with each copy of the transcript."

The judge paused again until both attorneys had voiced their agreement.

"On receipt of both your copies of the transcript, I will then review and consider any corrections or objections you have offered, and make my decision. Each of you will then receive a typed copy of that decision within sixty days after your copies of the transcript have been returned to me. Are there any questions?"

When both attorneys began to shake their heads and reply in the negative, the judge gave a slight nod and reached for his folder. "Thank you, gentlemen. This hearing is adjourned."

Herschel unconsciously pulled his coat together and turned, fingering the torn lapel into place as he watched Walter Hardesty hurry off to retrieve his briefcase from the plaintiff's table and head for the door. The man had every right to be huffy, but surely he realized that even circus exhibitions were sometimes flawed. All the maneuvering and finagling, all the planning and rehearsals in the world did not necessarily guarantee a winning performance.

At the sound of Hiram Jordan's voice, Herschel turned to see that the man was approaching the defense table, graciously introducing himself to Judy Hamilton and beginning to put the glad hand on her husband.

"We never doubted you for a minute, Ron, but I'm sure you understand how particular we have to be about observing the rules and regulations with these contractor complaints." Hiram turned, smiling graciously as he took Judy's hand, patting it as he talked. "Bill Warden and I were there for your husband all the way even though we couldn't openly show any partiality."

The man's accomplished mendacity made Herschel's stomach begin to churn, causing him to turn away as he placed the file in his satchel and fastened the leather straps. He breathed noisily through his nose as he listened to the lying sonofabitch moving in on Ron and Judy, giving them his own glib rendition of the Dance of the

Seven Veils. It apparently wasn't the first time the pretentious sonofabitch had to retrieve someone's head from a sacrificial platter.

Hiram Jordan smiled nonchalantly as he warmed to his subjects. "This one did get a little hairy, Ron, but we knew Herschel could handle it. And now that it's over I'm going to put you on administrative leave for a couple of weeks so you and your lovely wife can put this all behind you. So you two can get away, go somewhere to relax and enjoy yourselves."

He turned to give Judy a quick smile before he continued. "Then, when you get back I want you to come into the office. I've been talking to C.J. Donaldson about expanding that fuel savings program of yours. We had already been considering a new position, something like a Manager-at-large, to keep an eye on our entire transportation budget, and C. J. and I both feel you would be the man to move up, the man who could certainly handle it. Okay?"

When Judy Hamilton beamed proudly at her husband, and Ron began to nod, Hiram Jordan turned to Herschel and stuck out his hand. "Congratulations, Herschel. We had every confidence in you. I couldn't see any reason to bother the Legal Department in Headquarters with this when we had you right here in our own bailiwick."

Herschel pulled his worn leather satchel from the table, ignoring the proffered hand as he turned away. "You'll have to excuse me while I go back here and *puke*."